D1414291

THE
BANYAN
TREE

Alan Bartlett, whose professional and business experience
formed the basis for his first two controversial books, "Profile
of the Entrepreneur, or Machiavellian Management" and
"Power, Prejudice and Pride", believes that a book should
merit careful reading and serve several purposes. It should
entertain through light-hearted observations, provoke by
challenging convention and give cause for thought by taking
an unusual view. In short, attempt to reflect life as it is which
is often stranger than fiction.

The Banyan Tree is a factional story. For obvious reasons,
the contributions made by and the names of individuals have
been changed. The events remain true and are truly stranger
than fiction.

Charles Asprey, an English businessman, is asked to
mastermind the salvage of a sunken German U-Boat which is
known to hold some very valuable and highly dangerous
secrets. His efforts arouse the interest of British and German
Naval Intelligence as well as the attention of American and
Israeli Intelligence services.

Knowledge proves to be a deadly commodity and people
who acquire too much quickly disappear.

There are those in power who wish Asprey to fail and those
who want him to succeed. If he does hold the key to the
puzzle, will he use it or throw it away? But the most intriguing
question is why he does what he does and that can only be
answered by reading the Banyan Tree.

THE
BANYAN
TREE

ALAN F. BARTLETT

ISBN No. 0 9507646 2 0

Published by Schumacher & Cie, Geneva

Contributions made by and the names of individuals have been changed.

First published by Schumacher et Cie, Geneva

Republished 1987 by

Ashford Press Publishing

Cover design by Anne Glenn
Typeset and printed by Hayden Consultants in association with Drayton Ford
Published by Schumacher et Cie, Geneva
Distributed in the UK by Schumacher & Co. PO Box 1, Portishead, Bristol.

Contents

Prologue

The banyan tree grows in India. It is a fig tree with a peculiar method of self-propagation. Its branches send down limbs to the earth which take root when they make contact with the soil and gradually develop as new trunks.

As time passes, the tree can in the right conditions impose itself around its neighbours and ultimately become a self-perpetuating forest with a unique characteristic – its canopy of foliage is common to all its trunks.

Should a limb land on infertile soil, then that is its bad luck. The tree will just send other limbs to the ground so that sooner or later new growth is attained.

Until a limb strikes roots it is indistinguishable at first sight from the many and varied tendrils which casually hang down from other trees. Even in its form as a slim new trunk, it still appears to be relatively insignificant and vulnerable. It is only when it is obviously a sturdy member of a much larger and more powerful growth that its stature and importance can be seen for what it truly is. But by then its roots are deep and far spread. It is extremely difficult to cut down and virtually impossible to destroy. And if each trunk represents such a problem for others interested in the development of a pleasant and balanced forest, what chance have they of eliminating or even controlling the whole tree? If you like a diet of figs then the prospects could be quite attractive. But if you do not then you will need more than a sharp axe.

Chapter One

The Heavyweight

It was a smooth curve. If anything, too smooth. Charles Asprey's casual glance focused. Good Lord, the young lady was not wearing pants! His mind, suddenly activated, galloped on. He began to recall wall posters in the London Underground rhapsodizing on the fact that all good female undergarments produced a smooth top finish. At the time, he had thought it to be nonsense – obviously written by a woman. Foundations were for buildings! The line of the pants, provided the underlying curve was interesting, added to the sensuousness of the vision. It introduced a third dimension, visual touch. Success in obliterating any outline could only lead to suspicion rather than anticipation. Maybe because of the absence of resistance to the eye, her slim body, sheathed in a close-fitting dress slit almost to the waist and her near perfect features did not arouse any basic response. The young lady immersed in the preparation of his Irish coffee could easily have been a model for Sir Gerald Kelly and created little more excitement than she might have done had she been on canvas. His initial reaction to the poster brainwashing had been confirmed. Nevertheless, she was very good to look at, so Asprey did just that.

The girl went about her task in a very professional manner. She had already warmed the goblet using the spirit lamp placed somewhat precariously on top of her trolley. She poured into it a liberal measure of Irish whiskey. Two spoonfuls of brown sugar together with boiling black coffee completed the basic mixture. Very carefully and deliberately she poured a layer of cream completing the finished product which visually had a remarkable similarity to that of Guinness.

3

It was a work of art, putting the original concoction as produced in English pubs and restaurants to shame. Having moved rapidly from the erotic to the philosophic, Asprey picked up the hot glass placed in front of him and sucked the mixture of coffee and whiskey through the thick layer of cream. He would have to remember to wipe his mouth when he replaced his glass, otherwise he would undoubtedly sport a white moustache to rival his grey hair.

Still in his late thirties, the family tendency to turn white by middle age was catching him up at a disturbing rate. At least the thatch was still there and he had no doubt about the fire beneath.

So much for British innovation and speciality coffees. Seated in the lounge of the Marco Polo Hotel in Singapore, comfortable and relaxed, it seemed only natural to philosophise. Although he had made relatively few visits to the Far East, he had already seen many examples of the Anglophile attitude of the Chinese. In the basement of a Singaporian home he had discovered reproductions of London Street signs, restaurant menus and memorabilia of days long past in the sceptered isle, topped off by a large collection of original "78s" including all those made by Vera Lynn.

By this time the Irish coffee was taking effect. He relaxed deeper into the soft chair. Perhaps he would have a second glass. Although it was evening he felt completely wideawake – probably the effect of time distortion. He had been only two days in Singapore and the time difference between that state and London was eight and a half hours. So his metabolism had no idea where it was. The clock was no longer important when it came to effective thinking. Opportunity had to be grasped when it appeared.

A little knowledge can indeed be a dangerous thing. He had worked and indeed was working with the Chinese yet he could not pretend to know and understand their way of thinking. He was more than aware of their secret police and therefore quite convinced that had the nature of his mission been known to those close to the centre of political power he would have the greatest difficulty in leaving Singapore other than horizontally.

His first visit to the state had left an indelible mark on his memory. Singapore had just begun to blossom under the leadership and control of Lee Kwan Yew. The physical effect of the new policies was for all to see. The shanty towns were fast disappearing, being replaced by concrete high rise buildings. But similarity with European planning ended almost before it had begun.

Just as the eyes of a person reflect the soul and personality, so the windows of a building can translate the impassability of an otherwise blank wall into a living edifice. The windows of the new buildings were frank and open – unglazed and brightly lit. The occupants and their colourful belongings were on view, inviting neighbours to call as and when they felt so inclined. It was as if the horizontal conglomeration had simply been relocated vertically. The friendliness overtly remained. So much for the city planners of Europe! To be fair, Lee's achievement owed much to a happy combination of climate and character. Nevertheless it was an excellent start to a transformation that was to astonish many nations and create envy amongst most.

The Marco Polo lounge was large and very comfortably furnished. Those entering the hotel were admitted through sliding glass doors which opened automatically as the individual approached. Having entered the lobby, the guest could either walk directly across to the reception desk facing him or turn right, climb carpeted stairs and select one of the many seats scattered between tables in what used to be euphemistically termed the residents' lounge. The dais effect gave Asprey an advantage. Whilst seated almost at right angles to the entrance, he could see newcomers before they could see him. He concentrated his attention and eyes as he would need every benefit he could gain, however slight.

The large man's entrance was magnificent. It was without pomp but with much circumstance. He was preceded by a westernised oriental of youthful appearance who was obviously respected in his own right. But it was the white man who sailed through the eagerly opened doors like a fully rigged clipper welcomed by a host of beetling bumboats who commanded attention.

He was Brash, Q.C., a man whose physical presence admirably confirmed his commercial importance.

Those who can recall the actor Sidney Greenstreet will have no difficulty in visualising Mr. Brash. He was big. His cross section was that of a bell. His head was small, his midriff large, and his feet appeared to be hinged at the ankles. He had no knees, or at least, gave that impression.

Murray Brash was one of the two remaining English Queen's Counsels in Singapore. He had been educated at Clifton College, Bristol, and retained the self confidence of one who acknowledges daily the respect that nature had ordained should be accorded to him. He had many attributes which encouraged the Chinese to play their part in his order of things, not least that of being an outstanding trencherman. That, coupled with his capacity for liquor of all categories, placed him at the head of any table. He had only one true gourmand competitor in Singapore – also an Englishman named McCormack. He was a senior partner in one of the leading international firms of chartered accountants that had a number of branches scattered throughout the Far East. The combined capacity of these two gentlemen was not only to be found at the laden table. Whilst one directed, the other audited a number of important local concerns. Whether in dining or board rooms, they represented a formidable combination, one that justifiably put many of all nations in awe of them.

Murray Brash, Q.C., was a man of many parts. In addition to his directorships in a number of local companies, he held a significant interest in the Adelphi Hotel, one long regarded as more beautiful and certainly more comfortable than the celebrated Raffles. The Adelphi offered as wide a selection of fine wines as any hotel in the world and the best were reserved for Mr. Brash.

But perhaps his most interesting commercial involvement was with a substantial shipping line which enjoyed a special relationship with Peking. He was a man about whom many

6

metaphors would well be mixed.

His forerunner, Thomas Chua Boon Lee, knew Asprey and therefore led the way up the steps and across the lobby. Charles stood up. To remain seated would not only suggest impertinent disrespect but would undoubtedly place him at a grave disadvantage. There was the possibility that Brash would continue his advance to the point where his convex profile would effectively pin any seated adversary almost out of sight without any undue effort on the part of counsel. Stand up had to be the order of the day. At least Asprey would then have the advantage at eye level.

Thomas Chua Boon Lee was a Christian – his first name confirmed that. To the westerner his family name was Chua as indeed was Boon and the Lee was the Chinese equivalent to a forename. He wore glasses and suffered from sinus. Tommy, as he was generally known by friends and foes alike, was a member of a wealthy and influential Chinese family which controlled a Singaporian public company, Orchard Carriages. As its name implied, the company had established its reputation and business in personal transportation.

Tommy's father had not been a Christian. Consequently he had had a number of wives, Tommy's mother being the youngest. Two of Tommy's colleagues were brothers but of a relationship that was difficult for the Western mind to appreciate. Chua Boon Peng was the eldest and therefore the Chairman of Orchard Carriage. He was the image of the inscrutable Oriental. Smooth faced, calm, friendly but aloof, he presided at table whether board or luncheon. Inevitably Asprey had found it impossible to determine his age. Sheer logic and arithmetic insisted that he was well into if not past middle age. Yet with the exception of concern as to his alcoholic intake, he gave no outward sign of being other than at least 20 years younger than his actual age of 60.

Some people emanate a colour. If such an association of ideas exists, then Boon Peng exuded a warm almost glowing gold. Rather like that of a teddy bear. But he was certainly no toy and like the real thing could hardly be classified as cuddly.

Chua Boon Unn looked rather the worse for wear. He

suffered from eye problems and therefore viewed the world through dark glasses darkly. Yet he seemed to miss nothing. His complexion was quite different to that of his elder brother. If one looked for a colour identification then it had to be dark brown. Less inviting yet still somehow warm – but hard. Boon Unn was the Managing Director. Whether he had made decisions or not was almost irrelevant. He carried them out. Indeed he gave the impression that if circumstances warranted, "to execute" would be taken literally. If something or someone had to be done then they were simply "on the list". A man to be treated with considerable caution and respect.

Thomas Chua Boon Lee appeared to be so different from his two elder brothers that it needed time and concentration to identify common characteristics. Yet there was no doubt that such existed. Tommy could be very nervous, given to noisy throat clearances or alternatively quite positive, making clear and concise decisions. His appearance and attitude reflected the merger of two quite different backgrounds, the first being of an established and wealthy Chinese Singaporian family and the second the Western influence absorbed through education and business training. It would be neither unkind nor derogatory to suggest that he was a mixture of yellow and blue, a combination producing green. Such a colour code has no significance other than illustrating different external personalities.

Tommy was both bright and ambitious. He was potentially the largest shareholder in Orchard Carriage and should make managing director.

Those who believe that all Chinese look alike are as ill informed as those Chinese who believe that all Westerners are similar so Charles Asprey and Thomas Chua had no difficulty in recognising each other. Thomas introduced Brash to Asprey. The men shook hands carefully and firmly. All three sat down. Asprey opened the batting.

"Can I offer you something to drink?" "Thank you, a Black Label Scotch," replied Brash.

Asprey summoned a young girl. At least he intended to, but

he need not have bothered. A bottle of Black Label Johnny Walker Whisky miraculously appeared complete with glass on a small table by Brash's chair. It was unopened. Brash nodded. The girl quickly removed the top, poured the whisky into a glass and then filled it up with water. Almost simultaneously, but not quite, a tumbler of ice discoloured by whisky appeared at the elbow of Tommy Chua. Since there was no doubt as to who was footing the bill, the question had been superfluous. The respective tastes of Messrs. Brash and Chua were obviously widely known and acknowledged. Asprey sipped thoughtfully at his Irish coffee. If he was able to do business with them he would have two formidable colleagues. On the other hand if they finished up on opposite sides of any opportunity in that part of the world then he would rate his chances of succeeding pretty low.

"Nice to see you again, Charles," said Tommy. "Glad to be back Tommy," responded Asprey.

Tommy leaned forward. "May I introduce Mr. Brash, he is a director of our company and many others in Singapore and Malaysia. I felt you should meet each other, particularly in view of your mutual interests in finance. Mr. Brash, Charles, is a man of many parts and whatever your plans in Singapore I know he can help."

Asprey turned towards Brash. "Jolly glad to know you." (No harm in over-playing the English idiom – indeed idiot). "As Tommy knows I am looking at the possibility of establishing a private merchant bank in Singapore on behalf of a small English public company. I understand you have a similar plan?" Brash sipped his whisky. Whatever his original background he was now thoroughly Oriental in thought and deed. In fact as the evening progressed, even his face adopted a Buddah type mask – or perhaps it was the other way round. The European face was the disguise and the true man emerged as he relaxed. Brash continued to sip and look, eyes hooded, at Asprey. His face was quite expressionless. He could have been thinking anything or nothing. Asprey did not attempt to guess.

Finally –

9

"This is not your first visit to Singapore."

Brash paused.

It was not a question or even a statement. Asprey had been admonished. He should have known how to open up a business discussion, obliquely, carefully and with patience. It was by no means his first visit as both he and Brash well knew. Therefore there was no excuse. Asprey had been deliberately clumsy, even insulting and would now have to suffer the consequences. Brash could keep him waiting at least all evening, if not until another meeting. But should he? Brash weighed up the pros and cons. His first reaction had been to dismiss business from the evening's agenda. Lean back and enjoy the foolish man's hospitality. Or was he that foolish? He looked intelligent. His record was outstanding although he was relatively young. Above all, he had worked with the Chinese and Japanese in a number of successful joint ventures. Brash played bridge. He looked at Asprey and decided that he did also. In which case the call had been deliberate. Not a bluff, not a mistake, but a forcing pre-emptive statement.

Perhaps the stakes were much higher than he had been told. That was possibly because Tommy could well be unaware of the whole story. He might not even know the real purpose of Asprey's visit.

So Brash opted not to pass. Instead he responded.

"As a matter of fact you may be too late for that opportunity." (Just the slightest emphasis on "that" – the bid, if bid it were, had been doubled.) "I have just concluded heads of agreement with an Australian company for a joint banking venture."

Brash had left the original door slightly ajar. He felt it was still conceivable that he might have misread Asprey's opening gambit and that his sole interest was indeed in a banking operation and his anxiety to get down to business reflected the extent of his desire and more importantly his resources. Brash was not one to leave things to chance.

Asprey responded to the double.

"What a pity. Perhaps I might still have the opportunity of seeing if we could offer an attractive contribution to a possible partnership."

The answer was quite clear. Brash was now sure that he had been right. The joint venture had been dismissed – but something else existed. It had been agreed that that hand could be played later.

So Brash continued the bidding.

"I am always interested in improving my condition, but shall we now take advantage of our introduction to consider the more important things in life, those that are essential for living?" As if by further magic, a menu appeared suspended in front of Brash. Asprey had been fully aware of the bilingual capacity of all Singaporians but this was quite something.

The staff and management of the Marco Polo were so much in tune with Murray Brash that they anticipated his every whim with uncanny accuracy. Maybe he had a ritual. Or perhaps Tommy had a system of signals. Whatever the mechanism the results were both effective and awesome.

Without glancing at the menu and certainly not deigning to take it in his hand, Brash looked carefully at Asprey and said, "May I, even as a guest, take the liberty of suggesting that which we might all enjoy. We need not feel bound by any of the limitations of the menu so my advice may well be helpful."

Charles felt it unnecessary to reply and merely nodded his acquiescence.

Brash continued – ignoring Tommy completely. "The oysters or cherry stones are very tasty. Small but succulent. The beef here is excellent but I must admit that I have a preference for pigeon pie freshly baked." Tommy picked up the menu, apparently pigeon pie was not for him. He pushed his black rimmed glasses up the bridge of his nose and stared intently at the open page. Asprey was slighly puzzled. Tommy would have known the menu off by heart. So why the hesitation? The answer was not immediately forthcoming. Then Asprey caught sight of a small dark haired man abruptly turning on his heel, changing direction almost completely. One moment he had been walking towards the three seated men. The next he was walking away. He had been instructed not to join them as had been his intent – by Tommy?

Curious thought Charles, in fact curiouser and curiouser. First Tommy was obviously not privy to all Brash's activities and now a lower order associate or friend had been turned away. Perhaps the evening had more in prospect than eating or drinking however succulent the pie and fine the wine.

Chapter Two

Temptation

The dinner was excellent. Food and wine had been complementary, service miraculous. Conviviality reigned, and conversation
was relaxed. The debris had been cleared, superfluous cutlery
and condiments removed and the table cloth restored by
assiduous scraping to its original pristine state.

The port, brandy, cigars and coffee having been distributed,
it was no surprise to any present that it should be Tommy who
broached the subject uppermost in their minds.

"What exactly are you looking for, Charles?"

"Money first – influence second," responded Asprey almost
too quickly.

"Why money? I always thought that your philosophy was
that the first requirement was opportunity, the second timing
and a poor third, finance?"

"Absolutely so."

"That means that you already have the first two covered?"

"Right again. Obviously you know me too well."

Charles smiled at Tommy who began to look embarrassed.
Even his western training in business did not allay his natural
reaction that perhaps he was jumping too many hurdles too
quickly and much too early. It was time to back off.

"How much do you need?"

The backing off was confined to the more sensitive element
– the opportunity. Clearly Asprey would not even attempt to
declare his hand until negotiations had made considerable
progress and there were firm offers, albeit with conditions.

"About a million pounds, sterling."

"When?"

"Over the next few weeks."

"Security?"

"Tommy you are beginning to sound like a banker." Brash had intervened. Tommy turned towards him. Any intervention by Brash must have a purpose and Tommy had to be clear as to what that was, otherwise he would be quickly demoted to the role of spectator or even worse, excluded altogether.

"Ah," he said, "you wish me to be the entrepreneur." (This was one of Tommy's favourite words.)

"Business man certainly. After all money is only a commodity." Brash then looked at Asprey. "I'm a little disappointed. I would have thought that you would have been interested in much higher stakes."

"I am, but the money is not a little important. The real contribution is the influence that its source can bring to bear. Money is the key but we still need lubrication in the lock."

Brash had not had the answer that he wanted. A gamble has three elements – the Stake, the Risk and the Prize. The greater the Risk relative to the Stake, the larger the Prize. Even if he could not identify the latter at such an early stage in the discussions, he could at least get a feel for its size. If Asprey was not prepared to indicate that, then he must provide some idea as to the odds – and that would give Brash his answer.

"So it needs more than mere money to open the door. Will the key fit easily? How sure are you that it will do its job without being forced?"

Brash had gone as far as he could. It was now up to Asprey.

"Nothing is certain – certainly not success. We have had one attempt, but for reasons which at the time were quite unforeseeable, we failed. This time I am confident that we will not – but, by definition that which is unforeseeable is always present. So we could fail again. If we did, we would try a third time. We are nothing if not tenacious."

Brash could not make up his mind whether Asprey was referring to the royal "We" or whether he sought to impress.

Asprey continued just to make it quite clear.

"Yes, the opportunity is well worth the effort of risk. On

the other side of the door we have something much, much more valuable than the cost of the key."

Brash relaxed as far as his frame allowed. Detailed discussion could be best left to a private meeting with Asprey.

"Very interesting – but I'm afraid that pleasant though the company is, I must return to my abode. Thank you for a most delightful meal. May I reciprocate? Perhaps you would care to join me for lunch tomorrow, say 1 o'clock at Raffles?"

As he offered the invitation, Brash levered himself out of his chair. It was just as well that he was successful at his first attempt since at the movement signifying his intention to rise, the ubiquitous head waiter had rushed forward and pulled counsel's chair smartly away. Charles visualised Brash collapsing backwards through a surfeit of food and wine coupled with a lack of muscular co-ordination. But in reality it was difficult to see how even that emergency would catch this staff napping. There was not the slightest doubt that Brash would have received whatever support he needed. He would never have been allowed to fall, although he would have undoubtedly crushed a few Chinese in its avoidance, a small price to pay for the maintenance of face.

"Delighted to join you," Asprey replied as he rose to his feet. "A few more meals like this, however, and I shall have to watch my waist-line." Charles had done it again. It was not exactly the right thing to say to a gentleman who obviously had not seen his feet for many years other than in a mirror, the use of which was equally unlikely. It was a clear sign of Asprey's inexperience. He felt he had to say something, so the words were promoted from his subsconscious without prior thought. Inevitably they were associated with matters that had been deliberately restrained, otherwise they would have been expressed in careful conversation. It would have been far better to have confined his comment to one of thanks. Superfluous or gratuitous remarks are seldom if ever clever, but because of their unthinking nature are usually misplaced, capable of misunderstanding and sometimes downright rude without the calculated pleasure of intent.

Brash understood and was slightly disappointed. Asprey

had much to learn and Brash preferred to work with experienced associates. However, he was still intrigued. If Asprey
had indeed something of real value, then perhaps his inexperience could be turned to advantage. Nevertheless, Brash concluded that he would have to be cautious, but that had never
been a hardship.

The large man nodded towards Tommy, saying goodnight
to both his companions at the table and gathered himself
together for his journey through the restaurant. As he
accelerated staff fussed towards him.

Guests looked up and followed his progress with their eyes,
continuing their activities of eating, drinking, talking or
listening. Brash appeared to see no-one so that there were no
acknowledgements or signs of mutual recognition. He disappeared from sight and the diners re-focussed their eyes.

"Well, I think . . ." began Asprey, but Tommy interrupted
him.

"I have arranged a table at the best night spot in Town. A
little company and a little drink. Both carefuly selected. Shall
we go?"

Why not, thought Charles. It's probably about 8 o'clock in
the morning back in England, so I've missed a night's sleep
already. In for a penny – still no reason to be stupid.

"O.K., Tommy, but I don't want to be late, particularly as I
am meeting your friend again tomorrow and I am sure that I
shall need all my faculties to even stay with that gentleman."
But Tommy was already well on his way to the exit and gave
no sign that he heard anything other than the acceptance of
his offer.

As soon as the lift had jerked to a stop, Tommy pushed
open the door.

Both men stepped into the white glare of a concrete box.
Asprey narrowed his eyes and peered about him. Their way
seemed blocked by a mass of Chinese men and women. The
men were simply larger editions of the schoolboys waiting for
their buses in their white shirts and grey trousers. But the
ladies bore no comparison with their younger counterparts.

They had emerged from their school uniform chrysallises as strikingly colourful butterflies, their wings moulded around them accentuating the sensuousness of their lithe curves. Blessed with almost flawless complexions, their only weakness in the eyes of the westerner was the wig-like appearance of their hair. Sleek and raven-like it might be, but certainly not a crowning glory. But even this flaw was little compensation for the European lady in the competitive stakes of male attraction.

It was little wonder that western visitors looked in vain for gowns which fitted, tried with disastrous results to obtain a smooth bronzed complexion by sitting in the boiling sun and eventually relied upon diaphonous creations that left little or sometimes nothing to the imagination.

The locals had the overwhelmingly advantages of chosen ground and natural weapons. Their only weakness was that time would prove to be cruel to most of them and that almost overnight wrinkles would appear in abundance and waistlines would disappear to give a general impression of collapse. But until that final transformation, in their country they were the unopposed reginas. Asprey had little time to indulge in such speculation. Tommy's path through the crowd was fast disappearing and he had no wish to get lost even in that maze of interesting bodies.

He thrust forward to be struck physically by a blast of noise directed towards him by a door that had opened at Tommy's approach. Tommy had already been absorbed by the darkness beyond the threshold. Charles lowered his head, took a deep breath and fought his way through the cascade of sound into and across the doorway. He was totally engulfed by caucophony and air-conditioning. His senses were utterly useless. He just stood, shut his eyes and counted slowly up to ten – a trick learnt at a very early age when entering a cinema on a Saturday afternoon. Then he had been able to avoid reliance upon the inadequate torch of the usherette. Now he could move forward without dependence upon his guide, Tommy.

They were in a lobby. To their right was a counter behind which stood the inevitable check-girl. Yet, thought Asprey, what on earth could she be checking? No-one, not even Englishmen, wore top-coats or hats or even carried umbrellas in Singapore! In certain U.S. states it might still be guns, but surely not in the state governed by the omniscient Lee?

Tommy had walked on. As Charles moved to follow him, he realised that the check-girl was standing at the entrance to another room into which he could see through a glass panel as he stepped forward. It appeared to be a rest room for ladies, being heavily populated with young women in various stages of relaxation. Some were sitting. Some were freshening make-up. All appeared to be smoking. For some reason which he did not understand, the latter activity seemed to relate to intercourse although the general impression was that of being back-stage and able to see the chorus girls waiting for their call.

Charles was naive, but even he had worked out the answer to his initial questions by the time he had passed through the lobby into the club proper. The check-girl supervised the companions for the evening – or the night. Unaccompanied males could look through the window, make their choice and pay their dues. It was unlikely to be one way glass – not because the Chinese were insensitive to such matters, but rather because normal plate was so much cheaper. They were nothing if not frugal.

The club was illuminated by tiny glow lamps, each pin-pointing the centre of large circular tables scattered around the room. The end furthest from the entrance was obscured by a heavy undulating black squid. As the men walked towards it, Charles began to distinguish human forms playing the role of tentacles, writhing and twisting. He was looking at the dance area. It could hardly be called a floor. For a moment he had forgotten the all-embracing sound. The amorphous mass of people were responding as it washed over and around them. They were bereft of all but two senses. Speech was impossible. Communication had to be by touch, a limitation of considerable attraction. Even sight was of little use other than for the most obvious gestures. It was rather like sitting in the boiling surf on a Pacific shore with eyes tightly shut.

Tommy had stopped by one of the many tables. He was standing behind a vacant chair. He motioned to Charles to take a place opposite him. Both men sat down. Asprey could see that Tommy was flanked by two young ladies. Glancing to his own left and right, he was not surprised to discover that he was similarly supported. Around the table there were four men and five women, seated alternately. One face he recognised. It was the small dark man who had been turned away by someone – it must have been Tommy – when approaching them in the Marco Polo lounge. Whether or not he could actually see the look of recognition in Charles's eyes, he saluted him with his glass in greeting. Tommy, as always, was not slow in noticing the wave and shouted something. It sounded like "Johnny". Charles nodded across the table and smiled.

Despite the general gloom, the light was more than sufficient to reflect teeth and a show of welcome was at least a start.

Gradually his eyes became more accustomed to the darkness and he could study those around the table. All but one man appeared to be oriental. The women were of various nationalities and mixes. They varied from the pleasantly featured to the very beautiful. The one seated on Tommy's right was quite outstanding. Even in such poor light, Charles could see that she had perfect featues with dark luminous eyes. She was also very attentive towards Tommy. That in itself was not really remarkable as it soon became clear that each male was being looked after by the female on his right. Food and drink were placed at his hand, replenished or removed according to his need. Charles found himself to be no exception. A voice close to his right ear whispered:

"What would you like to drink?"

Charles turned towards the young lady and forced himself to shout in order to overcome the caucophony and avoid the alternative but intimate method of communication adopted by her: "Whisky and water, please." "Ice?" came the response. "No, thank you," responded Charles relying upon a shake of the head with which to bridge the distance over which his voice was undoubtedly lost. His glass was filled with the two liquids. Almost immediately Tommy stretched across the table and struck his tumbler against Charles's.

"Cheers, bottoms up," he shouted and dramatically drained his. The inference was clear. Charles was expected to respond in like manner. So, with a slight inadvertent shrug and taking several gulps, he drank his whisky and water. As soon as his glass touched the table, it was re-filled. Whilst that was being accomplished, "Johnny" or whatever his name was leaned across the table, tapped glasses, said "Cheers" and with a flourish, swallowed his drink.

Ah, thought Asprey this is a set-up. They are going to see if they can put me under the table. It's said that the Chinese cannot hold their liquor, but with these odds it could still be onesided. But, what else?

"Cheers," he said, raised his glass and then took several mouthfuls of whisky before it was empty. Odd, he thought. They drained theirs at one gulp and their glasses looked full. Here I am struggling to do the same with four or five swallows.

He held the glass above the table top and watched Tommy's girl friend fill his glass. The girl's movement was slick and short. And then he could see the reason. All the glasses around the table, other than his, were full of ice – large lumps. The amount of alcohol in each could only be minimal.

Asprey turned to his companion, "I'll have ice this time, please," he shouted. He watched with some relief as the girl dutifully filled his glass with a mass of cubes. The bottle only paused above it, and the operation was complete. He leaned back and relaxed. This was not going to be too difficult.

Whether or not Tommy had come to the same conclusion he was never to discover, but after only one further round, the game ceased. Whatever the object, it was no longer interesting.

The noise made conversation impossible, which was just as well as Asprey's command of small talk was somewhat limited. As he looked about the club, he felt amazed that anyone could regard the oriental as quiet, reserved and unemotional. When amongst their own kind, suitably warmed by a relatively small amount of alcohol, their combined efforts would rival that of a Saturday night knees-up down the Old Kent Road, with perhaps something less of the middle-aged leg-waving and stomping. Nevertheless, a boisterous loud and happy affair dominated by the males. Charles was beginning to feel a little more than tired. It was impossible to see the time by his old fashioned Omega with its plain dial, but it was merely a guide to good manners.

It was really a question of how long before he could indicate to Tommy that he ought to start making tracks for bed.

When the moment came, Tommy was surprisingly ready. He immediately stood up which was a signal for everyone else around the table to do likewise. They all followed him to the exit, where Tommy's driver was patiently waiting.

The uncomfortable contrast between the humid night air and the refrigerated atmosphere of the night-club was more than compensated by the loss of the head-splitting noise turned off by the automatic closing of the door behind the party as they left. It was only afterwards that Asprey realised that no-one had attempted to pay for anything they had consumed – and more significantly, perhaps, that no-one had tried to exact payment. He still had a lot to learn as to the power of the rich in Singapore.

Tommy led the way to his Mercedes. Charles followed, almost tripped by the driver who scampered around him, anxious to reach the vehicle first to open its doors. He succeeded which was just as well since there seemed little doubt that his job turned upon his ability to prepare the way for his master, whether in the car or out.

Tommy slid across the back seat. As Charles stooped to enter, he realised that one of the girls was ducking in between him and the car door. He paused, and without any further ado, the girl sat herself beside Tommy. Charles still hesitated which gave a second young lady just enough time to emulate her companion. The back seat of the car was full. Tommy laughed, grabbed the one nearest to him and sat her on his lap.

"Not to worry, old boy," he said, "there's plenty of room here even for a lanky Englishman." Asprey took his point and squeezed into the car.

"Ah, but our laps are most uncomfortable," he replied to pre-empt the next recommendation. There was no need for him to put the second girl on his lap as the Mercedes was quite wide enough to accommodate three posteriors, none of which was particularly broad.

Tommy laughed from behind the back of his girl. He knew better than to press the matter – at least for the time being.

The driver jumped into the car, closed his door and immediately switched on the air conditioning. He turned around to Tommy. "Marco Polo," said Tommy. The man swivelled back to face the front, started the engine and then whipped the car down the spiral ramp within the car park.

They retraced their route to the hotel. The traffic had abated a little. The number of people walking along the pavements had also diminished. Yet whatever the local time, whether late or very early, Singapore was still very much alive.

They were met at the entrance of the Marco Polo by the tall dignified Sikh who had the Mercedes' door open before the car had come to rest. Doubtless the driver would be taken to task later that day for allowing this to happen. As it was he endeavoured to make amends by rushing round to the other side of the vehicle and helping Asprey to fall out from his cramped quarters.

Tommy had long since preceeded his guests into the hotel lounge where to the complete lack of everyone's surprise a table and four easy chairs awaited his arrival. "What will you have?" The inevitable question and the customary answer, "Thank you, whisky and water," "No ice?" grinned Tommy.

"I think not, thanks," Charles laughed with his host. "T'is my night cap and it will set me up nicely."

"Ah," said Tommy, mysteriously, "that's already arranged. You will sleep very comfortably tonight." Charles looked at him quizically. The two girls had seated themselves at the table. They were the two who had sat each side of Tommy in the night-club. In the light of the lounge, Asprey could see that both were quite beautiful even to western eyes, but the one who had been and indeed continued to be attentive to Tommy was striking. She had a flawless complexion, pale but not white, very dark eyes that matched her raven hair and a slim petite figure. Her name was Marie.

The second girl had a rounder face and a slightly fuller figure. She could have been a year or two older than Marie. Her name was Lisa.

Tommy ordered the round of drinks from the ever-hovering waitress. "Would you like to borrow my driver later today?" he asked. "He can pick you up at any time and you can keep him all day if you wish." Charles was duly appreciative, but firm. "That's very kind of you, Tommy, but I have yet to confirm my arrangements and meetings. In fact I may have most of them here and that would mean that your chap would be hanging around doing nothing practically the whole day. Perhaps I could have a rain-check on him for another time, if that's possible?"

If Tommy was surprised, disappointed or offended, he did not show it. "Perfectly O.K. Just ask and he's yours at any time."

"Thanks very much," Charles leaned back in his chair. He truly did not have any ideas as to the final details for his plans for that day, but in any event he had no intention of providing Tommy with an up-to-date report of his activities. He had learnt many years previously that those engaged in the most intimate and secretive conversations seemed to ignore completely the presence of waiters, chauffeurs and door-keepers. The absence of faces, whether replaced by the backs of heads or lost in the gloom of expressionless service appeared to be accepted as evidence of the lack of hearing facilities, interest and intelligence. Whilst he had no doubt as to the sensitivity of Brash in such matters, others may not be so discreet. There were many things to be discussed with a large number of people whose existence and connections he certainly did not want to disclose to Tommy, at least at that stage of the proceedings. Whatever the motivation for the offer, it had to be declined – gracefully.

Tommy wasted no time in finishing his drink. He leant across the table and held out his hand: "If you will let me have your key, Marie can go ahead up to your room."

Asprey was really taken aback. It had not been difficult, even for him, to work out what Tommy had in mind, but he had certainly not anticipated that he would be offered Marie. There had not been the slightest doubt throughout the evening that she was Tommy's and there was considerable mutual interest between them. He looked at Marie as she stood up. She gave no sign at all whether she was happy at the proposal or not.

Charles had a problem. He had no intention of sleeping with even Marie, yet he did not want to upset Tommy at such an early stage when he might well need his help on a number of fronts. He had no idea as to the depth of relationship between Tommy and Marie and therefore whether a polite refusal might be secretly acceptable to Tommy even though it would be regarded as a loss of face. Finally, he had already decided, on the incorrect assumption that it would be Lisa, that he would appear to accept Tommy's offer when it came and rely upon his ability to buy the young lady's agreement to silence over the intended absence of action.

To insult Tommy by not accepting his offer would be bad enough but to have it known that it had been accepted as a charade would be unforgiveable. It would be worse than cheating at golf and being found out and that for the Chinese would be intolerable. Could he rely upon Marie's agreement? Perhaps the purpose was to simply gather information?

Tommy had misunderstood to the reason for the lack of response to his offer. "If you have left the key at reception, it would be better for you to collect it first and then give it to Marie. Although the management are fully aware of what goes on – and comes off – it doesn't like its guests to let on that they know they know! Discretion, even if unnecessary is still desirable in Singapore."

Asprey had had time to think. He actually had no alternative. He put his hand in his pocket. He always carried his hotel key about with him in the belief that room thieves would note its absence at reception and wrongly assume that he was in occupation and look elsewhere for their loot. It was arguable as to logic but not as to experience. So far he had escaped the attention of such villains but even that was not certain. Professionals could turn a room over without leaving the slightest trace of their visit – so he would never really know.

He handed the key to Tommy who smiled as he passed it on to Marie. The girl kept her eyes lowered and walked across the lobby towards the stairs.

"She is very good," said Tommy. "She will catch the lift on the first floor and leave the same way. She's also very good in other respects." Tommy grinned broadly. Charles could not decide whether he was embarrassed, amused or upset.

He was inclined to guess the last as he was still convinced that Tommy was truly attracted to Marie. Certainly Tommy was determined to impress him, perhaps to put him under an obligation? Whatever the reason, he was sure that Tommy was making his play with some reluctance, albeit carefully hidden. The stakes had to be high to justify the concealment of the extent of his personal sacrifice.

Tommy stood up. Lisa levered herself from the depths of her chair. "Give me a ring later on, Charles. If you change your mind and you find you need a car and driver – no problem."

"Thanks again." Asprey was genuine in his response. "I'll telephone you towards the end of the day. You must join me for a meal."

Tommy grinned broadly, "Not while you are in Singapore. Here you are my guest. Perhaps when I come to London you can turn the tables. But here is here, and here we look after you – and all your needs."

The last phrase was his parting shot. The two men had shaken hands. Charles had remained standing by his chair whilst Tommy, followed closely by Lisa, had moved towards the main entrance.

Asprey watched them go through the doors and disappear

amongst the waiting willing helpers on the steps of the hotel. He looked across at the lifts. The door to one was open. He walked across the carpeted floor slowly and deliberately.

He was surprised to find that he was neither worried or excited by the thought of Marie waiting for him in his room. Suddenly a thought struck him – You idiot – if she wants to go through your papers, what better opportunity than now! But as quickly as it occurred to him, he realised that it was inconsistent with Tommy's actions. If such had been the plan, then Tommy would not have departed so rapidly.

Tommy would and could have kept him talking for considerably longer than he had done. No, if there was an ulterior motive, it was much more subtle and projected into the future.

Nevertheless Asprey accelerated and stepped into the lift, pressed the button for the twelfth floor before turning round to face the doors which were already closing. As the lift climbed smoothly, he smiled wryly at the thought that there would be considerable embarrassment if he forgot his room number. Before he had had the chance of working out a solution to the highly theoretical problem, the lift had arrived at his floor.

Marie was waiting for him, seated on the large bed. She made no attempt to undress yet greeted him with a bright smile. "Tommy has arranged everything. When you wish, I will go home by taxi." She quickly added: "I can stay as long as you like."

Asprey smiled at her and walked across the room, taking off his tie. She followed his progress with her eyes, not turning her face or body. He slumped into the arm chair near the window. "Now" he said, "precisely what has Tommy arranged?" She was uncertain as to his meaning. "It's all right, he has paid for everything – anything," she said. Her English was excellent, only the "lisping 'r's" giving an indication that it was her second language learnt without the benefit of formal tuition. This seemed to be her cue for undressing. She began to unhook the back of her dress. Asprey sat up. "Momento", he held up his hand.

26

He wasn't sure if that was at all the right word, but it reflected the fact that he was fast getting out of his depth. "I appreciate very much what Tommy has done – is doing – and I think you are very beautiful, but I really am whacked – I meant – tired." (Translation of "whacked" was essential!)

"But Tommy has paid."

"Yes, I understand that, but what I really appreciate is that he has offered you (Asprey deliberately emphasised the "you") to me and I would not like him to be upset by finding out that I have not – er – taken full advantage of his generosity – if you understand what I mean."

Charles felt he was making a hash of the situation from every point of view. Why hadn't he had the sense just to accept the offer and have done with it?

But Marie had relaxed visibly. She had the message. For whatever reason she was not being asked to perform. Instead she merely had to be discreet – and silent. She was nothing if not philosophical. She had heard that the English – unlike the Germans whom she knew well – could be soft and lacking stamina in bed. Indeed, their public schools tended to encourage them to indulge in homosexual habits. She could not pretend disappointment.

"You have no need to worry. I am here simply to do as you wish, from everything to nothing, and if you prefer to talk then I would not tell Tommy. If he asks, I shall simply laugh – but he will not because he will not want to know."

Her last words confirmed that she at least believed that Tommy really cared and that that would make it easier to avoid descriptive explanations. Perhaps she might be right. On the other hand, the temptation to relieve Tommy's mind would be difficult to resist.

"There's only one problem," she continued. "What's that?" asked Charles. "I cannot go home too quickly as Tommy would then know we had not slept together."

Asprey understood what she meant. Her departure from the hotel would undoubtedly be noted and if immediately after his retirement must cause comment which in turn would undoubtedly be passed on to Tommy. So she had to stay, at least for part of the few hours of night left. As if in answer to his thoughts, Marie suggested. "It will be quite alright for me to leave in two or three hours. I can sit here quietly and let myself out. You can go to sleep."

It was quite ironic. Charles suddenly felt wide awake. Perhaps he was being an idiot again. The girl was beautiful. She was undoubtedly hand-picked – whatever that meant! But he had committed himself. He had not the slightest doubt that if he changed his mind she would still be on offer, but he could easily imagine her immediate reversion to her previous tense and anxious attitude. She would probably freeze and become quite mechanical.

It would be like making love to an alabaster model – not that he had actually had the experience of that – but the thought was enough to deter him. So he sat down on the edge of the bed.

"Tell you what," he said, "let's talk. Tell me about yourself – where you live – what you do." (As soon as he had said it, he realised how ridiculous a suggestion that was! He hurried on hoping to swallow the faux pas in a flood of words.) "You know what I mean, your family, your hobbies, where you were born . . ." He gave up. He could suddenly see himself playing the role of the English teenager on his first visit to Paris, naive, nervous and very foolish. Marie gave no indication other than attentive interest. She nodded, folded her arms in her lap and almost demurely complied with his request.

She was one of eleven children, born in a village in Malaysia and volunteered by her parents into prostitution like so many other youngsters in that part of the world. Being exceptional even at the tender age of eight, she was groomed for stardom, taught English and some German, some European etiquette and a lot of hygiene. By the time she was fourteen, she also understood how to please men.

In Singapore, prostitution was an essential element in business. It could be used as an inducement to encourage a buyer to place a contract. It could cement a relationship between organisations where one was determined to act as an agent for

the other. It was regarded as an important part of entertainment with a capital "E", the lubricant of the wheels of commerce and industry throughout the civlised World.

The more wealthy companies employed a Madame whose
job it was to provide those whom the company nominated
with interesting companions. The largest companies often
rented luxurious flats to provide permanent accommodation
and the provision of all the amenities so essential for the tired
businessman.

In addition to the Madames employed directly by companies, Singapore was the home of a select small number of
entrepreneurial Madames who specialised in fresh young
debutantes. For a number of obvious reasons, their services
were very expensive, but in a country where wealth was no
inhibitor and of as little consequence to those who enjoyed it
as was the inheritance of the landed gentry in Europe, their
wards were in great demand.

Each Madame was expected to understand the idosyncrasies
of the various nationalities and therefore to provide young
ladies who were not only prepared for such contingencies, but
expressed delight in their confirmation. Above all, she had to
have the latest and loveliest recruits to the profession. These
were made available, when suitably prepared, first to her
"sponsors".

Such young blossoms were not expected to be virgins. Even
if that were possible, which it was not, sponsors were men of
experience as well as taste and in no way would they wish to
express themseves with novices let alone noviates. But young
ladies were expected to be fresh and unspoilt and that in
Singapore with its good housekeeping, was quite practicable.

So Marie had been presented by her Madame to Tommy,
one of Madame's sponsors and he had been delighted with
her. So much so that she had remained his exclusive companion, a rare event in that sonority. Asprey appreciated
therefore that he had indeed been honoured.

As Marie told her tale, she grew less and less aware of her
surroundings and began to chatter quite freely.

She was the wage earner for her entire family. Every month

she sent home quite substantial sums, that is by the standard of her village, and carefully invested the balance mainly in precious stones. These were easily realisable and simply transportable.

Her ambition was to become a Madame, then earn enough to buy herself her own hairdressing salon, having first studied with Sassoon preferably in London!

Asprey was more than interested. Marie's clear thinking, her clinical approach to her career and the logical way in which she developed her goals and ambitions would have left many a Harvard business graduate gasping in her wake. She was not in the popular vernacular selling herself. She was using her limited resources to create wealth which in turn would be re-invested ultimately in a business that would create greater wealth and in so doing provide her with social acceptance and above all, economic independence. At the same time she remembered her family which ironically she regarded as disadvantaged as compared with herself. Indeed a potential case study with enormous possibilities!

It was Charles who looked at his watch first. Good heavens, it was past four o'clock in the morning. Marie although still enthusiastically continuing her story, immediately noted his re-action. She looked at the bedside clock.

"Is it O.K. for me to go?" But she still did not move. "If you like I can stay with you a little longer."

Charles thought that he had interpreted her correctly. In telling her story she had decided that she would be prepared to trust him. Perhaps she hoped for advice on her business interests. Women were far more pragmatic and realistic than men. He had something to offer which might be of considerable value to her. For her part – well that was obvious!

Oddly enough, however, the confidence she had shown in him, his awareness of her hopes and ambitions had created a relationship that seemed to be incompatible with sex for the sake of sex. Possibly it might develop into a friendship that would encompass intimacy. But that morning it was much too soon – and morning it truly was.

Charles made a point of looking at his watch.

"Good Lord, if I don't get to bed soon, there will be no need to go to bed at all." (He had an unhappy knack of saying the wrong thing even in those circumstances). "Let me show you to the lobby."

Marie stood up. It was difficult to see whether she was happy or sad at the dismissal. Regardless of race, inscrutability is the prerogative of women. "No thank you. It would be better not to. I can get a cab now very easily. Tommy's driver might even be waiting for me."

That re-emphasised the necessity for her to stay in the beginning. She only had her handbag, so she was at the door before Charles had straightened up. Marie gave him a long deliberate stare, opened the door just enough to slip through and vanished with no more than the click of the lock as it fastened behind her.

Asprey stared for a moment, watching her image fade against the dark mahogany of the door. Then he turned abruptly towards the bathroom. This would never do. There was much to be done and women had not figured in his plans at all. They could only be a complication and his venture was complex enough.

Chapter Three

Things ain't what they seem

The bedroom was quite chilly. As with most things in Singapore, the airconditioning worked extremely efficiently. So much so that Asprey woke up feeling decidedly cold. There was no point in checking the time. He was awake. It must be morning as it had been when he want to sleep.

After showering and shaving, he rang down for breakfast and then telephoned Brash to confirm the arrangements for lunch.

Breakfast arrived, fresh fruit, coffee, croissants and marmalade, the last being the concession for the Englishman. All beautifully prepared and presented with spotless linen and cutlery.

Charles admired the view from his window. This was the life, he thought. Perhaps one day he would return for a holiday and really enjoy Singapore. He then telephoned Tommy who suggested that he would pick him up at the Marco Polo early evening and they would go first to a Russian restaurant, then on for some entertainment which brought Tommy naturally to the question. "Did you enjoy yourself last night Charles?"

"Yes, very much indeed – and thank you, especially for the piece de resistance." Asprey had done it again. He really had stuck his neck out and almost anyone would have taken the gravest exception to the various interpretations of his phrase.

Now the telephone is at best a poor medium of communication. It eliminates the nuance of eye and facial expression. It isolates and emphasizes the hesitancy and uncertainties of speech. It encourages ambiguity but discourages repetition by request. Add to that awe-inspiring list the unfortunate ability to say the wrong thing at the wrong time and the result is a foregone conclusion. Catastrophe.

There was an inevitable pause. Tommy to try to assess what was meant. Asprey to decide whether to rattle on in an attempt to retrieve the position or to ignore any adverse interpretations and conclude the conversation as quickly and smoothly as possible. Whilst he was deciding, Tommy got in first.

"Well, I'm glad you enjoyed it. I have something quite different in mind for this evening."

"I shall look forward to that very much, but hopefully we shall have a chance to talk business first, as by the end of the day I shall have made some progress." Asprey felt it was essential to bring the conversation and indeed the relationship with Tommy back to the easier and more relaxed arena of commerce.

"Of course, and I am sure that we shall have many matters of mutual interest." Tommy's response was automatic. Both men could converse in this manner without effort or thought. The conversation was quickly terminated, Asprey replacing the receiver thoughtfully. He had to be very careful and avoid almost at any cost making an enemy of Tommy. His careless comments could easily undermine any trust that existed between them and all that would remain would be the attraction of wealth that would ultimately be attained by one at the expense of the other. Partnerships were seldom if ever mutually profitable.

Charles Asprey took a cab to Raffles, the hotel nominated by Brash for their luncheon meeting. The taxi was the usual black and yellow Austin Cambridge, not air-conditioned, but otherwise in very good working order. Having instructed the driver, Asprey took advantage of the man's excellent English to add to his scanty knowledge of Singapore. The driver was full of praise for the way in which the city had grown and prospered since the second World War. Cleanliness was the order of the day.

Street traders were closely watched and their produce critically examined. Sanitation was beyond reproach. Unemployment could not exist and there had ever been any strikes.

Utopia would have appeared to have arrived. But there were problems. It was expensive to own a car. The annual road fund tax on a large private vehicle could easily exceed £1,000. Families were discouraged from having more than two children.

When Asprey enquired how such objectives could be enforced, the driver concentrated on the traffic. If its undoubted density required his whole hearted attention, then he really had had no time for the earlier questions, but logic was irrelevant. There was a line beyond which the driver would not be drawn and that was any criticism of the system in general or Lee Kwan Yew in particular. And this caution was still very much in evidence, although he was seated in a taxi cab surrounded by vehicles all contributing to a traffic noise comparative with that of any city in the world. The Prime Minister's influence was almost of voodoo proportions. Respect for his achievements was more than matched by fear of his power and that had to be real.

Asprey did not pursue the topic. It was not only a waste of time but could also have unfortunate repercussions. Too many enquiries might encourage a report if only to protect the reporter from a planted informer. He therefore took the opportunity of getting to know Singapore at least by sight.

Despite its density and phrenetic urge, the traffic generally was very orderly. Occasionally cars or cabs would cross each other's paths, the streets being mainly one way. Then there might be some honking of horns, but generally the shirt-sleeved drivers would wave their free arm through the window in a general gesture of despair at their colleague's lack of technique, timing or direction. The drivers all looked alike. Small, dark haired, brown skin and white teeth. The last feature dominated Singapore.

The indigenous population, without exception, looked happy and content. However strong the element of fear, it obviously had a positive effect. It had created an atmosphere of confidence in themselves, their system and their achievement.

Nowhere was this more obvious than in the school children, waiting cheerfully and patiently for the yellow much battered and unreliable school bus – the brightly coloured brother of the grey public transport ramshackle conveyance. The children were all dressed alike, grey shorts or skirts and white shirts or blouses. All had raven black hair, bright eyes and cheerful smiles and carried carefully their satchels, full of eastern promise of work to be done. The schools worked a two shift day, early morning to mid-day, mid-day to early evening. Each shift had it's own teaching staff. Buildings were therefore fully occupied – not quite twenty four hours a day, but certainly twice as long as their European counterparts.

Education is the cornerstone of prosperity, providing it is tailored to the economic objectives of a community. There was not the slightest doubt that in Singapore this was precisely what was being done. The school children represented the investment in Singapore's medium term future. For the next twenty five years each young person would be bi-lingual, prepared to contribute to a technological society and conscious of the strengths and weaknesses of a nation that had only one natural resource, namely people. And they had to be unique if that nation was to prosper. Asprey had no doubt that they would be and to that extent he was much impressed.

Raffles disappointed. Certainly it retained its colonial atmosphere with ceiling fans, glassless windows and Victorian furniture. It was truly an epitaph to a society that had in many senses missed the boat. It provided no service to the past or the present.

It only served to remind those who cared of the opportunities identified and carelessly thrown away, of the ill conceived missionary zeal of those who sought to impose themselves and their ways of life on a country and a people who needed to be met at least half way.

Having created a chasm between the invaders and the conquered, the colonisers then sought to ignore any need for mutual adjustment and development. The whole philosophy was tragically but effectively exemplified in the infamous Singaporian fortifications. The guns defending the City pointed the wrong way. Those responsible for political and economic development had done precisely the same. They looked and went in the wrong direction. They therefore had no alternative but to capitulate when the time came. So the British threw away the dream of Raffles, leaving the old hotel a reminder of their stubborn resistance to the translation of vision into a new reality. The ideals of yesterday remained the foundation of tomorrow. The past and the future full of hope, the present the evidence of failure in implementation.

Brash – as a good host – awaited Asprey.

"I trust you slept well?"

Asprey would not interpret any more than the superficial intention of the words.

"Yes thank you. The air-conditioning is marvellous. In fact almost too good."

"Which is more than you can say of this place," responded Brash. "However, the food and wine and service are not at all bad."

Brash led the way into the dining room. Everything appeared to be brown. The tables, the chairs, the walls and the ceiling were all of timber, plainly varnished and apparently mellowed by the passage of time. The staff, although pleasant enough, blended obsequiously into the background. Even their smiles shone less brightly than those in other restaurants and hotels.

But as always in Singapore, Brash was right or perhaps he had ensured that it would be so. Everything was of a high standard. Asprey enjoyed the cuisine. This time he left it to Brash to determine when business would be introduced. Sure enough it came with the brandy and cigars.

"Now you have a need and an opportunity. Can I satisfy the first and can you provide a worthwhile second?" Asprey responded carefully. "I believe yes is a fair answer to both questions."

"Very well," puffed Brash. "Let's be specific. You mentioned last night a million pounds – for what exactly?"

"To hire a lifting vessel."

"So you want to salvage something?"

"Yes."

"How big?"

"Several thousand tons."

Brash looked up at the ceiling. His resemblance to Sidney Greenstreet was unbelievable. Charles Asprey felt an insane desire to emulate Humphrey Bogart – "Yeah, so what?" – but he held himself in check.

"Quite big – why not dismantle it first and raise it piece-meal?"

"It would destroy the value."

"So it's some kind of treasure?"

"Yep" – Asprey had succumbed, the word had slipped out before he could extend it into a less curt affirmation. Brash glanced at him casually. There was little doubt that he was quite aware of his appearance and its affect on others. It also became obvious that he revelled in it. It was equally certain that there was no way that he would allow any other character to share his place on the boards. Asprey's thespian inclination had to be cut short and quickly – "Why come to me?"

"One geography, two influence, three time. We need some-one who can get things done quickly, quietly and economic-ally."

"So you need to hire a salvage vessel. For how long?"

"One month."

"That will not cost a million."

"But we need to lubricate a few palms to ensure that it can be operated."

"I see, and what's in it for me?" Brash was direct – so was Asprey.

"Ten per cent of what we get – about ten million pounds."

"After expenses including the million of course?"

"Yes."

"I take it, Mr. Asprey, that as an Englishman you don't believe in bargaining."

"No, I offer what I believe is a fair price and that's it."

"Of course, that I heartily commend, so I will respond like-wise. You can have your vessel and influence – I have no doubt as to the effectiveness of either – for one million plus twenty percent of the proceeds of the project or twenty million whichever is the greater. Like you I do not believe in bargaining."

Brash looked quizically at Asprey. Then he returned his gaze to the ceiling. Charles was not surprised. He had offered what he believed to be a reasonable deal, but Brash had no need to be reasonable. Even if they came to a formal agreement there and then, Brash could up his demands as soon as he knew what was involved and even attempt to take over the project himself. The purpose of the discussion was keep the ball in play, hold Brash's interest and give away as little information as was possible. Charles had a choice. He could adopt the time honoured posture of halving the difference between them or he could simply accept.

He chose the latter because he did not have to pass over any further details which might have been unavoidable had he continued to bargain.

"Very well, you satisfy me on those two counts and I will satisfy you on the question of what the pot's worth."

Brash lowered his eye-lids. He appeared to lose interest in the immediate surroundings. Considering the volume and quality of that which he had consumed for lunch, it would have been reasonable to assume that he had nodded off. But Asprey preferred to think otherwise. He had not he slightest doubt that Brash was now pondering as to what he wanted to know, how he could find out and when.

"I think you should put your proposition on paper," he said. "There appears to be a lot of money at stake. I will need to involve others and if something happens to either of us, the opportunity might be lost forever."

Asprey was not sure how to take the last comment. Perhaps Brash suffered his own weakness as to throw away lines.

"I take your point. I will give you a summary of what we need, when and for what purpose. I can also give you references to confirm that we are at least good for the million."

Brash nodded – then he opened his eyes and looked directly across the table.

"Why did you fail the first time?"

"We made a number of basic mistakes. We tried to cut the costs, hired the vessel in the wrong country, the captain proved to be unreliable and our funds had been dissipated before the vessel had even reached its destination. It just never got started. By the time we had sorted out the problems that had been created, new ones had arisen and we needed a local influence to resolve them for which we had made no provision."

"The lessons we learned therefore, and they were extremely expensive, were that we had to get our resources as near to the point at which they were to be used as is possible and further that we not only had to have the agreement of those who mattered, but also ensure that there would be no intervention by those who did not."

Brash nodded. "So you are starting from a different base and with an additional capability. Is time still of the essence?"

"Yes," said Asprey. "Too many people know we are on to something and if it becomes public knowledge, politics may prevent it's realisation."

"Could that happen after we are committed?" questioned Brash.

"No I think not," replied Asprey. "We either go in with a political guarantee or not at all. We shall know whether we have it and once given it will be virtually impossible for it to be withdrawn."

Brash rubbed his nose with his forefinger. "I hope you are right. Now I suggest we defer discussing the detail, that is, what it is, where it is and why it is worth so much until we are in a more private place. For the moment we have an agreement. If you can persuade me you are good for a million, that you will have access to at least my twenty million and that the whole affair is practicable, I will arrange for a large vessel to be at your disposal for a reasonable period of time and use my best endeavours to persuade – peacefully? (it was a question to which Asprey nodded agreement) those who need to be persuaded that what we are about to do can be done."

"Fine," said Asprey. "I agree with all that. Now when shall we meet again and where?"

"Tomorrow evening at my place, say about seven." As Brash handed over his card, he looked directly again into Asprey's eyes.

"You have no partners in Singapore or in, as you would say, the East?"

Charles thought of Tommy but decided that his involvement would only lead to complications at that stage.

"No we have none. I shall look forward to filling you in tomorrow at seven pm." He had almost done it again. It was hardly the appropriate phraseology for a very corporate gentleman. At the very best, it could only be described as slack speech.

Brash was slightly confused. He was fast coming to the conclusion that basically Asprey was naive. For all his experience in industry and commerce and his knowledge of the ways of business in many countries, he had a large streak of immaturity. Brash was encouraged. Sooner or later he would have sufficient information to decide whether Asprey was necessary. He had a feeling the answer might be in the negative.

He made a move to indicate that he would like to leave the restaurant. The performance of the previous day in the Marco Polo was repeated, only this time the procession included Charles who felt entitled to a place in it, although naturally in the wake of Murray Brash Q.C.

After exchanging the usual pleasantries at the entrance to Raffles, Asprey and Brash parted company, the latter squeezing himself into the inevitable Mercedes. Asprey decided to take a look at the shops as a means of clearing his head and digesting the excellent lunch, so he walked towards the old financial centre of the City.

Shop fronts in European terms were non existent. The places of retail business resembled the dark pigeon holes in a Victorian desk, edging each side of the streets. Passers-by had to thread their way between shop assistants squatting on the pavement, such as it was, assembling bicycles, toys, household utensils and similar products and at the same time resist the blandishments of currency dealers waving wads of dirty notes under their noses.

Asprey was struck by the antiquity of the posters advertising consumer products. He could vaguely remember them in his early childhood – Ovaltine, Horlicks, Beechams Powders, Bile Beans, Pears Soap and so on. The most surprising aspect, however, was that the goods were in the shops supporting the visual campaign! Where on earth did they buy them? Surely not from England, but if not, where else?

As he stopped outside a drug store advertising many brands of aphrodisiacs which complement the vast consumption of brandy which the Chinese believe adds considerably to their fertile capacity, he happened to glance upwards. From every glassless window, a pole festooned with multi-coloured garments and cloths signalled the status and wealth of the occupants. The heat of the sun not only dried the efforts of the meticulous washer women, but also aired and ironed in a way that would be the envy of any English housewife.

The visual effect was to transform the streets above shop level into kaleidoscopes which changed their patterns according to the perspective of the pedestrian.

As Asprey approached the financial part of the city, the character of the shops changed dramatically. They were now peopled by Indians, swarthy and solemn. The visitor had to climb two or three steps in order to enter each shop. On one side stretching from just inside the front right through to the back, a row of grey gentlemen squatted like monks at prayer. A tiny table was placed in front of each. Facing some of them across the tables sat an assortment of Chinese, Malaysian and Indian men and women of equally solemn countenance.

This was indeed a serious business, money lending. Lounging at the entrance of the shops were small groups of burly men, whose nationality was as confused and difficult to define as those of the supplicants.

They were the bully boys, the unwelcome visitors in the event of back sliding. Failure to comply with commitments was not a sin, it was simply a case for hospitalisation or in repetitive circumstances an opportunity to assist in the wellbeing of the fish in the harbour or in the construction of highways or high rise buildings. Singaporian society, having no national resources, naturally regarded re-cycling as an essential element in it's evolution and development. It therefore seemed both logical and desirable that those who could not conform to the essential rules for day to day living, should at least contribute to the long term well being of those who did.

Repayment was not simply a matter of honour. Failure to keep a promise did not cast a doubt as to credit worthiness and the ability at some future date to borrow again. Those who did not pay up had no need to worry on either score. In truth they would be in no condition to worry at all. They would simply cease to exist and that in a confined and teaming population could even be termed as an advantage to those who remained behind.

It was curious that this aspect of money lending appeared to be controlled by Indians rather than the Chinese. Perhaps the latter performed the more prestigeous of commercial lending where the bully boys were more subtle yet equally as effective. The principle if it could be classified as such was the same, the ultimate deterrent equally frightening.

Within half an hour, Charles began to regret his tour on foot. Although the temperature was only in the low eighties, the sun and the humidity were starting to take their toll. He hailed one of the constantly perambulating cabs and returned in its relative cool comfort to his hotel.

A bath, a shower, change of clothes and then to await Tommy's arrival.

The phone by the bed rang. Asprey started. He was actually asleep and yet it was still only early evening. He picked up the instrument and Tommy's voice confirmed his anticipation.

"Are you ready and fit Charles?"

"Yes thanks, I will be down right away."

He replaced the receiver and picked up his coat. As he moved towards the bedroom door, he weighed the garment in his hand, thought of the temperature outside and then rather reluctantly took his wallet from the inside pocket. He then hung the coat in a wardrobe, removed his tie and left the room feeling a little naked but curiously relaxed in mind and body.

Tommy was waiting for him in the lobby. He led the way out into the humid evening air and then into the cold of the waiting Mercedes. Asprey began to regret the absence of his coat, but Tommy unknowingly now alleviated his worry – at least on that score.

"How nice to see you without a coat and tie, we shall make a Singaporian of you yet."

"I am sure there are many worse things to be."

Asprey's response was neither witty or appropriate. However, it could not be withdrawn and simply put a stop to that particular subject for further discussion.

After a few moments Tommy tried again.

"I hope you like Russian food. We are eating at the Troika. If you don't like the special menu, they do a very good fillet steak."

Asprey felt that honesty was surely the best policy when it came to food and drink.

"I've never had Russian food, I've had Vodka, but that's all – once I had some caviar which could have come from Russia, otherwise I am completely ignorant. I would like to try it just to see."

"Good," said Tommy. "It's also a very discreet restaurant, so we can talk business – if we want to. Afterwards we shall go to Boogie Street. Have you been there?"

"No," replied Charles. "Is it where people dance?"

"Sometimes," said Tommy. "That's not the main attraction, but I must not spoil it for you. You will see."

Charles was intrigued. Whilst time and inclination dissuaded him from tourist activities, he was by no means averse to broadening his knowledge with interesting facets of life in any part of the world. If nothing else, it made for good conversation, an activity for which he needed every assistance he could muster.

The Troika was on the second floor of an unimpressive concrete building. Asprey was not altogether surprised to find that the freehold belonged to the Mercedes marketing empire.

The restaurant's decor was equally unremarkable but quiet and cool. The only outstanding feature was an unequal distribution of round concrete columns between which tables of varying shapes and sizes were scattered. About half of the tables appeared to be occupied.

Tommy was ushered across the restaurant and presented to a table guarded by three columns. He had no other guests, so Asprey assumed that the intention this time was to get down to brass tacks. This meant that he had to decide quite rapidly how much he was going to tell Tommy both as to his conversation with Brash and, more importantly, as to the project as a whole.

Tommy ordered the inevitable whiskies – Asprey asked for ice – and then set about choosing the meal. That accomplished, he leaned back in his chair and looked over his glass at his companion.

"Now, how much are you going to tell me. I assume that you still need my help and Murray Brash hasn't provided everything already."

"No," responded Asprey. "Brash knows what I want and when. I know what it will cost. He knows roughly why but he has little or no idea for what."

"Well," said Tommy, "suppose you tell me the when and the why and then make up your own mind if you will tell me for what. We can agree before we start how much I will tell Brash so that we don't cross our lines there."

"Good idea, I would certainly not want to upset him, particularly at this stage. I will tell you precisely what I have told him. Then anything beyond that must be strictly between us." Tommy nodded, "Agreed".

So Asprey recounted his conversation with Brash as accurately as he could. Tommy listened intently keeping his eyes focused on Charles.

It was only when Asprey indicated that he had got to the end of his discussion with Brash that Tommy relaxed. He settled back in his chair and casually looked away beyond Asprey. As Charles raised his glass to his lips he became aware that Tommy had stiffened and that he was concentrating on something or someone behind his, Charles's shoulder.

"Don't turn round," Tommy said, very gently, "I believe that we have an audience. For how long I'm not sure. Please carry on as before." As he spoke, Tommy lifted his left hand just above their table. The waiter arrived at the double gliding rapidly between tables and pillars. Tommy turned his head towards the approaching minion so that he was looking away from Asprey and therefore the listener. He spoke to the waiter. Whatever he said – and Charles had no idea even as to the language let alone the content – caused the waiter to retire even more quickly than he had responded to the original summons.

Tommy turned back to look aross the table at his guest. "Perhaps now would be a good time to settle down to enjoy the food." Asprey agreed with alacrity. Whatever his metabolic clock might indicate, his stomach was quite convinced that it should make its contribution to the bodily function.

It was difficult to carry on a conversation and resist the temptation to look behind him and discover just what had caused Tommy's concern. He looked around for a mirror-like surface, but without success. He did not smoke cigarettes so that ruled out one obvious ploy of using the inside of the case. He could hardly ask Tommy for a loan of his. So he forced himself to mouth pleasantries, at the same time watching Tommy's eyes intently. Suddenly he realised that Tommy had again relaxed.

"O.K.," he said, "whoever she was, she's gone now. We can carry on talking."

"How far away was she?" asked Asprey.

"Near enough with the right equipment," replied Tommy, "but the idiot had been so engrossed in what you were saying that she had forgotten to eat."

So that was how Tommy had spotted the eavesdropper. Charles decided not to ask who the woman might be. He doubted if Tommy would tell him even if he knew, which at that moment was most unlikely. There was still a very basic need for security. Without it he did not have a snow-ball's chance in hell of retaining control of the project. Tommy –

and now one other – knew as much as Brash, but that was still limited knowledge. Even so, there was a real danger that the growth of the circle of those who were aware of the existence of the venture might in turn cause ripples to spread far beyond the present horizons. He had dropped a relatively small pebble in the Singaporian pond but already it had not gone unnoticed. Time was indeed of the essence. The sooner Asprey could conclude his deal with Brash, the quicker he could organise the recovery and dispense with secrecy.

Charles looked at Tommy thoughtfully. "Well, I'd better accelerate matters with our mutual friend. The wider the interest in what we may have, the more likely we are to encounter delay or even competition."

Tommy reacted to the last word. "I thought you had the monopoly – that you and your associates have an exclusive and irrevocable license to salvage any vessels in those waters?"

"We do, but the best way of protecting a personal right is to use it. The sooner we demonstrate our ability to take advantage of our privilege, the less chance there is that those who originally gave it to us can be persuaded or influenced to change their minds. Once we are on our way, we cannot be stopped – but failure to get underway can only invite interference."

Tommy agreed. "I understand that. If you feel that I can help you in persuading Brash to come across with his support, then just ask. Indeed, if you find that he is dragging his feet, perhaps I might even get the finance for you."

Asprey had foreseen the possibility of such an offer during the evening. "I certainly appreciate your help, Tommy. May I have a rain check? What we need from Brash is not only his money but also his undoubted influence in certain circles – particularly concerned with shipping. On the other hand any real delay would outweigh all those advantages and if he does fail to deliver within the next few days, I should be more than happy to have you as our sole partner."

He had chosen his words carefully and Tommy appeared quite pleased. As long as he remained ahead of the conversation, Asprey could be very effective with words. It was only when he felt obliged to make unconsidered and casual comment that he more often than not achieved precisely the opposite effect to that which he sought – and that, unfortunately was not infrequently.

Tommy was on the move. "Come on Charles, we will go to Boogie Street." As they walked across the restaurant, Asprey glanced towards the table at which the listener must have been sitting. It was now occupied by four men who were also on the point of departure. Asprey followed Tommy, both men threading their way between pillars and tables towards the exit, there to be greeted by Tommy's diminutive driver.

Their car journey down Orchard Road was as interesting as ever. The evening air was moist and warm. The pavements were busy with chattering young people. Up to middle age at least, the Chinese retained their remarkably youthful appearance, unlined in the face and slim body. Age when it showed itself arrived as unexpectedly and as unwelcome as the first frost in an English Autumn, the visited having been lulled into a false sense of never-ending youth by the mirror of a long and very pleasant summer.

The road was, as usual, as thickly thronged with traffic as the sidewalks were with people. Under the bright lights, the colour and cheerfulness combined to create a four dimensional reproduction of humanity at its best. The brilliance of the constantly changing combination of hues pleased the eye. But it was the overriding warmth of smile that transformed the scene from the possible work of an outstanding film director into an expression of all that can be good in the human race.

The buildings with their neon signs were but backdrops to the focal point of the action. It was the colour, movement, cheerfulness and chatter of the people that dominated the Singaporean stage. They were the wealth of the state. It had no other resources other than its global position. To the onlooker they represented more than adequate compensation for the absence of oil, diamonds or the more acceptable foundations of an ambitious nation.

47

The Mercedes pulled into the kerb. For once, the driver had no difficulty in fulfilling his function, which he did with alacrity. Tommy led the way into a side-street, bathed in light but devoid of traffic. Even so, progress down it was quite difficult, first because of a maze of tables and chairs spread from one side to the other and secondly because of waves of small boys who presented themselves at frequent intervals along the length of the street and in faultless English offered "the best table in the street". Since all looked alike and none commanded a better position than any other, Asprey was at a loss to understand the basis upon which such recommendations could be made. Perhaps it was service, but if so, of what?

The profusion of tables, chairs and boys was flanked by two lines of mobile stalls each specialising in a particular offering of food. As yet there were no customers, so that the majority of the owner-cooks were busily engaged in preparing their ingredients in anticipation of some later demand. Pots and pans were being scrubbed, polished and oiled, vegetables washed and swept into bowls of water. The only sight that jarred was the array of very dead and very naked ducks that hung like white ghosts, the antithesis of their final presentation as succulent dark brown, almost mahogany coloured "finger licking" morsels and their previous experience as lively quacking inquisitive characters.

Asprey felt a twinge of sympathy for the unfortunate birds but that was quickly lost as the two men allowed themselves to be seated at a table which obviously pleased Tommy. Other than the fact that it appeared to be in roughly the middle of the street both as to its length and width, Charles could not for the life of him identify its attraction as compared with its numerous fellows. Even the lad who chattered away between them was but one of a host of peas in the pod of Boogie Street.

"What happens now?" Tommy smiled. "What would you like to drink, whisky?"

"With ice," Charles responded automatically. So it was going to be a surprise, whatever it was. The trickel of people entering the street had swollen into a bore. The competition between the young boys for customers was transformed into races between newcomers for fewer and fewer chairs and tables. Prime positions were soon engulfed and it was only the inherent politeness of the Chinese that avoided outright physical conflict in establishing ownership – albeit temporary – of the sites remaining. The warm air was stirred and circulated by the chattering and laughter of happy and eager pedestrians. The tinkle of glass and cube added a very pleasant dimension. Over all hung a buzzing air of expectation – but for what? Asprey did not have to wait too long for the answer. The stage had not been set for more than an hour when the first of the players percolated amongst the audience. They were small in number and not immediately distinguishable from their equally colourful onlookers. Yet they had one hall-mark which made them easily identifiable to even the most casual observer. They were tall and slim. They were also beautiful, but in that they were not unique. It was their grace of movement that set them apart from all the other women present.

The source of attraction undulated from side to side across and then down the street. Some were smoking cigarettes, others were carrying small open parasols which had the effect of emphasising their swaying hips. The young ladies were quite something. If they were prostitutes then their display could only mean one thing – they were expensive, particularly since they were obviously western. If they were actresses then they could only represent an extraordinary collection of talent. That train of thought brought Asprey to the possibility that they were the oriental equivalent to the Bluebell girls – perhaps the Lotus lasses?

As the leading girls approached Tommy's table, Charles suddenly felt decidedly uneasy. It was not beyond the bounds of probability that Tommy had arranged for two of them to join them for a drink and "entertainment". The nearer the girls the more inadequate Charles became. They were not only exquisite, they were confident, experienced and expensive. Charles looked across at Tommy who was thoroughly enjoying himself. Tommy caught his eye, raised his glass and

49

saluted him.

"What do you think of them?" he asked.

"Marvellous, absolutely stunning," replied Asprey.

"They leave our girls miles behind," Tommy's admission did not seem to cause him any real grounds for complaint. Asprey felt obliged to compromise for the benefit of his host and perhaps to appear something less than completely enthusiastic for that which he believed Tommy had in mind for them.

"Oh, I don't know, oddly enough I really prefer the young ladies of eastern mystery." Charles's choice of words left something to be desired but still hopefully conveyed his intent – to praise local products and to discourage sampling of that presently on offer. His words seemed to have the opposite effect.

By now two young ladies were almost level with their table and looking straight at them. Tommy was one huge grin.

"Which one would you like, Charles," he asked, "the blonde or brunette? Just say and I'm sure they will stop. They make jolly good company."

By now, Tommy was looking positively mischievious and Asprey was feeling increasingly uncomfortable. Entertaining sophisticated call girls in public presented a completely new and daunting prospect. His smile began to ache. He could feel the sweat accumulating under his shirt. He was mesmerised by the luminous eyes of the leading girl. There was no way in which he could respond to Tommy's question. All his faculties had departed. The situation had hypnotised him. The best that he could hope to achieve was to lean back and like Confuscius enjoy it.

The leading young lady walked past their table. The spell had been broken. She was followed in quick succession by her companions, undulating like beautiful but deadly snakes between the seated groups of men who cheerfully applauded their progress without apparent lust or leer. It was indeed a gala performance.

Charles looked closely at Tommy. Had nothing been arranged? Or had he been expected to make the running?

Tommy's glee provided no answers, but only confirmed that he was enjoying himself hugely, as indeed was everyone else.

"Let's get some food," said Tommy, levering himself out of his chair.

"No-one will take our places." He led the way towards the stalls. "What would you like, something tasty? I can thoroughly recommend the Malaysian curry."

Assuming agreement, Tommy made a bee-line for a stall which, by the number of people pressed around it, was obviously very popular. Asprey followed thoughtfully. The girls had been quite strikingly beautiful, but the entertainment had been confined to goggling and banter. Yet to be fair, the Singaporians were not given to lasciverous oggling as were their western counterparts. Striptease yes, but undressing in a public place – definitely not. So what was the interest? Were the girls returning? Asprey looked round for a clue but could see none. The noise – a babble of laughter and voices continued unabated.

Tommy had achieved his objective. He turned to face Asprey with a plate in each hand and offered that in his left. It was covered with pieces of steaming meat sliding about in a thin brown sauce. As he took the plate by its edge, Charles included with his thanks the question: "Are they returning?"

"Good lord, no," replied Tommy. "That's it."

"But don't they perform – or do something?" persisted Charles.

Tommy sat down and grinned at the Englishman. "They have a show in town, but the food and drink here is much better and we can see them here face to face. But if you really want to go?"

Charles quickly interrupted him: "Oh, No. No. Since we've seen them and that's what we came to do, there's no point in repeating the experience."

Tommy looked over his plate at Charles. "On his last visit here, your friend George brought his wife. She insisted on doing the show rather than the street. In their last act they strip in unison – completely. We had to carry George's wife out."

Charles looked incredulous. He knew the lady in question and they didn't come any tougher.

"What on earth upset her?"

"The 'girls' were all men!"

Chapter Four

Money and Intelligence

Asprey enjoyed a love hate relationship with what is generally termed as the City. As an entrepreneur he tended to do his own thing and to rely on no-one. That of itself was anathema to the bowler hatted gentry. But to add a poorly disguised prejudice in economic and financial theories which were unfashionable was to attract a hearty dislike. However, the City was nothing if not realistic. Its purpose in life was to make money. As long as Asprey was reasonably successful and created wealth either directly or indirectly for those who supported him, it was prepared to indulge him in his idiosyncrasies. Should his star start to fall, then it would be an entirely different matter. His continued success or inevitable failure would give rise to almost equal satisfaction. On balance, the former was to be preferred, since it might not last over long.

As the opportunities represented by Asprey increased in size and profit, one City introduction led to another. Such a chance sequence resulted in a meeting between the entrepreneur and an equally young rising star in the stock-broking firmament, one Sandy Gilmour.

Sandy, even at an early age, was a senior partner in one of the largest firms in London. He was the very epitome of an English "Someone in the City". There was a second nationality that could and often did "make it" in that confined space. These were the alternative to Eton, Cambridge and the Guards. Gents who had made their way from some vague mid-European origins, travelling upon an accent that smacked not a little of Maurice Chevallier with inferences of Heidelberg and/or Versailles. Sandy's firm was a force to be reckoned with since it combined both happy breeds and could therefore open almost any door that really mattered in the field of finance. It seemed natural enough that when Rossi was introduced to Asprey that, having carefully considered his requirements, Charles should in turn take him to Sandy.

Basil Rossi was large, florid and Australian. Unlike the generally accepted image of those of his origins, he was softly spoken with only a trace of an Antipodean accent.

His slow and deliberate movements belied his intensity and dedication to work. Travelling thousands of miles each week was a necessary investment in his business and raised no more comment than that of the average British commuter when speaking of his daily sardine act. The concept of a daily exchange by air of Australian beef for Malaysian fruit and vegetables seemed no more out of the ordinary than the collection and distribution of similar products from Smithfield and Covent Garden.

He was also a man of vision with the extraordinary capacity of being able to spread his enthusiasm like a contagious disease. Those who came into contact with him found it impossible to resist his infectious confidence in untried and unproven ventures, a confidence that Rossi consolidated with the solid assurance of personal commitment. It was therefore not at all surprising to discover that, almost single-handed, he had persuaded leaders of Malaysian commerce and industry that he could introduce and develop profitable new industries in their country.

By the time he met with Asprey, Rossi had become frustrated almost to the point of desperation. He had two needs for finance. The first was the creation and expansion of companies that would complement his activities in Malaysia. That country had become famous for its exports of hardwood. Rossi had recognised that rather than selling the timber as such, the Malaysians would benefit greatly if they could add value to their exports through conversion into semi-finished products. To be successful, he had to set up complementary organisations in or near their ultimate markets for the assembly and final finishing operations as well as the distribution and marketing. To him the opportunity was gilt-edged. He did not anticipate and could not understand the resistance and lack of interest in that which he now offered. His opinion of London as the world's centre of venture capital was as low as that which he publicly voiced on the English qualities as cricketers. It may well be that he had kept his views on that matter more to himself during his perambulations in the square mile, he might have enjoyed some success in achieving his objective. Possibly, but not likely.

The meeting of the two entrepreneurs took place in Bristol – the established home of merchant venturers. The financial centre of that city is unique in the British Isles. It flourishes without any real Jewish influence. It jealously guards the wealth that its forefathers made in the ruthless trades of bodies and drugs – slavery, spirits and tobacco. It maintained its anonimity and avoidance of moral responsibility by keeping it commodities out of sight and thus out of mind.

Despite these obvious attractions and the possibility that Rossi's plan could well find a sympathetic audience, Asprey felt that having considered his proposals a final approach should be made to the sanctum sanctorum of money and that, in particular, Sandy Gilmour would be the ideal person to translate the problem into an opportunity. At that stage Asprey was unaware of the one element in the proposition that would have caused him to proffer different advice. As it was, it seemed to him that the sum of money required was reasonably significant and it could best be obtained through a consortium of private individuals based in London.

Asprey's assumptions proved correct. Gilmour was intrigued with Rossi's proposals and undertook to find the required finance. At that stage, Asprey bowed out leaving the two men to translate their agreement into fact.

Nearly twelve months had passed since he had even thought of the Malaysian venture. August had almost slipped away and the sun on one of its rare visits that summer to London was already clearly indicating by its desire to disappear far too early in the evening that autumn was anxious to take over. It was just hovering over the tops of the trees as Charles walked down Park Lane.

He had long developed the ability to identify two types of London pedestrians. The first were English and the second "the Others".

The former detested physical contact, especially with strangers, and their passage would have qualified them as rugby threequarters at the highest level of the game – even Cardiff Arms Park. They side-stepped oncoming opponents whether of their own category or of "the Others" with split second timing. The latter had no such inhibitions. For them physical contact was more than acceptable – it was to be enjoyed – particularly with ladies (the cads). Collisions could become acceptable as unavoidable excuses for manual support. The English insisted upon an untouchable cocoon of air with the radar reaction of bats to pre-empt the undesirable.

As an expert exponent of the art of physical avoidance, Asprey achieved his isolation automatically, with no conscious thought. Consequently he could and often did make his way unaware of those he met and passed on the pavement, being accused thereafter of ignorance, bad manners or an over-inflated ego. When so challenged, being usually unaware of his assumed transgression, he simply confined himself to abject apologies. The excuse of having his mind elsewhere had long been recognised as totally unconvincing. It was the perversity of human nature that having so apologised, the accuser inevitably assumed that he had in fact been thinking of other things so that that which would have been unacceptable as an excuse was readily offered gratuitously in his defence.

Whatever the normal state of affairs, it was a practical impossibility even for Asprey on the teeming pavements of London W1 to pass Rossi and remain oblivious of his presence. Their eyes met, widened in disbelief then smiled in welcome. Both men stopped, to the consternation of those immediately behind each. Rossi held out his hand.

"Well, well, Dr. Asprey I presume?"

Charles responded with an equally unoriginal greeting. "Hello, sport. What are you doing here and not in Malaysia?"

"It's a long story. Can you spare the time?"

"Surely," replied Asprey. "Let's pop in there for a drink and exchange news in comfort."

"There" was the Grosvenor House Hotel, outside whose entrance they had almost made physical contact.

Except for four Arabs, wedged like striped bolsters under and around one table, the lounge was empty of customers. Faced with such a wide choice of location, Asprey and Rossi chose the corner furthest from the entrance and settled themselves into large armchairs.

"How much do you know of the outcome of my meetings with Sandy?" asked Rossi.

"For all practical purposes, nothing," replied Charles.

"Right, so I will start at the beginning. You know I made a presentation to Sandy. Well, that was unsuccessful. Whilst he understood and appreciated what I could do, since I had no track record in Europe there had to be something unique, exciting, glamourous or whatever to encourage real venture finance. That which I had was interesting etc., but no more. You will recall that I had a mixture of businesses under one umbrella, Consolidated Industrial Holdings, and these consisted of hydrophonics, garden buildings, oil reclamation and salvage. If one could add a little spice then it might be different. As it was, sorry. It was my last shot and I was more than desperate. So I took Sandy completely into my confidence. I told him of the true potential of the salvage rights that C.I.H. had to all the wrecks in Malaysian waters, including a mysterious and unacknowledged German U-Boat. That did interest him. He wanted more details than I could give him, so we agreed that we would engage two investigators, two men called Davis and Foster, to find out more about the U-Boat and its contents. By good fortune and using Sandy's contacts at the British Admiralty, they confirmed that the U-Boat would be extremely valuable if carefully salvaged – and that became the raison d'entre for the fund raising."

"So what was the essence of their report to you?"

"U-134 had been specially fitted out in Bremen in late 1944. All its armaments had been removed, including torpedos, and it was equipped with the latest diesels and underwater running gear. Early in 1945 it had been re-commissioned with a completely new crew whose number we don't know for certain but we believe was much smaller than the normal complement for a boat of that size, even allowing for the lack of gunnery crew. We don't know the exact date of departure from Germany or even the port, but working on the supposition that it made a bee-line for its ultimate grave it must have been about the day that the Russians entered the bunker in Berlin. We do know that the U-Boat had four or even five passengers but we have no positive identification of them. Finally we know that it carried an extremely valuable cargo but again we can only guess at what that is . . . and so far that is literally anyone's guess."

"But," queried Asprey, "you must also know for certain the condition of the wreck, the probability of its being successfully salvaged and therefore whether you can get at its contents."

"True," replied Rossi, "because we had been down and had a really good look at it. But there was something else which we didn't understand, yet it must have been important because of the attitude of the Germans."

"What's that?"

"We had been warned that we had to lift the U-Boat in one piece. That we could not enter the vessel whilst it was still submerged and in no circumstances should it be allowed to break up either before raising it or during the operation. The Germans insisted that they must have an official standing by to ensure that we would comply with those conditions and furthermore, that they would reserve the right to stop the salvage at any stage if they felt there was any possibility we couldn't carry out our undertaking. Finally that they would supervise the entry into the sub and remove bodies and all contents other than the cargo before we would be allowed to get inside.

"The last requirement presented no problem because the boat was obviously a war grave and the Germans were more than entitled to bury their dead as they wish. Nevertheless their firmness seemed to go beyond the interests of sanctity, but we were not worried on that score. Whatever the value of its, shall we say, general contents, the fact that seemed incontrovertible was that we had been given confirmation that the cargo itself was virtually priceless."

Asprey summed up. "So, the facts seemed to add up to that some high ranking Nazis, realising that the war was coming to a disastrous end, had made preparations for a last minute get-away, taking their ill-gotten booty with them on a fast one way trip to their last haven, apparently, Japan. But on second thoughts that destination doesn't make sense. If they were high ranking, and they must have been to be able to arrange such an exit, they would have known about the atomic bomb, its probable use in Japan and therefore that that ally would at best be only a temporary respite from their conquerors and at worst a potential death-trap. So why not the favourite, South America, nearer across the Atlantic and for many reasons much more attractive both in the short and the long runs? But why Japan? Perhaps it never intended to go there. Perhaps it was en route to somewhere else, but where?"

Rossi was not really interested in that line of speculation. Yet he didn't want to appear rude at the critical juncture. He needed finance. Asprey could be useful once again. So he gently tested the logic. "The most important thing is that we and only we know exactly where U-134 lies and only we have the right to get it up."

"True," said Asprey, "so why haven't you done just that?"

"We didn't even get started. No, that's not quite true. Having obtained the reports through Davis and Foster, confirmation from the British and German Admiralties, Sandy had no difficulty in raising enough money to charter a salvage ship in Rotterdam and providing the funds for its use in Malaysia. The attitude of the lenders was quite simple.

"If the venture was as good as it was made out to be, they would support it. Out of its share C.I.H. would have more than enough to finance its own commercial and industrial enterprises. So the money was raised entirely for the salvage of U-134."

"Our vessel left Rotterdam for Malaysia. En route the captain called in for supplies at a friendly West African port, but generated some personal problems which resulted in his acceptance as an unwilling guest of lodgings for an indeterminate period. In short, they threw him into the local caboose. There he stayed and no-one thought fit to tell us. The local authorities were encouraged in their silence by the fact that the port had an interesting scale of escalating dues and costs for ships tied up to their quays. The longer the captain enjoyed their hospitality the greater his bill. By the time we became aware of what was going on the sums involved were enormous, so much so that in the end we had to pay off the charter and cut our losses. Our venture died thousands of miles and pounds sterling away from its intended destination. Its most significant lift was that of the captain's elbow. So, here I am, ready, eager and willing to go again. Are you interested?"

Asprey had had no difficulty in anticipating the question. "Yes, but on one condition."

"Name it."

"I have complete control not only of the fund raising, but also of the project itself."

"Agreed. So where do we go from here?"

"Firstly Germany, then Singapore," Asprey replied after a brief pause.

"Why?"

"Before we can even contemplate starting again, we must first be absolutely certain that we have the full support of the German Admiralty, whether that is overt or unofficial. We cannot afford to have them against us. They could even be competitors for the salvage rights.

"Then we must have new money and I would much prefer to have that available to us from a source that is near but not too near to where it will be used. It must be near enough to be able to exert some political influence but far away enough to be independant of local politics. I believe that such a place is Singapore. I also know some interesting people there."

"Fine," said Rossi. "No problem with any of that. And you

would be prepared to mastermind the whole thing from start to its profitable finish?"

"Yes, as I said that is the only way in which I would accept involvement. I must be the leader."

"Good, good." Rossi looked and sounded very pleased. "I'll drink to that – better still we will both drink to that." As he spoke he raised his hand and triggered the take-off of the waiter hovering near the entrance to the bar adjoining the lobby. "What would you like, if it's not too early?"

Asprey hesitated, but only as to choice and not the hour. "In the circumstances a launching glass would seem appropriate. We'll leave the celebrations to when we have completed the course. A Campari soda, please."

Rossi added his request for a large gin and tonic and the waiter wheeled about to return to his base.

"Why do you lay so much emphasis on the co-operation of the German Admiralty? We had to drag it out of them last time," commented Rossi.

"Very simply because if they say no to you they will undoubtedly convey that decision to the Malaysians who would take note of their reaction and restrict your licence to exclude the sub. They would not wish to upset the Germans and would only regard you as being greedy."

"As a matter of fact that is exactly what the Germans are," countered Rossi. "Their agreement also contained the right to 50 per cent of the net proceeds. When Foster and Davis reported to me in K.L., they made it clear that the Germans wanted everything to be done their way. That was reasonable enough. Then they blackmailed us for half the profits!"

"But you agreed."

"We had no choice. I asked Davis and Foster to see if there could be some give and take and to call at Frankfurt on their way back to England, just in case. They obviously had no joy as we heard nothing from them at all. As a matter of fact I have been trying to trace them whilst I have been back this time in London, as I thought one approach might have been to get them to return to the Germans and see if they would be prepared to help more positively second time round. Fortunately, we met instead, so there's no need. Still, it might be useful if we could look them up, but they simply seem to have disappeared. No-one knows whether they even got back here from K.L.! Curious, but," with a shrug of his shoulders, "we don't need them anymore."

"They were also the ones who obtained confirmation from the British Admiralty that at the right time and place a British Sub had logged the sinking of an unidentified U-Boat which in turn ultimately forced the Germans to admit to the existence of U-134?"

"Yes, in fact they probably knew more than any of us about the whole affair. I felt that they were keeping something back so that they could earn a little more than their fees."

"Perhaps they did."

Rossi looked sharply at Asprey but could gain nothing from the latter's expression, which was one of thoughtful concentration. His next comment was equally unhelpful.

"This might be the missing link. To know the end is to be able to see the beginning."

Basil shrugged. If the Englishman wanted to make clever remarks then he was quite prepared to indulge him as long as it did not waste valuable time.

"Maybe, but first you should read their reports. Those with your own knowledge should give you a pretty fair summary of the whole story, at least so far. If you will let me have your London address I will have them delivered to you this evening."

Charles agreed. "O.K., if you can let me have them as early as possible I can then get on the telephone tomorrow and arrange to meet anyone that might still be helpful here before we leave for Frankfurt."

Basil stood up. "It will be done. Give me a ring when you're ready to go to Germany and I will arrange the flights." He held out his hand. "Perhaps fate decided that we should meet again and is saying that my luck has changed."

Asprey grimaced, partially from Basil's tight grip and partly at the possible irony. "Let's hope so. Will be in touch."

Rossi was as good as his word. Charles had the reports as

he had been promised. They were four in number and very well cross-indexed. The first covered the initial briefing of Davis and Foster and included copies of all Rossi's original notes. The second detailed their meetings in London, and Frankfurt concerned with the identification of the U-Boat and its possible contents, including a Commander McGregor of British Naval Intelligence at a Whitehall address and a Herr Eisendorf who was in the German Admiralty in Frankfurt. The latter's role seemed identical to that of the British sailor's. The third summarised their efforts in Kuala Lumpur and the last was incomplete. It appeared to be an attempt to piece together information gathered from unscheduled meetings and anonymous conversations.

By the time he had absorbed their contents it was early morning. Nevertheless he did not call it a day until he had completed the list of those he wanted to see in London. It started with the merchant banker and the naval commander.

*   *   *   *   *   *   *

Getting to know "the City" is rather like peeling an onion. As each layer is removed, a smoother harder skin is discovered. To pursue the process to the bitter end is to encounter a strong odour and the possibility of discomfort. A happy breed to be found almost in the centre of the vegetable is that of the merchant banker, whose texture of skin is entirely commensurate with his position in the scheme of things. Whenever there is a need for a consortium to provide finance, there is a merchant banker. He is an essential endorser of uncertain ventures and recompensed for his occasional risk by involvement by invitation in those far more numerous gilt-edged opportunities to which he lends his name. His price is high.

Charles Asprey knew that Robert Fitzpaine had been the city catalyst in putting together the money required by Basil Rossi and that before accepting that role he would undoubtedly have conducted a very thorough investigation into the proposition. Had there been any warts, visible or invisible, he would have found them. So Charles decided that a meeting

63

with Bobby, as he was universally known, could only be a positive investment of his limited time. A telephone call to Bobby's secretary resulted in a 3.00 p.m. appointment, late enough to allow for the usual business lunch and early enough to avoid an impediment in the plans for any evening social commitment.

It was a Wednesday, still in August and the weather was warm and sticky. London is not an attractive excursion when there are alternatives, but when it comes to questions of business and money, there is no choice. The mountain must be visited. So the occasional supplicant is encouraged to fill his day with as many meetings as he can and thereby reduce the number of forays into such uncomfortable surroundings. This can best be achieved by judicious use of the Underground.

The Tube, as it is usually called by the locals, is a world all of its own. Dirty, dark and germ laden, at peak periods it is populated by robots who have taken over human beings. They avoid eye contact, speech and most natural functions. Long accustomed to unexplained delays, these travellers close their minds and concentrate on anything other than their immediate surroundings. Even problems are more attractive points of focus than the carriages and their occupants.

Throughout the summer holidays, this unwelcoming world is invaded by hordes of school children, oblivious to the attitude of its inhabitants. They are bent upon exploration in much the same way as they would pass through a zoo or the chamber of horrors at Madam Tussauds. As Charles sat on his torn seat on the Inner Circle train, brief case safely tucked under his long legs, he felt swamped by the incessant vitality of a gaggle of children detached by the length of the carriage from their two teachers who clearly had no intention even of acknowledging their responsibilities, let alone applying discipline. To look at, the kids were a multi-coloured, polyethnic cross section of nationalities from every deprived corner of the globe. Yet if he closed his eyes, the aural image bore no relationship to that which he thought he had seen. "Please, Miss, t'aint arf 'ot (hoots of laughter), cor blimey where the bleeder are we? My plates of meat aint arf killing me," and much more in the same vein. To the listener, phrases and mode of speech synonymous with the Lambeth Way and the Old Kent Road, but in this instance the genuine article. Asprey became lost in his own thoughts. A radio interview cannot be colour conscious. Speech becomes the divider of class and location. Vision is the weapon of the politician. The visual image eliminates the pleasure of private imagination. It is thrust into the viewer's eyes. So to look at the children was to confirm the impossible. They were the modern Britain, the English of tomorrow, as potentially pure a combination as that of the Anglos, Saxons and Danes. Luckily for him, his conclusion arrived simultaneously with the platform of his destination. He pulled out his brief case and propelled himself between the opened doors.

As Asprey emerged from the Tube, he felt as if he had been an unwelcome guest at a party promoting Smarties, over-whelmed by cascades of colours and sound. The change in scenery was hardly for the better. Cannon Street mid-weekday afternoon is also full of noise but adds a physical dimension – dust. Ears are blasted by a constant stream of traffic and eyes making the mistake of looking skywards are quickly filled with grit. Pedestrians are numbed by the one and desperately avoid the other by keeping their heads and eyelids lowered. Since Charles was looking for a building of which he had only the address, he was forced to compromise and risk the painful consequences of gazing around.

The numbers 39/47 affixed to the first building indicated that he was on the side of the street that boasted odd num-bers. That was progress. But the next edifice was apparently known as number 51. So, where was 49? The answer was by no means obvious and required a certain devious logic for its identification. Letterheads need to be impressive both as to layout and location. Certain thoroughfares are universally recognised as the centres of specialist services. Addresses therein confirm respectability and competence. In somewhat similar conditions, when some squares and streets were re-garded as fashionable in the West End of London, it was discovered that main entrances to property lurking in minor roads could masquerade as side entrances for a more prestigious but fictitious number in the superior street. That there was no such door was irrelevant since an entrance a few yards off the main stream is no real inconvenience and quite overwhelmed by the advantages to be gained. The City is not above adopting tricks from the trades of others if they have proven to be beneficial.

Having applied his mind to the task, Asprey soon found the address he sought. The entrance to the building was not impressive. Yet it seemed to attract throngs of people vying with each other to enter or to exit. Charles instinctively avoided the revolving doors which swallowed and spat out individuals at an alarming rate. Their speed of deposit upon the pavement was obviously greater than their normal pace of walking so that they gave the impression of having left a fast moving escalator at right angles to their intended path. Synchronisation had to be the secret of a successful entrance or exit. So Asprey entered by the side door, with safety and dignity – just like a tradesman. Not knowing the floor number he looked about for the usual indicator board and made his way towards the bank of lifts.

As he crossed the entrance lobby he was struck by the apparent lack of any correlation between expense and use. The annual rent of the floor space must have been astronomic. The building itself dwarfed its older brethren within a radius of at least two hundred yards which in the City of London represented a vast area of land. Whatever the business of its tenants, the landlord would want his pound of flesh and that in E.C.2 was a unique measurement of weight. Nowhere else in the world could space command the level of prices set and paid in the golden square mile. Furthermore, no number of Portias could deny the rights of the lessors had they the necessity to recourse to judgment.

Business conducted in such premises had to be highly profitable. There was no connection between effort and return. The object of the exercise was simply to make as much money as was possible in as short a time as was practicable. A monument to the ideal example translating principle into practice was to be found in one highly respected City boardroom in the shape of a fine glass goblet engraved by Whistler commemorating a deal which had taken about three minutes and had realised for the benefit of those whom the board represented some five million pounds sterling as a result of government bond placing. Truly it was not a question of what but of who you know. Conform, do that which is right and one day you too will do a deal, my son. After all, the corner-stone of banking is nepotism.

The lift deposited Asprey on the top floor but one. The final rung in the ladder of success was exemplified by a small very private transfer lift that shuttled between the landing upon which he had arrived and the inner sanctum, the collection of offices and luncheon rooms located in the penthouse. Invitation there was restricted to those who had made it and those to be made. The rest had to make do with the rest of the floors identified on the main entrance indicator board.

Charles had no such invitation so he sought Fitzpaine's office – or rather Bobby's secretary, who had been patiently waiting for him and led the way cheerfully and efficiently to that abode.

Bobby did not bother to stand up when Charles was ushered into his room. It was not a question of bad manners or class. It simply was not expected of him. They had met on several occasions before and hand-shaking was a practice not to be encouraged.

Bobby Fitzpaine was a chief in his tribe. He shouldered the risks created by the slings and arrows of outrageous fortune – and made his own. His was the gentle pursuit of wealth at the expense of others.

Bobby's physical appearance was the very epitome of his profession. He was slim almost gaunt and definitely languid. Dressed expensively but not too carefully. Blue and white striped shirt with white collar and cuffs. Grey suit and hand made grey shoes. His most critical feature was the length of his trousers. Too high and he became a clerk. Too long and he developed bags, the wrong kind of course. In all respects there had to be a fine balance between the best and the casual. It had to be an attire that did not give the impression that it had but recently been assembled. The tie was slightly untidy – the mauve handkerchief in imminent danger of being lost out of the top pocket.

The total image was one of an inevitable acceptance of wealth and influence, enough to remove the necessity for anything less than absolute integrity and sufficient to eliminate the pressure of having to accept unwelcome business. Bobby was one born to and with it. He could afford to turn away anything that others might attempt to thrust upon him.

"Nice to see you, Charles. How does it go?"

Asprey relaxed in his chair. When in Rome...

"Better than I deserve – and with you?"

"Mustn't grumble. Still earning the old crust."

"So I see," smiled Asprey, "any left over for the birds?"

Bobby looked sharply at him. Several years earlier they had bumped into each other in a dimly lit West End eating club. Their surprise and discomfort had been mutual. Neither had been accompanied by their respective spouses.

Charles kept a very straight face. There was no merit in trying to score points. Bobby came to the same conclusion and ignored the comment. Instead he asked: "To what do I owe this unexpected pleasure?"

"You will recall Basil Rossi?" Bobby responded immediately. "Do I not?"

"Well, I met him a few days ago here in London and he wants to have a second try."

Bobby laughed drily. "I wish him all the luck, but before you ask, the answer is No. I lost enough the first time, not only in money but in reputation. I introduced him to some of my friends and one day I will have to cover their losses."

Asprey decided not to comment on the extent of a friendship that required both guarantee and underwriting. "No, Bobby, the purpose of my call is not to persuade you to jump in again but just to make sure that you have had no reason to change your opinion as to the potential of the original proposition. Also of course to make you aware of what is going on so that afterwards you will not feel that you were deliberately excluded."

Bobby chuckled. He misunderstood Asprey in so far as to believe that despite his protestation Charles was still attempting to get him to invest again, the implied threat being "you'll be sorry".

"If this time Basil succeeds and raises a few million pounds worth of treasure, I will be the first to drink to his health – and indeed yours. Frankly you'll need more than a little luck and of one thing you may be certain, there's no way you'll be able to raise any money in London."

Asprey took it as a statement of fact rather than a threat. Bobby's sensibilities may well have been upset, but his personal wealth was such that the reimbursement of his friends would not cause him more than a temporary embarrassment.

"No, I appreciate that. We shall have to look elsewhere. But there's one question I would like to ask you before I leave you in peace."

Sandy waved a hand to indicate his agreement. Charles continued.

"Can I take it that you remain quite convinced that the U-Boat does exist, that it does contain treasure or whatever of considerable value, despite your experience?"

Bobby looked deliberately as Asprey. "As far as I am concerned, it's definitely there and definitely worth the getting – but I don't think Basil will succeed. He's honest, enthusiastic and energetic but he hasn't enough pull in the Far East and that he must have second time around." He looked at his watch. "I missed lunch today. What about joining me for a cup of tea and a plate of toast at the club. I must tell you about last night. It'll lighten your day, if nothing else."

Charles didn't object. He had no further meetings that day and Bobby was still someone to be cultivated. So they left the metal and glass box together, hailed a cab and directed the driver to White's of St. James.

It was the first, in fact the only time that Charles gained admittance through that august anonymous portal. Its members regarded the club as the most exclusive and therefore the most prestigious of its kind – anywhere. Applications for membership had to be supported by pedigrees that made those issued by the Jockey and Kennel clubs seem like short form birth certificates. It was not sufficient to be related to or proposed by the right people. It was vital not to be or have been even remotely associated with the wrong people. It was a reference in two dimensions. The first being obvious and therefore casually accepted as a matter of course. One just had to be a wholesome twig on a carefully selected and pruned tree. The second dimension was the minefield that not infrequently ejected black balls into the ballot box – that ignominious and unkindest cut of all, the root cause of the fateful cry, "out, out – black spot".

Many famous names, acceptable at the first hurdle, had had to be withdrawn, most in humane silence, some under the harsh light of gossip columnists, on the grounds of an un-washed connection, thereafter to be lost for ever in the halls of less favoured establishments with lower hypocritical standards.

But Bobby had been accepted, indeed welcomed, following in his father's footsteps who also followed his dear old dad.

The tea was pleasantly brewed, hot and presented in the best that came out of Stoke-on-Trent. The toast was an acceptable advance on that experienced in school studies, a feat hardly difficult to achieve. Even the stewards were aged versions of the college servants. The whole being an extra-polation of the past into the present to ensure the future. But Bobby was just itching to tell his tale and Charles was by no means averse to its telling.

"You must think that a merchant banker's life is pretty easy."

Asprey looked around the hallowed room. "Well, I must admit that there are times..."

"Absolutely," responded Bobby, glad of the opening, "there are times. I missed lunch today as I was still feeling the effects of a call of duty last night. Yesterday evening I had the chore of entertaining a large – in the account sense, you understand – American client. He is short and fat. What I

70

believe they call stubby. With a Christian name of Earl. He makes his money in candy. He was staying at the Carlton Tower and had invited me to join him for dinner in the Chelsea room. I must say the food was very good. Unfortunately the choice of wine was limited as he insisted on staying with the hard stuff. He made some amends by ordering an excellent brandy to go with our coffees, but suddenly excused himself and left me sitting there like a lemon. Naturally I thought that it was simply an unexpected call of nature but after about half an hour that seemed a little unlikely. I had just decided to pack it in when I was paged to take a house telephone call. Who should be at the other end but my client, Earl."

Bobby then produced a very fair imitation of an American drawl. Characterisation and mimicry inevitably enhance a good story and Bobby was doing more than a fair job of both. "Hi, Bobby, sorry to have kept you waiting. Time really does fly when you're enjoying yourself. Come on up to the suite, 617. I have a little surprise for you." Well, as I said he was and is a big client. I went up. The door was open, so I knocked and walked in. There waiting for me in the middle of the drawing room was a long-legged blond holding out a glass of bubbly. Quite a sight. As I took it – the glass of course – Earl's voice came out of what was clearly one of the bedrooms. "Is that you, Bobby? Meet Christine. She has something for you with my compliments." I had the distinct feeling that Earl was referring to more than the bubbly. So I shouted back: "That's very kind of you." He must have guessed that I was being deliberately ambiguous and relying upon a charade in absentia, because the next moment he came out of the bedroom wearing one of the most tasteless bathrobes I have ever seen. "Now you know what I mean, Bobby. There's a second bedroom there. Why don't you make use of it?" Well, she was beautiful and if I did have any trouble with my conscience then the size of his account and my responsibilities to the firm provided a reasonable salving mixture. I had been with her about half an hour when his voice interrupted again. "Bobby, are you going to take all night? The idea is we exchange and

71

I'm well and truly ready." Well, what I hadn't bargained for was that he had not two but three young ladies. I looked up and there he was framed in the doorway, still wearing his garish garb, but this time with one on each arm. "Are you left or right-handed Bobby?" he asked. "Which one would you like first?" By then, my conscience was beginning to twitch, but I quelled it again though with some misgiving. So I took the one on his left as I assumed he was right-handed. He had a lead on me which should have given me something in hand – if you will excuse the implication. Now I am sure you will guess what happened next.

About half an hour later, there he was again. "Two down and one to go, Bobby." Well, I had always believed that if not a man of the world at least I was a man about Town but it had gone beyond a joke. There is, after all a limit – if not to decency then to physical capability. Besides it was getting late. His account might well be of a size as to cause incredulity and greed and he might be similarly endowed in other directions, but yours truly had had enough. Give Earl his due, he was not slow in sizing up the situation and I mean sizing it up. "I know exactly what you need, Bobby." With that he picked up the telephone and ordered four very large brandies in balloon glasses – "right away".

Now we had three ladies and two gentlemen so unless one of the ladies was teetotal, Earl's arithmetic was slightly adrift. Either seemed unlikely and I was not wrong. After the waiter had delivered his wares and departed, Earl handed me one of the glasses and took one for himself. "Bottoms up," he said. Whilst he did not down it in one gulp, his adam's apple only moved about three times. I endeavoured to emulate him. T'was very good and I must admit I felt quite a bit better, but still determined to get away at the first decent opportunity. But it wasn't going to be that easy. Earl wiped his mouth with the back of his hand then handed me the third glass of brandy, picking up the last again for himself. My immediate reaction was to think, my God if I drink all this then there will be no question of any great expectations or Oliver Twist, it will simply be curtains. Earl must have seen the look in my eyes.

"Gee, Bobby, I'm not expecting you to drink that as well. This is an old Chinese remedy. Surely you must have heard of it?" I have to admit that I just stood there and looked completely blank. So Earl continued my edification and uplift. "Just dip your little end in this and boy, you're right back in business."

"Well, we learn something every day and I must admit that last night my education was, shall we say, extended."

Charles felt that the story merited a more detailed ending but he had a feeling that any request with that in mind would fall on stoney ground. As he sat pondering his reaction, a head and a voice suddenly appeared above the back of a deep leather armchair situated behind Bobby. "I say, Bobby, I knew you spent some of your evenings on the tiles but it sounded as if you jolly well nearly fell into the guttering. There's a limit to what a chap has to do in the call of duty even for the unselfish benefit of his colleagues." The voice and the features bore a distinct resemblance to Bobby's.

"Only a politician would have the gall to listen and the nerve to pontificate and then to top the lot with such a corny comment." Bobby turned to Asprey. "Charles, you've not met my brother Michael, though you might have seen him on the box or even reported upon in the news-sheets. In the old days we always sent the weakest member of the family into the church. Nowadays, he is ideally qualified for the Party. Michael would have made an excellent Archbishop. Not so sure about P.M., but you never know. The most unlikely people seem to get that job."

Michael winked at Bobby and disappeared behind the chair back. Charles suddenly felt rather like Alice. It was a tea-party of sorts. Equally unreal in a world all on its own, where time and relationships responded to rules long established, nonsensible to the temporary guest but abundantly clear to the permanent participants. There was no half-way house. You either joined the game, or like Alice you went on your way as soon as you decently could. So Asprey did just that.

*　　*　　*　　*　　*　　*　　*

73

"Commander McGregor will see you now."

Charles Asprey responded to the Wren officer's invitation, stood up and marched through the doorway which she had opened for him. As he passed her, he wondered why he had yet to meet an attractive member of her occupation and class. Ordinary ratings, sometimes pert, often pretty, but officers? Well, he found then rather frightening. He had gained the impression that activity in bed with them would be punctuated by shrill whistle blasts and he would have to respond, if not by numbers then by a specified sequence of movements each to be held for a satisfactory period of time. Come along side and be berthed – distress flags completely ignored and everyman expected to...

Asprey was brought to an abrupt halt in his mental meanderings by a sudden impediment to his physical progress. He had walked into a desk at which a dark haired man was seated, looking at him in cold amazement over the top of his gold-rimmed half spectacles.

"Er, Commander McGregor?" Asprey spluttered.

"Yes," meaning "Who else?"

"Er, thank you for seeing me."

"I am not short sighted. Would you please take a chair." The Commander indicated accommodation that looked distinctly uncomfortable. He was obviously worried that unless he made his intentions absolutely clear, Charles might decide to perch on the edge of his desk.

"Now, what can I do for you?"

Charles positioned himself carefully and placed his brief case on the floor beside him. His eyes were temporarily dazzled by the bright green of the carpet. Possibly a colour to remind McGregor of his original calling, but more likely to discourage visitors from overstaying their welcome.

Three Christian names had been de rigeur when Commander C. A. M. McGregor had entered Dartmouth at the tender age of thirteen. Four would have been ostentatious and two quite inadequate, unless of course the second was St. J., or St. Something. As for hyphonated surnames, they had virtually disappeared after the last aristocratic intake in 1913,

74

known as the Exmouth term. Only landlubbers referred to years of entry. Navy men identified themselves as members of a named class, rather like the old fashioned steam engines of yesteryear.

But the Commander was very much a man of today, a professional sailor with deep set brown eyes that told nothing and thick beetled brows that in contrast could hoist gale signals. He had been in the administrative branch yet still seemed ill at ease behind a desk.

The brows had united over the eyes. McGregor was not noted for his patience and what little he possessed had become sorely strained. He thrust his torso forward, resplendent in gold braid and multi-coloured ribbons.

"Do I have to repeat my question?"

Charles hurriedly collected himself. "It's about U-134..."

"What about it?"

"My associates and I wish to raise it."

"I am fully aware of your hopes and your attempt to date." The tone of the Commander's voice clearly indicated that he was not impressed by Charles as a person or as a member of a salvage team. "So?" The single syllable was far from inviting.

"Well, we would like to make sure that we have all the available facts and that we have them correctly before re-approaching the German Admiralty for confirmation of their permission."

"I see," said the Commander, leaning back into his chair, "so probably the best idea would be for you to reel off the facts as you know them and for me to correct or confirm, where I can."

"Fine," Asprey was now concentrating on his task. "The extracts that we were given from the log of the British Submarine involved indicated that early one morning (Asprey just managed to restrain an idiotic urge to break into song) in May 1945 it torpedoed a U-Boat which it had sighted steaming on the surface in Malaysian waters. The U-Boat sank immediately after being hit so that there were no survivors and no wreckage to confirm its identity."

"Absolutely right," smiled McGregor, "and with that information your colleagues were able to get the German Admiralty to confirm that that U-Boat did exist, to offer its identity and ultimately their approval for its salvage. I can reconfirm the facts as you have just stated them."

"So far, so good," Asprey smiled in return, "but we still have a number of loose ends which could trip us up in Germany if they are left untied." The Commander stopped smiling and crossed his arms. "And they are?" he enquired softly.

"How did the British know it was a U-Boat?"

"That's easy enough, by the silhouette of its conning tower."

"Then knowing it was German and not Japanese, why sink it when hostilities were over? V.E.-Day had passed."

"We have a procedure for such circumstances which is internationally recognised. Whilst keeping ourselves protected we first signal such a vessel to heave to. The German might well be on its way to port to surrender or making a run for it. So we keep our armament trained. If he does not respond we fire a warning shot. If he then continues to ignore us we then sink him. Quite straightforward and universally understood."

Asprey interrupted. "But not, in this instance, followed through."

There was a long pause. The Commander looked over his spectacles at Asprey who calmly returned his stare. Eventually the Navy man spoke, quietly and clearly.

"No, it was not."

"I thought not," agreed Asprey, "there was no mention of such a procedure in the extracts from the log. So why not? Had the British submarine commander instructions to sink on sight?"

"It would appear so."

"Then," pursued Asprey, "it would also appear that the British sub. not only had intructions to sink that U-Boat, but knew pretty accurately the time and place, the when and where to intercept. To find a U-Boat by accident in Malysian waters would have been quite exceptional."

Asprey was now warming to his theme. "We believe that U-134 was one of a number of U-Boats that left Germany at about the same time bound for different destinations. Could it be that they were also intercepted and sunk?" The Commander was looking thoughtfully into space.

"What might or might not have happened to other enemy ships is not really relevant, Mr. Asprey. As I understand it your only concern is with U-134. I have confirmed to you that it was sunk on sight and you can draw your own conclusions from that if you wish, but whether they will help you in your negotiations with the Germans, well, that frankly I doubt."

Asprey frowned. "You mean that if the Germans became aware that their U-Boats had been intercepted they might begin to wonder how their plans had become known to their enemies when secrecy even amongst themselves had been of paramount importance?"

"Precisely, you will start a quite unnecessary hare that can only confuse your hunt."

"Mmm," Asprey pursed his lips. "Nevertheless I feel it is important that we should have as many of the facts as we can put together if only to be sure we don't unknowingly put our proverbial foot in it. So now we believe that U-134 was deliberately sunk, that to achieve that one of a very small number of top-ranking Nazis passed on to someone at the highest level in the British Admiralty or Intelligence enough information to ensure that some if not all of the U-Boats would not escape. No, further than that. That they would be destroyed." The Commander had followed the speculation. He interrupted, "Why at the highest level?"

"Because action was taken very rapidly and a damaging instruction issued which was obeyed without question – although it was virtually murder." Asprey suddenly changed course as a new thought struck him. "I wonder if I could see the British log?"

"Certainly not." The Commander's reaction was short and sharp. "We should not have given your colleagues extracts or sight of it in the first place."

"Well, that's your prerogative, of course," replied Asprey, "but someone in your organisation knew who provided the information in Germany and who his opposite number was here. But why sink the U-Boats? Why not just capture them? That should have been quite simple, especially in the case of U-134."

"But we were not to know that."

"Did you know the nature of their cargo?"

There was a pause. The Commander's eyes remained unfocussed. "Not for certain. We guessed the usual things, gold jewellery, etc."

"And people?"

"The same applied. We guessed."

"So someone here and in Germany wanted it all put away for good. Sunk quietly and without trace."

McGregor pushed his chair away from his desk. "I think we have had enough speculation for this morning. Unless you have some more facts that you would like to air, perhaps you would excuse me."

Asprey had no alternative. He picked up his brief case switching off the tape-recorder concealed in it, stood up and offered his hand to the Navy man.

"Thank you very much for your time, Commander. It has been a most interesting and rewarding meeting. Perhaps we could continue it on another occasion if I can uncover any more facts which could be of mutual interest."

"Perhaps," smiled McGregor, returning Asprey's handshake, "but I have a feeling that further facts as such will be even more difficult to raise than your famous U-Boat – and that's going to be quite a task. Anyway, good luck."

"Thanks," responded Charles, "you never know." It was a parting comment that could mean a lot or nothing. Both men were convinced it was the latter.

The Wren officer conducted Asprey to the outer door and unsmilingly wished him a good morning. There was no suggestion in her voice that she was doing other than closing the door behind him both physically and verbally.

She had hardly completed her manoeuvre before her intercom buzzed stridently, propelling her smartly into her boss's office. "Sir?" she asked.

McGregor was standing behind his desk, hands clasped

78

against his rear and legs wide apart. She knew it was his quarter-deck posture, that heavy weather was expected and everything had to be battened down. She braced herself for the instructions.

"Ask Adams to check out our Mr. Asprey thoroughly and urgently. Get me Swan on the phone. And Kelland-White, never again let a visitor bring his brief case into my office unless he is on our staff or known to me. Our friend tape-recorded our conversation and that I don't like at all. That's a prerogative, as he would say, entirely reserved for us. I want a typescript of our tape before you go tonight."

"Yes, Sir," the Wren officer looked more than disturbed. Her dominance had been threatened by error. "Sorry, Sir, it will not happen again."

The Commander made no reply but instead looked pointedly at his telephone. The response was as he intended, immediate. His phone rang. He picked up the receiver and pressed the scrambler button.

"Ah, Swan, just had an interesting visitor, a Mr. Charles Asprey. I'm having him checked out by Section Three. You might look through your records and see if any of your chaps have come across him. Real purpose of this call is that I thought you ought to know that he has cottoned on to the old link between M. and his counterpart in the Fatherland. I appreciate that both are dead but the channel is still open and very useful. How did he stumble across it? Well, you remember the gaggle of U-Boats that M. disposed of before V.J.? Asprey's trying to raise one of 'em. You better advise our end to lie low for a bit. If he makes even routine contact now he might expose the other end and that might be disagreeable. Right. Now I want someone reliable to go to Malaysia at short notice. It would be preferable if he has had some experience out there. I will make arrangements for his cover. It shouldn't be difficult because of Asprey's intentions. No, I agree. After all the trouble that was taken to put them down, it would be more than a pity if our sleeping dogs were not allowed to lie in peace."

There was then a long pause as McGregor listened intently.

"Excellent – that's agreed. There's too much at stake, both past and future. I'll report personally to the chief. You maintain our file. No, I don't think we need involve the other departments, but I may get over-ruled on that. Yes, I'll see to the log. T'was a pity that its significance was not understood, but you can't have it both ways. Yes, it should have been destroyed. Fine, see you tomorrow at Temple."

The Commander replaced the receiver and looked thoughtfully at nothing.

Abruptly he reached across for his diary. "Kelland-White," he called – he had decided he couldn't write and buzz at the same time – "get me extension one. I shall be out this afternoon and tomorrow."

He completed the entry and pushed the book back across the desk. The Commander's mind was obviously turning over his recent conversations. Without breaking his line of thought, he inserted his finger and thumb into a breast pocket and pulled out a gold toothpick. Again using only touch he removed its case and absently stuck the pick into his gum. "Damn."

Chapter Five

Power

Frankfurt-am-Main in the winter is far from attractive. In the absence of snow, the city is grey, the colour of industry and policemen. It is a utilitarian conurbation, a concrete representation of teutonic effort and power. It has very few features, being almost a deliberate faceless entity disguising its achievement and potential.

The brightly neon-lit shopping centres provided beacons of attraction supplemented by shop windows crammed with goods to satisfy any conceivable want. Frankfurt was really a city of contrasts. The old and the new, the Germanic and the Americana, the dull stone and the gleaming glass, summarised as the conservative and the garish. The city combined the qualities of the Germany that were universally recognised, portrayed and caricatured. It also contained the other face of a nation that was patiently biding its time.

Its common denominator was the God of power. Sometimes he was worshipped through wealth, sometimes through beauty and often through brute force. He was ideally personified by a mixture of all three attributes. It had long been acknowledged that power was given and not taken. That was well demonstrated in Frankfurt. Those who wished to join the ranks of those who wielded that weapon could do so only by invitation. The price of admission varied only as to the coin chosen. The cost was always high.

The airport conformed to the general impression given to the casual visitor, particularly in the rain that greeted Asprey's arrival. He squeezed into the rear seat of the first of the line of taxis patiently waiting in the dismal drizzle, thankful for its dry and warm interior. Now to brush up my German, he thought. Always the same problem, two or three days of stuttering nonsense, a mixture of French and the indigenous language, then without any warning the subconscious recovery of untranslated thought. He had never been able to fathom the idiotic tendency to think in French before translating into the intended German.

It wasn't as if he were at all fluent in the former, yet it remained his initial reaction to the challenge of making himself understood.

The instructions to the driver had been simple. Being an airport cabbie he was more than used to gibberish and sifting the only useful piece of information needed from amongst the foreigner's peculiar version of greeting and thanks.

Despite a fairly intimate knowledge of Frankfurt, dating back a few years after the end of the 1939/45 war, the only part in which Asprey felt at home was the old city. Even that with its memories of stern students had about as much warmth and welcome as the rebuilt Heidelberg.

The economic miracle of Germany's recovery in the early 1950's was still shrouded in secrecy as to its achievement, purpose and intent. Asprey knew that Western Germany had been structured with a determination to provide a springboard or at the very worst a bargaining counter for its merger with that part of Germany controlled by the Russians. The fact that it was based on survival and thereafter a return to European dominance provided a logical raison d'etre which was easily accepted by its neighbours and therefore gave them no cause for suspicion or enquiry that there might be any longer term objective. This singleness of purpose fuelled by fear and pride generated the irresistible force of a nation that was as potent as a nuclear reactor. And that was an accurate metaphor for the heart of Germany.

Charles arrived at his hotel – a modest, spartan and almost clinical establishment – above a furniture shop. Why waste valuable floor space in the provision of lobbies and waiting areas? Hilton had long ago led the way in designing hotels as hives of sleeping cells.

To gain entry he had to speak into the mesh of a microphone set in the wall beside the main entrance some six feet above the pavement. The implication was that the German race was tall enough on average not to be inconvenienced by such an arrangement. Asprey's German was quite adequate to obtain admittance.

Upon entry he found that the owner of the deep voice that guarded the outside door was the very antithesis of the mental image that his vocal chords generated. The hotel-keeper was small, slight and as bald as a billiard ball. Asprey's reaction was similar to that when he had first been introduced to an actor he had seen many times previously on the large and small screens – disappointment and egotistical improvement. He looked down at the smaller man, deepened his own voice and commanded attention. It worked. Despite his still atrocious mode of speech, nothing was impossible and everything necessary. At least he would enjoy his stay at the hotel.

He had arranged to meet Rossi that evening in the Brücken-keller, a restaurant rivalling Harveys of Bristol. As its name suggested, it was located in the cellars along the bank of the river Main in the centre of Frankfurt. The atmosphere of the cellars was almost romantic, with violins played by wandering musicians embarrassing diners by asking for requests which immediately occasioned complete mental black-outs, and then by standing within bow-shot of the pink faced customers and playing the inane tunes they had forcibly ejected. For the foreigner at least, any romanticism engendered by the small alcoves and low ceilings was completely overwhelmed by the absolute dominance of the food. It filled the plates, engulfed the tables and openly challenged the waiters as to their strength and balance.

The only persons apparently immune to its ubiquitous presence were the Frankfurters. They had one initial advantage. Almost without exception, whether male or female, they were large. As the overloaded trays staggered towards them, they gave no sign of any anxiety or the slightest suspicion of inadequacy. Each pile was thankfully thumped on to the table by its perspiring carrier and greeted with lustful enthusiasm. The only visible disappointment appeared when the column of bearers ceased and it became clear that the table groaned under an order completed. There was no more to come. But Frankfurters are nothing if not pragmatic. If that was all, then it would have to do until the next course when any material deficiency could be adequately compensated. So napkins were tucked into collars and bosoms and the one-sided battle commenced.

Asprey found their performance quite fascinating. If the way in which the Germans satisfied their physical desires was any guide to their approach to the achievement of national objectives then heaven help Europe yet again. Rossi enjoyed the whole atmosphere. He was certainly not dwarfed by his neighbours and if only through necessity in Malaysia of more than reasonable capacity as a trencherman. His natural intensity was already heightened by the exitement of their mission. He cast a cursory glance over the menu which occupied three foolscap pages, refolded it and placed it on the table. "My German is for all practical purposes and certainly for eating zero. I shall leave the ordering entirely to you. The only comment I would make is that I am hungry".

Asprey's knowledge of "menu-German" was not as extensive as he would have liked. Nevertheless he foolishly decided to take pot luck. He assumed that the prices indicated clearly quality and quantity and that as long as he steered a middle course, he would not get too much out of his depth.

In concentrating on the multi-syllable words, he omitted to notice the semaphor signals of the waiter's eyebrows as he took down his order. Failure to take note of the warnings proved a costly experience. The salvo of food when it arrived was more than enough to sink the Grand Fleet. It even gave cause to the other diners to pause in their shovelling and open their eyes at a sight which they could normally only expect to see when called to the happy eating place in the German equivalent of Valhalle.

Rossi was at first amused. "There was no need to take me so literally, Charles," he said. "I didn't say I could eat a horse or even what looks remarkably like a whole pig."

The continued delivery of food gradually erased his amusement and his expression became one of pink embarrassment.

It was beoming increasingly clear to Asprey that a number of dishes were really for two persons and those with Germanic appetites. He felt obliged to take some action to dam the flood. He therefore summoned the waiter who had taken his order, "Genug ist Genug," he said, "bitte, nur . . . " The waiter regarded him impassively. "You wish to cancel the, er, balance?" he asked in excellent English.

"If you please," Asprey looked the man squarely in the eyes. It made no difference whatsoever. There was not the slightest chance that the waiter would show any sign of compassion, remorse or indeed any reaction at all. The Englishman had brought it upon himself and as long as he paid for that which had been delivered, the problem was entirely with him.

Rossi and Asprey sat and looked at the various heaps. Some appeared more appetising than others. Colour was not a particularly strong point in the culinary efforts of the Germans and its absence discouraged visual anticipation. Nevertheless there was a job to be done, face to be saved and fed, so each took up his knife and fork, gripping each tool tightly and began to dismember portions for transfer on to the plates before them.

Fortunately Asprey had ordered wine rather than beer so that their liquid intake was more of taste than volume, easing an otherwise impossible task.

Nearly two hours later, the Australian and the Englishman staggered out of the restaurant, collapsed into cabs and returned to their respective hotels. As an "evening on the Town" it had not been a success. The expense had been anticipated as had the probable incapacity, but the total absence of light relief in any female shape or form coupled with the after effect of satiation with solids rather than liquids effectively eliminated any reference thereafter to that particular experience. In future Rossi would make his own arrangements.

In the meantime, their prime objective was to recover their health and strength since they would require all their faculties for their first meeting in the morning with representatives of German Admiralty Intelligence who would certainly be of no more assistance in their quest as had the waiter in the Brückenkeller. But this time, Charles had to get it right. To pretend to have knowledge that he did not possess would not lead simply to an indigestible shambles. The consequences could be far more painful and exceedingly expensive.

The following morning, Asprey and Rossi met as arranged at the Hilton Hotel. Over a cup of coffee they considered their programme for the day. Rossi had already arranged a meeting for them at 10a.m. with a Herr Eisendorf whose name had figured prominently in the reports of Davis and Foster before they disappeared. There seemed little doubt that Eisendorf was more than a civil servant. It was a reasonable probability that he was a high ranking officer in Naval Intelligence. The meeting had been difficult to arrange and Rosse had been advised somewhat curtly that its maximum duration would be thirty minutes. Since there was little doubt that the limit would be applied, it had been a simple matter then to arrange the second session of the day to coincide with lunch. Davis had mentioned in his reports a contact he had made with a Herr Muller who had been able to provide some supplementary information. Herr Muller was a tutor at the University who specialised in German history up to 1945 as far as his students were concerned. As a professional historian he had extended his researches to include the two decades immediately following that year. However, since the university syllabus did not extend beyond 1945, he was obliged to regard such studies as exclusively for present personal interest and, when completed, hopefully for posterity.

In the afternoon, Asprey and Rossi hoped to find a Frau Decker. Again, with the benefit of the notes provided by Davis and Foster, they knew where she was likely to be found but since she did not appear to have a permanent residence they had been unable to make contact and advise her of their intended visit. Asprey had planned to catch the evening flight to Singapore and Rossi wanted to return about the same time to London. These arrangements should still leave them ample time to complete their programme and find the lady.

Rossi glanced at his watch. "I think we ought to get moving," he said. "I'd rather arrive outside the building early and have to wait around instead of a few minutes late and give Eisendorf any excuse, however slight, not to see us."

"Agreed," replied Asprey. "From what I have read he sounds a tough nut and if we give him any opportunity of being difficult he will not only take it but also stuff it down our throats."

The two men paid for their coffee, collected their essential raincoats and exchanged the warmth of the hotel interior for the damp cold of the pavement. A common complaint in every major city in the western hemisphere is that the arrival of rain coincides with the retirement of taxies. When the sun shines the proliferation of such transport is usually embarrassing. The pedestrian has only to be seen to falter in his stride for a cabby to appear at his elbow offering his services. But the mearest suggestion of any precipitation is enough to send the cabs scuttling for cover with obvious disregard for the now dire needs of potential customers. The conditions were such therefore that the tip to the hotel doorman who condescended to hail a taxi and open its door was for once a reasonable investment and not the normal cowardly surrender to illogical social snobbery.

They arrived at 36 Friedrichstrasse with some five minutes in hand.

"Well, I don't think that he would object to us being a few minutes early and anyway by the time we have got through the door and made our arrival known, our timing should be precise enough even for our teutonic friend." Whilst making these observations, Asprey had walked up the short flight of stone steps and pressed the white button inset in a brass plate which reflected a distorted hand.

Whatever lettering there might have been on it had long since been completely obliterated by the constant polishing of visitors and cleaners. Its original information would in any event have been wholly misleading.

There was no indication that any bell had been activated

within the premises. The two men waited in the door-way feeling increasingly exposed. Charles glanced around then upwards. A small tube protruded like a barrel of a shotgun above his head aimed directly at him. He turned to Rossi and using his eyes as guides, made him aware that they were under scrutiny.

Rossi could not restrain himself. "I do believe that we are on candid camera. I wonder if they also record it on tape. Let's look up and give them a big smile." As if on queue, the tube swung slightly in his direction. "If we are going to be recorded, at least we shall show them our good side." Both men had failed to notice that whilst their attention had been diverted upwards the door had opened. There had been no sound of bolt or chain withdrawal, but any disappointment on that score was soon forgotten when they looked at the man silently framed in the doorway. He was tall, grey-haired with a large white forehead which dominated all his remaining features. His eyes were deep set, pale and expressionless. He could have stepped out of any video nasty except for an aura of evil that could never have been reproduced on film or tape. Whatever his given task, it would be despatched clinically without hesitation or deviation – and certainly without question. Suddenly Asprey understood how concentration camps had existed. The keeper barring their way was no ferry-man even in the underworld. He was the despatcher on the other side.

"Ya?" The voice fitted the part – disembodied. Charles deliberately replied in English. "We have an appointment with Herr Eisendorf at ten o'clock this morning. We are Messrs. Rossi and Asprey."

"Danke." The man was far from impressed. He could play the same game. "Kommen Sie mit mir, bitte."

He took two paces back and allowed them entry, then closed the door. They were in a dark hall, stone-flagged with mahogany panelling from floor to ceiling. Facing them was an imposing staircase which swept upwards and out of their sight. The steps were of white marble and more than compensated for the warmth of polished hardwood. The heels of their grey-haired guide clicked like castenets as he led the way up the stairs. As he reached the top, the noise ceased. The floor of the corridor into which the stairs gave access was heavily carpeted. The remainder of their passage was in complete silence. They passed several doors to their right and left. By such elimination, it became obvious that their ultimate destination was the pair of double doors facing them at the end of the corridor. The German knocked once and bent his head forward as if listening for a response. Suddenly he straightened, grasped the door knob with his left hand and made his entry, assuming that he would be followed. It was a reasonable assumption as neither Asprey or Rossi had any intention of waiting to be invited.

The room was large, well furnished, with walls completely covered with books. Once again the predominate colour was mahogany which ideally matched the leather upholstered chairs which were scattered amongst the incidental tables and assorted rugs. The dominant feature was a very large partners' desk placed in front of heavily draped windows at the end furthest from the entrance through which they had walked.

Seated with its back to the light was the black silhouette of a burly figure, that stretched its arms across the desk and propelled itself vertically as Asprey and Rossi paused having entered its domain.

"Please come in," the figure invited and gestured towards three large chairs conveniently placed in front of it. "And please be seated."

As they sat down, the guests became aware that their guide had already deposited himself in one of the three.

Under the pretence of making himself comfortable, Charles contrived to move his chair to one side so that he could look diagonally across the desk and therefore shield at least one of his eyes from the glare of light from the window accentuated by the gloom within the room. His efforts were in vain. The chair seemed to be screwed to the floor. Either that or it was so heavy that to move it even an inch would require an overt effort to avoid risk of injury. The alternatives were equally unattractive, so he subsided into the leather depths and tried to accomplish his objective by forcing himself into one of its corners. Although this resulted in a very uncomfortable posture, it did enable him to distinguish the features of the man seated opposite.

He had large eyes, a large nose, a heavy mouth and a thick neck. Everything about him was in proportion, but what proportions! He had the build of a heavyweight wrestler and a face to match. He was neither ugly nor handsome. Everything was in order and balanced. He did not project an image. He was solid and real like a lump of granite. His skin was lined but not through obesity. The impression was one of weathering and Charles could imagine rain sweeping across the face yet being guided down like rivulets on the side of a mountain. A man to be respected but not liked. A man to be feared but not disliked. He was Eisendorf.

He spoke. "Now, gentlemen, I am very glad that you were so punctual. We have thirty minutes and in that time I am at your disposal. I understand from your letter that you wish to re-open the question of U-134. As the letter was over your signature, Herr Asprey, perhaps you would like to explain precisely what you wish to know."

Charles realised that the German was looking directly at him and that therefore he already knew their respective identities without introduction. As that thought flashed across his mind he suddenly appreciated that in a very unteutonic manner there had been no formal introductions or shaking of hands! That could in no way be accidental as its omission on the Continent was virtually unthinkable.

"Yes, Herr Eisendorf, I understand that nearly twelve months ago you met with two of our associates, Davis and Foster, and provided them eventually with certain information which led to the agreement between the German Admiralty and the company they represented, namely Consolidated Industrial Holdings Behad, which included your permission to salvage one of your submarines, U-134. The terms of the agreement were that the contents of the submarine would be divided equally in value between the Admiralty and the company and that the company would observe at all times the obligations related to an official war grave."

Eisendorf nodded. "Yes, that seems to be a reasonable summary. Your only omission is that the agreement was for a limited period of time which has now expired."

Asprey raised his eyebrows. "We have, we believe, all the correspondence and the documents related to the agreement and I do not recall any time limit being specified or even suggested. The only limitation was the contract between the company and the Malaysian Government. As long as that existed and the company continued to have the right to salvage any vessels within Malaysian waters, it appeared that you were not worried as to when the submarine might be raised but rather how?"

"Whether or not it is in the correspondence, I made it abundantly clear to your associates that having given them our permission with the greatest reluctance, it could only be on the clear understanding that every effort would be made to implement the agreement as quickly as possible, certainly within a reasonable period. Now that was nearly twelve months ago and that is long enough to be more than reasonable. I would suggest that as experienced businessmen you would take exactly the same attitude. Such an offer cannot be left open indefinitely."

Asprey was beginning to feel that the interview was not only accelerating down the wrong track but they had clambered aboard at the wrong platform. Something was far from right. If they hoped to make any progress it could only be achieved by starting again.

"You will be aware," he said, "of the unhappy fate of the salvage vessel that was leased by the company. Consequently we have had to start again. This time we will succeed and we are here to give you an undertaking so to do. We can quite understand your irritation at the delay which for us was also very expensive. We know the mistakes that were made and these will not occur again. Rather than argue over the past, cannot we agree on the future? If you insist upon action within a reasonable period from now, then so be it, but I am confident that it is in our mutual interests to have another go."

"I can only re-emphasise," replied Eisendorf, "that we made it abundantly clear to your associates that we had considerable misgivings as to their capacity and capability and we would not wish one of our U-Boats to be salvaged other than in a most professional and efficient way."

"I can quite understand your concern," responded Charles. "For that reason we are approaching the opportunity quite differently. There cannot be any repetition of the disasters encountered before. This time our plans are well and truly laid."

"How can we be certain of that?"

"Well, first the salvage vessel will be obtained almost locally. Secondly, all the other resources necessary for successful completion of the job will be available on the doorstep. Control will be tight and effective."

This answer obviously gave food for thought. There was a long pause during which Eisendorf gently drummed on the leather topped desk with the fingers of his left hand. The silence was broken by the fourth occupant of the room, their guide.

"Have you arranged all that is required?"

Asprey remembered the waiter in the Brückenkeller and the consequences of his pretence. "Everything is not arranged with mutual commitment, as that can only be concluded when I can assure those involved that we have your continued co-operation and help."

"What do you need then from us," Eisendorf asked.

"We need your confirmation that we have your approval for us to raise the vessel. We are aware of its history, but we still do not know what precisely is inside. We understand that previously you were not prepared to divulge this but would only confirm that the cargo was extremely valuable and highly sensitive in a number of different ways. If you could now see your way to providing us with full details then I am confident that we can give you an absolute assurance as to the ultimate success of the operation."

Eisendorf replied: "We will let you know whether we are

prepared to give you that information since, as far as we are concerned, we shall be looking at the situation as if it were completely new. The history of your involvement does not encourage us to believe that whatever your assurances you will be successful. As to your second point I can tell you that we are not prepared to give you any further information as to the contents of the U-Boat. I will however reiterate that you will have to raise the vessel in one piece, that you cannot dismantle any part of it on the sea-bed and if we agree to let you go ahead we will insist on an observer being present at all times when the wreck is being lifted and that during the operation he will have absolute authority as to its conduct. If at any time he is not satisfied with any aspect of the work, he will have the authority to abort. On the other hand, should it prove successful, he will be the first to enter the U-Boat with only those whom we may nominate and no-one else will enter until he says so."

Asprey looked thoughtfully at Eisendorf. However restrictive such conditions might be, their listing was hopeful. He began to feel that the Germans would agree.

"We should be more than happy to accept those conditions which are entirely reasonable," responded Charles. "However, I am going to Singapore this evening and Herr Rossi is returning to London at about the same time. I appreciate that it may not be convenient (Charles did not want to suggest that Eisendorf might not have the authority) for you to reconfirm, as you put it, your approval at this precise moment, but it would be extremely helpful if it could be conveyed to me before I leave as this would allow me to conclude our negotiations in Singapore immediately after my arrival and save invaluable time?"

Asprey was taking a chance. His remarks could have been interpreted almost as an insult to Eisendorf, designed to raise his temperature and encourage him to give a decision as a matter of pride. If Eisendorf gave any thought to that possibility, then he could go the opposite way and deliberately extend the waiting period with the final thrust of a simple 'No'. Charles hoped that instead he would accept the request

93

at face value as confirmation of an anxiety to get the green light as quickly as possible.

A long silence ensued. Even if the room had been well lit, Charles would have looked in vain for any clue as to Eisendorf's thoughts. His fingers drummed again on the desk top. The beat syncopated with the deliberate ticking of a large ornate clock standing on a round table in the corner of the room to the visitors' left.

The intake of breath was the only warning that Eisendorf had made up his mind. "It is extremely unlikely that I can give you our approval to go ahead before you leave for Singapore. I can quite understand your position, however, and therefore I will undertake to let you have our decision within twenty-four hours of your arrival there. If you will let me know the name of your hotel, then I will see that it is arranged."

"That is very helpful," said Asprey. "I shall be staying at the Marco Polo. I shall look forward to what I hope will be your confirmation that we can go ahead." He almost added the merest suggestion that whether he received such approbation or not they would still make arrangements to raise the U-Boat which they were legally entitled to do. However attractive such a threat might be, it would have been quite superfluous. The Germans would be thoroughly aware of the options and would not need reminding. It could only serve to raise their hackles and that would not help. Far better to give them the opportunity of grandly approving their endeavours and using them as unwilling allies.

Eisendorf stood up. The interview was at an end. Asprey studiously avoided looking at his watch. Whether they had had the benefit of thirty minutes or not was now irrelevant. Rossi and he were leaving only a little more knowledgeable than when they had arrived, but there did appear to be a likelihood that the Germans would give their approval.

That would be positive. The Germans undoubtedly had influence with the Malaysian Government either directly or indirectly and if they did not support Consolidated in their official venture, that task might be offered to others. Asprey and Rossi could only hope that the Germans would be

94

attracted to the opportunity of virtually controlling the exercise without responsibility for its failure but with a major participation in its success.

The visitors followed Eisendorf's example and pushed themselves out of their massive chairs. The desk was far too large to permit any hand-shaking and to walk around it solely for that purpose seemed wholly inappropriate, so they simply followed the German's example and inclined their heads with the inevitable "Aufwiedersehen's", turned on their heels and walked across the room towards the doors. They found that they had been preceded by their guide who had already led the way into the corridor into which they could walk without hindrance.

In fact their progress was so smooth and organised that they found themselves standing in the rain without even the suspicion of a pause in the main entrance doorway at the top of the steps.

"That was the most sophisticated bum's rush I've ever had," laughed Rossi, "and I've had a few. Now where do we go?"

"You're darn right," acknowledged Charles, "I would suggest the University. We may be early but it will do no harm. We can have an early lunch and give ourselves more time in the afternoon."

He raised his hand as a taxi appeared out of the gloom. As it was still raining this was a welcome surprise since by the law of averages it should have been a straight choice between public transport and walking.

Having instructed the driver, Rossi turned to Charles. "There was something distinctly odd about that meeting. They not only knew which of us was which – hence no introductions – but whilst you and Eisendorf were talking I became increasingly certain that there was someone else in the room."

"You mean in addition to the chap who met us at the door?"

"Yes. There were two chairs that were facing away from the desk on your right," said Rossi. "I'm positive that one was occupied. I'm sure I could see a pair of shoes but that may have been a trick of the light which was pretty poor. There was something else odd as well."

"What was that?" asked Charles.

"I could smell fresh cigar smoke."

"So what?"

"Eisendorf was not smoking, neither were we or our guide and there was no ashtray on Eisendorf's desk."

"Curiouser and curiouser," mused Asprey, "perhaps that's why he drummed on the desk. He's by no means a nervous man. Perhaps he was afraid of the silence being too silent. The whole affair becomes even more intriguing. They will still not give us any idea as to the contents of the U-Boat, its present value, why we can't dismember it before the lift and why they must be the first and only entrants into the tomb. It's more like the treasures of ancient Egypt. Perhaps there's a guillotine that cuts the robbers' heads off as they enter!"

As his imagination started to run riot, Charles glanced at his watch. He was astonished to see that rather than being early, they were actually behind schedule. The interview must have lasted at least the full thirty minutes. He spoke to the driver; "We are a little late. I should be grateful if you could get us to the University as quickly as safety permits."

The driver nodded and leant forward over his wheel. Asprey frowned. On impulse, he had spoken in English. The man had understood. Unlike British cabs, their European counterparts had no internal division and thus no privacy. The absence of any language barrier eliminated the last obstacle between any eavesdropper, accidental or otherwise, and their conversation.

Charles looked at the back of the man's head. One effect of the aftermath of the second war had been the erradication of any visible signs of class distinction in Germany. Even so the driver appeared to be well dressed, wearing a quite expensive raincoat, the shoulders of which were remarkably wet. Perhaps the man's previous fare had required him to stand in the rain to help unload his cases, or perhaps the man had been waiting from them – ?? Whatever the answer, discretion appeared to be the order of the day, so he contented himself by pre-empting any further gratuitous information by suggesting to Rossi: "I'll tell you about our next session when we get there."

Rossi nodded. If he had understood the implication of the offer, he gave no sign.

Chapter Six

Treasure

Unlike Professor Higgins, Herr Doktor Muller was indeed an ordinary man. He was of medium height, slightly built, brown of eye and hair and eager to please.

Asprey and Rossi had discovered him in his rooms at the University busily worrying paper. The invitation to lunch need never have been made. As soon as they removed their raincoats, Muller started in on the subject that had brought them together.

"We know in great detail most of what happened during the last days of the Third Reich. We are discouraged from guessing that there might have been other activities not so listed. We can have as many post mortems as we like, but we cannot have the body. Perhaps that has been spirited away in the anticipation of the new rising, a new ascension. We have only to breath the words "Fourth Reich" to become lepers. But as a historian I have one major advantage. I know that people never change. Their pattern of behaviour, individually or in mass, is self repetitive. Only the environment changes. People do not respond to such change. They will try again and again to repeat what they have attempted before, despite failure. Unless at some stage they succeed, the evolution of the environment will defeat them. Their objective has ultimately been made humanly impossible. But between the identification of their target and its elimination by changing circumstances, people will be as stubborn and as obdurate as any other animal or insect in pursuing their self-imposed task."

Muller was obviously warming to a pet theory. Rossi settled back for a long session. His movement was quickly interpreted for what it was.

"Ah, but you seek the facts," Muller interrupted himself. "How much more have you learnt and what would help you now?"

"Thank you," responded Asprey. "Our problem is that we are no wiser than we were before and we shall be entirely dependent upon the German Admiralty."

"So," mused Muller, "let us briefly review what we know. Public records confirm that U-134 was completely re-fitted early in 1945 and converted to a high speed underwater transport, as indeed were four other U-Boats at about the same time. It left Bremenhaven early in April 1945 but there were no records of its cargo or passengers – if any. But we do know that it had an extremely small crew and no armoury. That was the sum total of my knowledge when I met with your colleague Davis. Now, if you will bear with me, let us turn from those facts to my theories and see if they can guide us towards further information or at least probabilities."

"I have studied the behaviour pattern of the German nation and its leaders during 1918 and over the years from that date to 1929. In 1918, many arrangements were made to redistribute the nation's wealth in various forms but mainly through accounts in Switzerland. Gold bullion disappeared and certain materials of international intrinsic value shipped overseas. Plans were made hurriedly and in great secrecy for obvious reasons. To have indicated such preparations would have been treasonable, regardless of legality. When you have time I shall be more than happy to give you the facts and figures. For the moment, however, it is sufficient to confirm that before that war ended, those who held the necessary power made preparation for the continuity of the fight, albeit at some future and unknown date. They did not hoard the wealth for their own comfort. It was to be the cornerstone of the Third Reich. That experience therefore existed in 1944/5. Plans could be made more thoroughly the second time, although the element of secrecy was still as important as ever. So again we have no records. It is for sure that those who helped in the arrangements but were not destined to participate to assist in their final implementation were eliminated.

99

But we now have the relaxed censorship of the period 1918 to 1929 to point us towards what might have been intended for 1945 to 1956. Again I do not wish to burden you with the details of my research, so I will take you immediately to my findings and how they might be interpreted in regard to U-134."

"I am confident that that vessel was the key to the Fourth Reich. It contained or was intended to contain the future puppets and enough wealth to ensure that they could independently re-establish first an organisation and secondly a control base outside Germany of influence and power that at the appropriate time could be linked with a new radical movement established within the Fatherland. It was appreciated that it would be a number of years before any overt moves could be made and that there was no way that they could be within the ridiculously short period of time between the end of the First World War and the' beginning of the Second. Nevertheless, patience costs little and is worth much."

Muller stopped and looked directly at the two men. "You'll probably be wondering why I, a German, should tell you this. Am I a traitor, a Jew or pacifist, perhaps? Well, I am none of those, other than a German. I am a historian and I believe that the circumstances about 1875 when all this started have now so changed that domination of Europe by any one nation, however powerful, is politically and economically impossible. That whilst Britain could have achieved that by subterfuge during the last quarter of the nineteenth century – and indeed nearly did – and whilst Germany might have done likewise during the first quarter of the twentieth century – and nearly did – it cannot be done now or any time within the foreseeable future. I could give you a list of all the reasons why not and the developments that have contributed to that conclusion, but that would be wasting your time. May I ask you simply to accept the statement. If you do so, then you will understand my lack of reluctance in putting to you my theories. However meticulous the plans, however successful they were or might have been, their time has passed – for ever. So any disclosure now is academic. It is what might have been but never was. What was intended but is now unachievable."

Asprey and Rossi nodded. Neither wished to interrupt the flow, fearing that to do so would only encourage further philosophising. The logic was interesting but it was the outcome that was fascinating.

Muller continued. "We know that these five U-Boats were designed to go to several destinations and that only one was completely unarmed, yours. Now I have also established that the cargoes were taken aboard in every case some time before the vessels were commissioned. It is therefore unlikely that the crews could have been aware of their contents – which would make sense. They were dispensible when the voyage was completed."

"Now let's assume that there is a desire to repeat history. The first and obvious course is the transfer of funds from Germany into numbered Swiss accounts. In 1945 that would undoubtedly have been done by the industrialists who would be already using such facilities, but unlike 1918, they would not represent the caucus of support for a political revival. They would be acutely aware that post-war conditions would almost certainly differ quite dramatically from those which had been experienced in the early twenties. They would transfer their wealth solely for their own protection and independence, to be withdrawn quietly and invested carefully at some future date. Secondly, the Americans virtually controlled Switzerland over the last two years of the Second World War and despite its international reputation for banking secrecy, it was extremely unlikely that any representative of the Nazi Party could rely on that to protect any funds that he deposited if the Swiss had the slightest suspicion as to its source. So Switzerland was out. Again, based on past experience, this left the Third Reich with only one tactic, the physical movement of assets that could be realised anywhere within reason in the civilised world without too much problem and too great a discount. The first choice would be gold bullion but this has a number of drawbacks, not the least being the need to minimise quantity and maximise value."

"Gold is surprisingly cumbersome. Precious stones, particularly diamonds, would appear to be more attractive but even they are not entirely satisfactory. The diamond market is controlled by de Beers and any hoard would be at jeopardy as far as its value was concerned. Art treasures just cannot be sold at will."

"The most likely scenario therefore is that those in power would have divided their spoils between them according to their pecking order and the most valuable cargo would disappear with the highest ranking members of the party. Since we are dealing with fairly substantial volumes, the method of transport was limited as to choice."

"Germany was hemmed in on all sides so that underwater escape was the only feasible proposition. So U-Boats were commissioned and prepared. In passing we should not overlook the probability that at least one of those U-Boats was earmarked for use as the slush fund and made available to those whose support for the planning of the operation was essential but who did not figure in the ultimate plans for the Fourth Reich. That would be their reward and indeed incentive to ensure that the escape was successful. That fund would have consisted of a mixture of art treasures, gold bullion, etc., which whilst very attractive to the greedy individual would be relatively insignificant when compared with the total hoard. That brings me back to U-134."

"I believe that the evidence we have so far points to the probability that that particular U-Boat contained the highest value treasure and therefore the highest ranking Nazis. Hence the German reaction to your request. I am pretty sure that I can guess accurately its contents but where I need further research is to obtain confirmation as to its ultimate destination. Returning for the last time to my basic theory, in which country would one expect the power base of the Fourth Reich to be inseminated? The first reaction is without doubt Brazil, followed closely by the Argentine. But Malaysian waters are hardly en route for South America. The second would be South Africa, or at least somewhere in Southern Africa."

"But again it's quite irreconcilable. The third but actually an unlikely destination would be Japan. The Nazis would know that it would be only a matter of time before that country would be overwhelmed. They were quite aware of the developments of the atom bomb and the implications of that research. So at the moment I am perplexed."

"I must, however give you one warning. Despite its value and the hazard that U-Boat cargo represents, that is not the inhibiting factor as far as the German authorities are concerned. I think it also unlikely that the identity of the Nazis in the U-Boat is at the top of their list of worries, even if it includes the mummified remains of Hitler and all that might follow from that discovery. So what have we left? In my view, it can only be the probability that somewhere in that vessel will be evidence as to its destination, the intentions of its passengers, but above all the names of those with whom the survivors intended to re-establish their new party. In short where it was going, to whom and for what purpose. That is the information that the Germans will seek to recover first and until they have succeeded in doing just that or convincing themselves that it does not exist, there is no way that you will be able or allowed to realise any benefit from the salvage. I am convinced that as a last resort, they would be prepared to destroy the cargo, whatever the consequences and cost, rather than take the risk that such evidence might see the light of day."

"Finally, if I am right, then, whilst your knowledge as to the location of the U-Boat and its possible significance might have put you in some danger in the early stages of this venture, even your realisation of the nature of the cargo would not now add significantly to the dangers of the enterprise. If you correctly guessed the identity of the passengers then you might expect trouble, but if the authorities felt that your attention was really focused on possible documentary evidence, then not only would you both be uninsurable, but you would be putting at risk the livelihood and health of millions in Malaysia."

There was a long pause. Muller had slumped further into his chair, with his beard enmeshed in his woollen pullover.

Asprey and Rossi looked at each other. There was no doubt as to Muller's logic, but there was one further question to which he appeared to have an answer. So far it had not been forthcoming. So Rossi asked it.

"We realise that you cannot know for certain, but would you give us the benefit of your conclusion concerning the cargo. What do you think it is?"

Muller did not look up. He gave no indication that he had even heard the question. Rossi persevered. "You said that that particular knowledge is not as much dynamite as other bits of information at which we dare not even hint. Anyway it would only be a guess at this stage and you may well be proved wrong. In fact no-one need ever know that you had put it forward even as a theory. You can rely on us to be discreet if only because it would be in our interests to keep it entirely to ourselves."

Muller looked up, brows wrinkled as he looked over the top of his glasses and smiled. "It will be known that we have met and that we could only have discussed one subject, the reason for your visit to Frankfurt. It will be assumed that I will have told you everything that I know (he gave the word just enough emphasis to make his point). What I know may well be known by a number of people. What I may guess may be guessed by some, but known to be right or wrong by possibly only one or two persons."

"If my guess is right and I tell you then we will have increased that exclusive club to the anger of its present member or members – and that would be most unfortunate – for us."

"But," insisted Rossi, "it is still only a guess and we will keep it to ourselves."

Muller smiled. "You're right, it is only a guess as I have been unable to find any corroboration. For what it's worth – and it would be a fortune by any standards – I believe that U-134 carries special glass containers full of mercury. Enough to upset the world commodity market and to pollute the fishing industry of Malaysia and that part of the Pacific for centuries to come."

"It is the only form of wealth that is consistent with the

facts as we know them and the intentions of those who organised the project so far as we can logically assume. Now you
will understand my fears and worries. If I am right, then you
truly have a tiger by the tail and my personal opinion for what
it's worth is to let sleeping Nazis lie. No treasure, however
valuable, could be worth such a risk – even to you."

The three men sat in silence, each occupied by a sequence
of thought triggered off by Muller's disclosure. Asprey's
immediate reaction was to question why the glass containers
had remained intact when the British torpedos had dumped
the U-Boat on to the sea bed. Then he remembered being
lectured by a glass manufacturer who had insisted that a door
made in an armoured version of that material was actually
tougher in certain circumstances than steel. So it was possible,
and its value could be enormous.

Rossi had arrived at the same answer by a different route.
He had started with the question how had the Nazis been able
to corner a large part of the world's supply of mercury, but
that could be explained. They had had years to prepare a
hoard of wealth for whatever purpose. They had increased the
importation of such materials to satisfy their production needs
and they had over-run many countries and so obtained control
of their stocks of mercury. It was just possible, but what
would an accumulation represent in terms of money?

Asprey got there first. "What would you say it might be
worth – if it existed?"

Muller had anticipated the reaction. "In present day terms,
about a quarter of a billion Deutsch Marks, say sixty million
pounds Sterling. But it could be more if that was all the U-134
carried as cargo."

Rossi whistled quietly. Muller's smile became lop-sided.
"So you will have a go?" he asked. "I don't see why not,"
replied Rossi. "If it has survived so far without contaminating
the sea then it will survive a careful lift."

Asprey could see another angle to that reaction. "We can
afford to ignore any other aspects of the venture. They would
only be embarrassing and certainly would not compare financially with the results of a simple salvage operation. If we

play ball with the German Admiralty, letting them have what they want, there's more than enough to keep us happy. If that is obvious then it would reduce the risk of the authorities believing otherwise. We should be allowed to go ahead even with that knowledge. Indeed (Charles was now warming to this theme) especially with that knowledge."

Muller could see the drift of his argument but he was not at all happy with its possibilities. "But that might encourage you to tell them that you have guessed its contents after you have met with me. They would immediately decide that I had put it to you and that since I was right – if I am – I had gone further in my researches. Either way we would all be at risk."

Muller's anxiety was becoming obvious. Asprey had visions of violence if the academic were allowed to develop his present line of argument. "You are absolutely right," he said soothingly. "We must give no indication that we might even have guessed at its contents other than the usual suggestions of gold, diamonds etc. The less we know the better. You can rely on us."

As he spoke, he stood up. Rossi took the hint and walked across the room to collect their raincoats. Muller remained seated, unhappy and not a little fearful. But he was calm and collected. Asprey took his coat and turned to Muller.

"I'm sorry we took up so much of your time. We are indeed grateful for your . . . (Charles was looking desperately for the right word) Muller interrupted. "I to am sorry that I could not really be helpful, but my real interest is in the history of Europe up to the Second World War."

"Now if you ever come across any situations related to events between say 1850 and 1925, then I am sure that I can provide you with some original research that will truly add to your knowledge and understanding. Say, for example, Mayerling." The tension in the room had been dispelled. So much so that Asprey felt that given time and encouragement, Muller would have propounded his theories on the murder of Mayerling there and then. Fortunately neither element was available so it was an easy matter for he and Rossi to take their leave of the earnest Doktor and find their way back to the world outside the University.

Both men were excited, so that their common desire was coffee to lubricate dry mouths rather than seek alcohol. Food as such did not even command consideration. Their need was easily satisfied as the normal lunch time had passed them by.

"What do you think of it now?" Rossi asked between sips. "It's raised some possibilities which are, to say the least, unpleasant," replied Asprey.

"For example?"

"What happened to Davis and Foster? What did they find out? Why did the German Admiralty change its mind? Will we be allowed to succeed?"

"I think the risk is worth the candle." Rossi sounded quite firm. "Anything could have happened to those two guys. We ran out of money so that we could not afford to reimburse them even for their expenses, let alone salaries. So they went off in a huff. Admittedly we have looked for them since but perhaps not as hard as we might have. As long as the Germans get what they want they will let us have our share. After all they not only have whatever they find, but also half of the treasure as well."

Asprey nodded. "True, they are better off if we succeed, if they want what is there."

Rossi frowned. "Of course they want what is there, if only to make absolutely certain that no-one else can ever have it."

Asprey nearly responded with the suggestion that it would be difficult to find a safer location for unwanted papers guarded by an enormous pollution bomb, all covered by a complete lack of evidence that either actually existed. That which was unwanted could be destroyed but first it would have to come into someone's possession and that itself was an unnecessary danger. However, it was neither time nor place for such fundamental disagreement and in the end he felt that he would still go along with the project. Such was agreed. The morning's experience had put him on his guard so that Charles could only have himself to blame if the outcome was other than very profitable.

"You may be right. Anyway, nothing venture, nothing gain

and it's surely worth some risk."

"Good," said Rossi. "Let's get on our way to see Frau Decker – if we can find her. According to Davis, she had a shop in Frankfurt selling flowers. He arranged to have a second meeting with her, but, for whatever reason, that never took place. We know the shop was near to the tram station or main railway station. How long have we got?"

Charles looked at his watch. "No more than two hours at the most. I have to be at the airport an hour before take-off."

"Right," said Rossi, "let's go."

Again they had little problem in collecting a cab which dropped them outside the Bahnhof. It was still drizzling and the light was beginning to fade. The only consolation was that it made the brightly lit shops more inviting and they stepped out briskly across the street.

The first flower shop they tried had never heard of Frau Decker. Their request had been received with some caution, probably because they had not identified themselves or their reason for asking. But the directness of the response and the care in its confirmation encouraged the belief that their method of approach was probably the most effective. Germany has a great respect for officialdom, whether identified or assumed.

It was not until they entered their fourth flower shop that they had any indication that Frau Decker even existed. Yes she had worked there but had left about six months before. No they did not know why. She had been an excellent assistant and had been with them over ten years. She was a divorcee so lived on her own. Where? The last address they had was in Wilhelmstrasse. Yes they would write it down for them.

Rossi and Asprey looked at their watches. They still had to collect their luggage from their respective hotels and there would undoubtedly be traffic problems in the later afternoon rush hour. Asprey turned to the lady behind the counter. "Did she have a particular friend here who might be able to help us find her?"

"Yes, Anne-Marie, the dark haired assistant over there."

She pointed across the shop.

"May we speak with her, just for a few moments, please?"

"If you wish. I will call her across."

Anne-Marie had a customer with her so that she could only give a cursory acknowledgement of the request. When she was free, she walked towards them, heels clicking loudly on the stone floor. Explanations having been given and received she looked calmly at the two men. "Yes, I knew Frau Decker very well."

"Knew," repeated Asprey, "so you have lost touch with her?"

"Yes," replied Anne-Marie, "when she left here she left Frankfurt. Apparently a relation died, and left her estate to Frau Decker. She said it might be worth a lot of money and would take time to settle. As soon as she had done that she would return to Frankfurt."

"Have you heard from her since then?"

"No, but she will come back. Of that I am sure."

"Why?"

"Because all her roots are here. In fact I always understood that all her family were or had been in Frankfurt. The aunt that died must have been the odd one out. Even Ger – Frau Decker was surprised to learn of her when she was told of her death."

"So it was an aunt that died. What relation exactly?"

"I believe it was her father's sister, or more truly his half-sister. She could not remember her father having mentioned a sister, but then she was very young when her father was killed."

"In the war? In the bombing?"

"In the war, yes. In the bombing no, although that killed her mother and two sisters. Her father was a Kapitan in the Navy, one of our very brave U-Boat commanders. She thought a lot of him. The tragedy was that he was killed after the war ended in Europe."

Asprey felt as if the rain had dripped down within his rain-coat collar. Could it be? If so he had better cut short the question and answer routine before he would be asked the inevitable – who were they and what did they want? And any answer might be incriminating.

"Thank you for your courtesy. Since you are sure that Frau Decker will return to Frankfurt we will, if we may, call again, say in a couple of months. In the meantime, once again thank you." Asprey included the first assistant in his nod of appreciation, glanced at Rossi and then quickly led the way to the door.

Outside the flower shop, they retraced their path back to the station where there would be a taxi rank. Rossi was naturally inquisitive. His lack of German had forced him to remain a spectator able only to guess at what was being said. "What the hell went on back there?" he asked. "I thought you were making progress with the second girl, then all of a sudden you closed it off and scampered out here. What did you find out? Do we know where to find this Frau Decker?"

"No," replied Charles, quietly but firmly. "No, we do not know where to find her and even if we did we probably haven't got enough time, so either way it doesn't matter. I think we know enough to make her either superfluous or exceedingly dangerous to us. Now is the time to leave Frankfurt, quickly."

"So what have we found out?" Rossi could not forebear to lean on the "we".

"Frau Decker's father was killed after V.E. Day. He was a submarine commander. After Frau Decker had met with Davis, she was told of the death of a hitherto unknown aunt, her father's half-sister, and had to leave Frankfurt to help in settling the estate about six month's ago. She intended to return. Her bosom friend has heard nothing from her since. Now I suggest we don't discuss this any more, especially in the taxi. Indeed you can arrive at your own conclusions on everything that has happened today and when we meet in Kuala Lumpur in a few days time we can then compare notes. The sooner we can get away from this city, the better I shall be pleased. It's been a very worthwhile journey, but only if we can get away from it and apply what we have learnt."

Rossi shrugged. "If you wish, O.K., but I believe that

you're overplaying the whole thing. Still, we now know it's worth it."

"I wonder," muttered Asprey.

Chapter Seven

The Eastern Aristocrat

The predominant colour of Kuala Lumpur Airport was green. Even the humid atmosphere added a pale green wash that drenched anything that moved and coated any object that had no option but to remain stationery. To those of artistic temperament the general impression was like a massive water colour held out in the rain, with blurred figures, confused colours and the gradual reduction to a mess of pulp.

Rossi was waiting for Asprey in the arrivals section.

"Glad to see you – good trip?" A perfunctory question, as it was less than an hour's flight from Singapore.

"Fair," replied Asprey. "Bit bumpy but I suppose that is to be expected this time of the year."

The exchange covered the handshake and exit from the building. Asprey had had no bags in the hold. Outside, Rossi indicated a nondescript Ford.

"Jump in, I'll drive. We have some business to discuss."

Asprey threw his briefcase on to the rear seat and clambered into the front of the car. Rossi lost no time in getting into the stream of traffic.

"We probably have a tail," he said, looking into his rear mirror. "But they won't be sophisticated enough to be able to hear what we are saying whilst we are on the move. No, don't look behind. Let's play their game and pretend."

Asprey slid a little further down into his seat. "Who are they?" he asked, emphasising the last word.

"Not sure – either the Tunku's men or government agents. Now you'll ask why either should be interested in us?"

"Yes."

"Well, it's very simple. I am Consolidated. C.I.H. has the

sole right to raise the sub. That sub is a potential bomb and the proverbial crock of gold. It could destroy the Malaysian economy or it could make C.I.H. very very rich. The Tunku, who is a Malaysian prince, finances and politically supports C.I.H. The government interest is obvious."

"Do either side know the precise location of the sub?"

"Precise, no, but enough to find it if need be."

"So why follow you?"

"Both sides want to know what I'm up to all the time – particularly with whom I do business."

"Charming – so now I'm on their list."

Rossi smiled dryly. "And you never would be missed. Is that what you're thinking?"

"Not exactly, but near enough."

"Well, not to worry. I have told T.K. what your role is. He's already seen all the papers and reports on our previous attempt, so he'll have no worries about you. If the Tunku knows, so do they."

Charles relaxed – a little. "Can we now discuss the sub's contents?"

"Not yet," Rossi frowned. "We will have a look at the spot, give you a feel for the place and then run over our plans."

"O.K. But I'm booked back to Singapore on the 6.30 flight."

"Plenty of time." The conversation then ceased as Rossi threaded the car through the bustling noisy traffic until they reached the docks.

Asprey had previously been quite unaware of the size and significance of trade between Malaysia and the rest of the world. The flow of goods into and out of K.L. was enhanced by the transhipments between it and Penang. He was much impressed, but there was no opportunity to stand and stare. Rossi drove through the dock area and on to an almost deserted quay. Waiting for them was a large powerful motor launch. Rossi waved to the figure behind the wheel in the covered bridge then ran up the narrow gang-plank linking the quay with the deck of the vessel. Asprey followed his example. It was obvious that Rossi had completely mastered the deck-hand's contribution to the operation of putting to sea and within seconds they were away, the launch growling its path between the assorted craft moving into and out of K.L.

Despite the brilliant sun, cloudless sky and bright blue sea, the breeze generated by the accelerating pace of the motor launch was distinctly cool and acceptably refreshing. Asprey and Rossi relaxed in the chairs set out on the deck at the stern of the boat. Hospitality was offered and accepted, Rossi obtaining the choice from a cabinet conveniently positioned within an arm's length of desire.

The launch was moving very fast. It suddenly occurred to Charles that if they indeed had any shadows they would now be obliged to declare themselves. He scanned the horizon over the stern. Rossi correctly interpreted his movement.

"You won't see them yet. They'll probably be waiting for us."

Before Asprey could attempt to reconcile the two statements, Rossi continued. "For the moment we cannot be overheard. I am sure that we are not bugged out here. Now down to business. The answer to the conundrum – What is it that could destroy yet could be worth vast sums of money?" Asprey did not dare to interrupt.

"We know that U-134 had something very special on board. It carried five passengers one or more being leading Nazis. In addition it carried something that had to be very valuable. We can only guess at its destination. The German Admiralty would give no indication of what that might have been although I'm sure that they know. So we can only assume that it was en route probably to Japan. The fact that that does not stand up to analysis as the top Nazis knew that the end of the war in the Pacific was imminent is interesting but not vital to our quest. Perhaps we shall find out when we raise the sub. For the moment, however, only the Germans know all the answers. As a result of our negotiations with them we have some – the ones that really matter to us, including the identification of the cargo. It was pure mercury – tons of it, in specially reinforced glass containers. Enough to spoil the world market in the stuff. Enough to finance a developing country. Enough to finance a new German Party. Enough to destroy the fishing industry of Malaysia and its neighbours and enough to damage the seas of the East almost irreparably."

"This answer poses another conundrum. Is the value of the treasure worth the cost that we might incur if we shatter the containers? At first we believed that it was not and therefore the risk was too great. That, we thought, was why the Germans had been so unhelpful, indeed deliberately obstructive. But it still didn't make sense. Glass can be as strong if not stronger than steel and concrete. Furthermore, the U-Boat had been sunk by a direct hit with a torpedo from the British sub. If the containers were going to break at all, that would have been the most likely time. But they did not. We know from our divers that everything appears to have survived – intact. Unless the original circumstances had been nothing short of miraculous, it was extremely unlikely that we, knowing the problem and taking all reasonable precautions for our own benefit, could create more damage in lifting the U-Boat, that is, more than the rupture that it first suffered. So the answer must be – Yes it is worth the risk because the greatest risk – the original sinking – has already taken place. When the Germans capitulated that seemed to confirm that assumption. But it wasn't as simple as that. Despite their agreement, advice and removal of any further impediments, there still remained a strong feeling that at some moment critique they would again intervene and the U-Boat would remain where it was . . . which is where we are now."

As Rossi came to the end of his review, the launch dropped its bow into the water, its forward motion transformed from an impatient thrust into a gentle sidle through the waves.

"We are at the edge of our box. Somewhere within its co-ordinates is the sub. To some extent, we have created a nuisance for ourselves because when we want to visit the wreck we literally have to find it each time. On the other hand it avoids giving its precise location to any observers."

Whilst he spoke, Rossi stared up into the sky. As if on cue, a tiny helicopter buzzed into view, some twenty feet above sea level. It came directly up to the launch, hovered astern then

115

circled.

"No doubt they are looking in hope?" Asprey asked.

"Probably," replied Rossi, "but not in expectation. Let's go into the wheel-house. I'll introduce you to our skipper."

Rossi led the way around the side of the launch and up the short flight of steps to the bridge.

"Herr Strauss, may I introduce Charles Asprey."

The man standing behind the wheel turned to face them. He was of medium height, solid build with, in naval parlance, a complete set, beard, moustache and whiskers. The three-quarter frame of black hair was topped by gold-rimmed sunglasses and a tanned brow from which his original hirsute gear had retired leaving him virtually bald. He emanated confidence and competence.

"Pleased to meet you," he said with no hesitation or accent. Charles responded with word and hand. It was commonplace courtesy, although the situation was anything but. Asprey suddenly felt that he was simply an observer. That in actuality he was not involved. There almost on sufferance, being deliberately excluded. Rossi had taken command. "No point in hanging about, let's get back to K.L., Strauss.

"Right," the skipper agreed, "why don't you take advantage of the main cabin. I've spread the charts on the table."

"Good idea," said Rossi. "See you later."

As they stepped outside, Asprey echoed Rossi's promise thoughtfully. Rossi caught the mood but made no comment as they descended on to the deck. Instead of going directly into the cabin as recommended, Rossi made his way again to the stern. The launch had gathered speed and its wash was quite impressive. The helicopter flew a few half-hearted circles, orbiting the launch, then turned its back on the vessel, departing with a distinctly disappointed air in the general direction of K.L.

As both men leant over the stern rail, Rossi looked sideways at Asprey.

"Surprised to find our captain German?"

"No, not really. Makes sense that they should want someone on hand to see that we are keeping our side of the bargain. It's the chap himself that worries me. He has an air of authority that rings a bell."

Rossi looked at Asprey. "You're not wrong. Herr Strauss commands a lot of respect from a lot of people. That's why we are here before we go into the cabin. I wanted to tell you that he is the other part of the bargain with the Germans. He is the chap who will supervise the lifting. He will be the first to enter the U-Boat and he will say what is to be done and when with its contents. Therefore, he knows what is inside, and my guess is that's the way it's going to remain. Now I'm equally sure that the cabin is bugged so be warned – we still have to play the game."

With that Rossi moved away from the rail and walked into the main cabin. The charts were fascinating. Someone had marked out the broad limits of the company's salvage licence which in fact were the territorial waters of Malaya and within these had outlined the individual wrecks, each identified as to name and date of sinking. The number far exceeded anything that Asprey had conceived. It included vessels of all shapes and sizes, representing many countries. Most appeared to be in relatively shallow waters.

Mindful of Rossi's last warning, he swallowed his immediate question as to the location of the U-Boat and instead asked: "Most appear to be in shallow water. What have you achieved so far?"

"Quite a lot. First we have used pearl divers and local fishermen who know the sea-bed intimately. So we have accurate knowledge as to what is where. The divers are young girls who can stay down for amazingly long periods without gear and their services are cheap. The fishermen are only too willing to help for relatively small rewards. For a miniscule investment we now know what is valuable, where it is and whether we can get at it. For example, we know that these cruisers have phosphur-bronze propellers which are relatively simple to cut off and raise. We know where we can sell the metal and for what price. The guns can also be taken out without too much trouble and they command a good price."

"So you would use the salvage vessel for this as well?"

Rossi was not impressed with that logic. "No, we can take our time raising the bits and pieces, doing it on the cheap. Wages are very low and we can help the economy more by employing people in preference to machines. But the U-Boat is quite another matter. We are forced to lift it in one piece. The salvage vessel will cost us a small fortune every day that it is with us. We will use it solely for the one operation and that hopefully very quickly. Whatever the outcome of that venture, there is no reason why we should not continue with our original objective and provide work and some profit for years ahead."

Asprey could see some of the force of the argument, but had the feeling that it might have been directed more towards the unseen listener than at himself. He nodded in agreement and leaned forward again to study the charts.

"Very interesting. You have quite a project."

"Yes," said Rossi, "but as you know, C.I.H. has a number of original businesses here, including oil reclamation, hydrophonics, building timber kits for export . . . Our target is to develop the largest conglomerate in Malaysia made up of highly profitable firsts. So far we are on course."

Asprey nodded again. "Yes, that's true."

The throb of the diesels suddenly slowed to a murmur. Almost simultaneously the angle of the deck dropped to the horizontal as the boat lost way. Rossi looked through one of the cabin port-holes.

"Ah, we are back in Kuala Lumpur." He looked at his watch. "We have plenty of time but you never know with our traffic, so it's just as well."

"Plenty of time for what," asked Asprey. His mind had already conjured up a night on the tiles.

"I am going to introduce you to the Tunku. He is the man who originally financed and promoted Consolidated Holdings. He is extremely rich and very powerful. His family has tremendous political influence in Malaysia. If he likes you then we literally have no problems in K.L. On the other hand, if he does not," Rossi shrugged, "well, let's see how you get on with him."

"If the downside is so steep," queried Charles, "why take the risk? Why should I meet him at all?"

"You – and I – haven't any choice. He's my boss. Anyway he's already had a report on you and with all the resources at his command, the only unknown as far as he is concerned is what you really look and sound like. Then he will make up his own mind."

The launch had drifted against a landing stage with a sideways shuffle. Rossi moved towards the cabin doorway. "Let's go. No need to take our leave formally of Herr Strauss. We shall be seeing quite a lot of him from now on. In fact you can regard him as one of the family."

The two men filed on to the main deck and had jumped from there to the landing stage before Strauss had finally cut the engines. Despite Rossi's direction, Charles felt it would still be politic to wave goodbye to the German although he did not bother to look for any response.

Basil drove the Ford back into the busy streets of the city. He had been right as to the possibility of delays and the absence of airconditioning other than open windows added discomfort to frustration as the car crept and crawled amongst every conceivable mode of transport.

Then without any warning they emerged from the teeming roads into a tree-lined avenue cooled by shade and serenity. Along each side, hidden by wall and foliage, defended by locked gates and deep storm drains, the mansions of the wealthy protected their owners from inquisitive eyes and unwelcome visitors. This was obviously the Beverley Hills of Kuala Lumpur as far as the status of its inhabitants was concerned. But there the similarity ended. There was no way in which tourists would be encouraged to invade such privacy or catch a glimpse of the famous.

Rossi pulled up outside an unnumbered and unnamed gate. "Here we are, just on time." He looked at his watch with evident relief. The prospect of being late had been uncomfortable. As Charles pulled himself out of the car, Rossi pressed an iron knob framed in the white cemented wall. The silence was almost as heavy as the humidity. Both automatic-

ally reached into their trouser pockets to bring out hand-
kerchiefs to wipe their faces. Then, without warning, the gate
opened inwards allowing them access to a pathway that disappeared between shrubs and trees covered in blooms and
blossoms.

Familiarity with the route from gate to house was no
advantage. There was but one path over which Rossi strode
purposefully and quickly. They no longer had any time in
hand. The final approach to the house was magnificient, with
carefully manicured lawns, splendidly maintained borders
festooned with mobile as well as set colours. Malaysia is
rightly proud of its butterflies.

The main door was open and standing on its thresh-hold
was a tall figure dressed in a long flowing garment of subdued
but clearly defined hues, brown, tan and buff. As the two
visitors came near, he placed his hands together in greeting
and inclined his head upon which was carefully placed a black
pill-box hat.

Charles dropped a step behind Rossi. He preferred to leave
the introductions to the Australian. He had had no experience
with aristocratic protocol outside Europe and now was not the
time to learn the hard way. It was just as well that he had
been cautious since the welcome was being extended by the
Tunku's major domo, a fact that became quickly apparent
when Rossi returned his greeting casually and with familiarity.

"Lead on, McDuff." The Malaysian's features remained
completely impassive. He simply bowed and turned on his
heel to walk back into his master's residence.

The interior was palatial. The two main colours were white
and gold. The walls were covered with paintings and tapes-
tries. Carpets and rugs acted as stepping stones across the
rivers of highly polished hardwood floors. To slip would
certainly have been human, but the damage to one's person
would have been anything but divine. In a land of gracious
living and immaculate manners, an undignified posterior landing, whether on two or three points, would not have been
regarded as an acceptable entry and introduction.

Charles proceeded from one room to another with increasing care. Each one appeared to be on a different level, so that in many instances the absence of a door was more than compensated by a series of steps, sometimes up and sometimes down, which, being of marble, also had to be negotiated with some concentration.

He soon lost count of the number through which they had passed and also his sense of direction. It became simply a matter of following the leader. He was therefore quite unprepared when the major domo suddenly halted in the centre of a large area which boasted a fountain at one end and an inlaid concert grand piano at the other.

"If you would kindly wait here, gentlemen?"

Rossi and Asprey stopped in their tracks and looked around. The immediate impression was of a mixture of the Waldorf-Astoria, the Dorchester Hotel and a set for the King and I. It was opulent, cool, calm but unrestful. There was no encouragement to relax and waiting around added to the tension, which was probably the wish of the owner.

Rossi strolled up to the piano. "Don't you play, Charles?" he asked.

"S'matter of fact, I do, but entirely for my own enjoyment and uplift."

The Australian turned and smiled at him. "Not to worry. I wasn't going to ask you to perform. The Tunku's father had this specially made for him so that they could have international artists perform here. It's a Steinway. I have always been amazed how little the Europeans know of the performers who are on our Eastern circuit, both classic and pop. We listen to some of the best musicians and groups in the world and you wouldn't even recognise their names – and vice-versa."

"What about the Beetles?"

"Ah, but they must be the exception to all the rules – although I don't recall seeing them beyond the West Coast of the States."

"But their records sell very well over here." The last comment was made by neither Rossi or Asprey. The Tunku had decided that his vistors needed to be interrupted before they

121

made themselves too much at home.

"Your Highness," said Rossi, "I hope I find you well?"

"As always, my dear Basil." The smile was perfect, just enough to disclose gleaming white teeth and not too much to confirm their angular sharpness. "I trust that you are also in good health?" Without waiting for a reply, the Tunku continued, "This must be your colleague, Mr. Asprey. How do you do?"

Charles stepped forward but kept his hands by his side. "Very pleased to meet you, Your Highness." A simple response that should give rise to no adverse comment.

"Let us sit over there. Can I offer you something to drink, tea, coffee?"

The Tunku had made his point. No alcohol. Rossi replied as they walked towards a cluster of cane furniture. "Thank you, tea would be fine."

Whilst they were seating themselves, the major domo reappeared and deposited a very large silver tray on a table some distance from the three men. Individual requests were made as to milk, lemon and sugar and suitably filled cups with saucers placed on small side tables ready to be sipped as and when the desire arose. It was all extremely civilised.

"Now, Basil. Tell me where we are now and where do we go from here?" The Tunku's questions were innocuous enough, but Charles still had the uncomfortable feeling that he and Rossi were taking tea with the Headmaster. Pleasant enough but essential to stay on the alert. The juggling with cups and saucers – fortunately without the impossible burden of cake – had to be performed with neither vocal nor ceramic chatter. But of prime importance had to be the choice of words. This arduous task had been allotted to Basil and he was obviously well versed in the ways of satisfying the Tunku.

"Well, first of all, Charles has been invaluable and we have been able to salvage the venture itself." He then summarised with great accuracy the past events. The Tunku sat motionless except when taking occasional sips of tea. Basil left nothing out and nothing to chance. Asprey recalled their "tails" in Kuala Lumpur with wry amusement. Honesty was not only the safest course, it appeared that in Malaysia at least it was the only one.

When Rossi had completed his report, the Tunku commented approvingly. "Well done. We seem to have made real progress this time. Perhaps our endeavours will now be rewarded with success. Mr. Asprey has made an invaluable contribution and we are most grateful. Perhaps he can make another."

"While you were away, Basil, I received a telephone call from a Mr. Sventloski who is in Singapore. He was most anxious to explore the possibility of making a bid for Consolidated Holdings. He understood that I and my family are the controlling shareholders even though it is a public quoted company and for that reason he had approached me informally first. I pointed out to him that the control of any company in Malaysia must remain in the hands of indigenous investors, but he did not feel that that would be an insuperable obstacle. Apparently, Mr. Sventloski has friends who can help in such matters."

"I asked him if he was aware of all Consolidated's activities and he said he thought he was. So I then suggested that he should meet our financial advisor who would be in Singapore shortly, and I took the liberty of giving him your name, Mr. Asprey and that of your hotel, the Marco Polo. I hope that is agreeable to you."

The Tunku paused for Charles to confirm; "Of course." He really had no alternative. "I would like you to find out," continued the Malaysian, "who Mr. Sventloski represents, what he wants and why. C.I.H. is a national company and, between ourselves I have no intention of passing control of it to someone else whatever the price offered. Neither do I wish to provide anyone with the opportunity of examining our merchandise on the pretext that he might buy. Nevertheless, I am intrigued."

"It should make for an interesting meeting," said Asprey. "What do you think is our friend's nationality?"

The Tunku laughed. "Well, his accent was certainly not American, and with a name like that you only have one choice

123

left. Now I am afraid that I have another commitment, so if you gentlemen will excuse me? So nice to have met you, Mr. Asprey. I shall look forward to your continued help in the future. Tomorrow we have a Board Meeting, Basil, so I will see you then. In the meantime, go in peace."

All three men were standing before the Tunku had arrived at his blessing so that the natural reaction of the Englishman and the Australian was to bow slightly and respond with simple "Good-byes". The major domo acted as the necessary substitute for a ball of wool leading them through the labyrinth of rooms and halls.

It was a silent drive back to the centre of the city. Both were immersed in their thoughts, Charles concentrating on Mr. Sventloski and Basil trying to adjust to the day-to-day management problems which he knew would inevitably be waiting for him on his desk.

*　*　*　*　*　*　*

On balance it is usually advantageous to be a regular customer at a good hotel or restaurant. While familiarity can have its drawbacks, generally speaking the customer feels more relaxed in surroundings which are known to him and the staff acquire a measure of his requirements. In the Marco Polo, there was the added advantage that such clients were not asked to sign in on their arrival or complete the usual formalities. These were carefully logged and abstracted so that the staff could take care of such inconveniences on his behalf. Even the key to the room or suite would be available on the desk top for the bell-boy to collect on his way up with the luggage. The only exception to that smooth routine was created by messages and these were handed personally to the customer as he was greeted in the lobby.

Asprey's flight from Kuala Lumpur had been short and un-eventful so he was still fresh in mind and body. His attitude to messages was therefore quite different to that which he might have had after the long haul from the U.K.

He took the piece of paper cheerfully and read it without

any change of expression. As expected, it was from Mr. Sventloski, inviting him to be his guest in the hotel restaurant that evening. The assumption was made that in the absence of a call to the number given that he had accepted. It would appear that Mr. Sventloski was a man of few words.

Charles paused at the entrance to the restaurant to give his name to the head waiter so that he could be directed to the host's table. The back of his guide obstructed any pre-view he might have had of the man waiting for him. Mr. Sventloski was standing behind his table with hand outstretched. Asprey's first impression was that he was about to shake hands with Winnie-the-Pooh, an illusion soon shattered by the hard vice into which he had thrust his hand. His host might have a large, round head with small protruding ears, a light brown complexion and short arms, but a favourite character in a child's fairy story he was not. The only true common denominator was the eyes, button black hard and sharp, glass and false.

"Ah, Mr. Asprey, you will not remember me?"

"No, I am afraid I don't."

"It is not surprising. It must be at least eight years since we met. You visited the offices of Intraco here when you were negotiating the sale of shoes to eastern Europe. These were being made in Singapore by a joint venture between your company and some Chinese investors."

"I recall the venture and the discussions, but to be absolutely honest I still cannot place you."

"You need not be anxious on that score. I was not amongst the principals. But please excuse my terrible manners. Please be seated."

The table was well and truly tucked away in a corner. The restaurant was on different levels and divided by partitions between almost every table. The result was that Mr. Sventloski had ensured their complete privacy. He did not waste any further time on pleasantries or memories and except for the breaks in conversation occasioned by the intrusion of waiters to receive instruction or provide service, he concentrated on the object of the meeting.

125

"I represent a group of substantial financiers who are anxious to help industry and commerce in the developing countries in the Pacific Basin. We have heard of C.I.H. and we like what we hear. If it is correct then it would seem to be the ideal sort of business for us. But we may have been misled and what we have heard may be out of date or only partially true. So, as a preliminary step, I would very much like you to explain to me what C.I.H. is all about, what it does and where you can see it going. So, over to you."

Charles quickly responded to the request and set out at some length all that he knew of C.I.H., its history, activity and personalities. In fact, the only part that he omitted was specific reference to U-134 although he did include in his list of wares the licence to salvage vessels sunken in Malaysian waters. His host listened carefully, asked a number of highly pertinent questions but raised no query that could be linked either directly or indirectly to the German boat.

The catalogue had almost been completed when Asprey became aware that Mr. Sventloski was looking past him and that they had a visitor. Out of the corner of his eye he could see a large white half moon. That could be part of but one profile in Singapore.

Murray Brash and Sventloski greeted each other cordially. Then counsel turned his attention to Charles. "How nice to see you again, Mr. Asprey. I see you are extending your circles in our fair state. Are they concentric or perhaps they are Chinese rings that one moment are joined together and the next, after a suitable hard knock, suddenly they fall apart?"

Charles looked up at him. It was certainly a disadvantage to be seated whilst Brash stood, particularly when fencing, but Sventloski had made no move to rise and Asprey could hardly as a guest do other than follow his host's example. It was clear that there was no intention to offer Brash any invitation to join them. So his response could only be to parry.

"It would appear in Singapore that the more people you know, the more people wish to know you."

"Ah," smiled Brash," perhaps, unlike England, here we

value what we know rather more than who we know. But I must not interrupt your meal. We shall meet again."

The last comment was addressed to both of the diners who each smiled their acknowledgement as a parting gesture.

Charles got in first. "So you know Mr. Brash?" Sventloski shrugged, "Who does not in this city? He and I have had many meetings, sometimes as associates and sometimes on opposite sides of the table. We have some common ground but we also have quite disparate interests."

Asprey recalled that Murray Brash did business with Peking. Whilst Communism and Red China had certain similarities as far as the West was concerned, there were undoubted differences of opinion and objective. Sventloski returned to the matter in hand.

"What you have said encourages me. I do feel that an investment in Consolidated would suit us very well. I also believe that it would be highly beneficial to the company itself. For example, we can provide external currency – I realise that the Tunku is enormously wealthy so that local money is of no importance, but more effectively we can provide overseas markets for all your products including the foodstuffs, oil and scrap metal. If you have need, we also have available technical as well as scientific expertise. Obviously you do not as a company need financial advice. (Charles took that as a compliment). So how would you react to a proposition whereby, subject to the usual safeguards, we would acquire either by rights or new issue a large but minority equity stake in C.I.H.? We would of course want Board representation, but I am sure that that will not prove a problem. Now, do you think that the Tunku would view such an offer favourably?"

Up to that point, Sventloski had appeared quite calm and self-assured, but the last question was put just that shade too eagerly. He was anxious to do business!

Charles pretended to think. He had already made up his mind. To mix Brash and Sventloski would produce as explosive mixture as bangers and beans. So that was out. Yet he could not afford to affend Sventloski at that early and critical stage. So he took the only course open to him. He lied.

"It sounds frightfully interesting. I am sure that the Tunku will welcome your involvement, but he is very much the boss. I will be reporting to him at the end of this week – may I say favourably. But the next step must be with him. If he does agree then I see no reason why we should not be able to arrange for you to visit C.I.H. to see everything for yourself and to take along any of your colleagues who might be interested."

Sventloski looked suitably gratified. "Thank you very much, Mr. Asprey. I am glad that you feel that we can work together. May I give you my card. Whilst I am not always at this number there will always be someone there who can contact me any time of the day or night. I do hope that this is but the start of a long and mutually profitable association."

From there on, the conversation degenerated into the normal business platitudes and it was not long before the two men went their respective ways, Sventloski to his car and Asprey to his suite.

Charles had hardly taken off his jacket when the phone rang. It was Tommy.

"Did you enjoy your dinner with our friend?"

"Is nothing private in Singapore?" Charles was really amused.

Tommy was serious. "Not when we take an interest. What did he really want? Did he mention the boat?"

"To your second question the answer is No, not at all. As for the first, an equity investment in C.I.H. with a seat on the Board.

There was a pause. "Odd," said Tommy, "so what was his game?"

"I don't somehow think he was playing," Asprey could not stop the automatic response and hurried on. "He went on at some length as to the potential of C.I.H. particularly if he and his friends got involved. How it could help the Malaysian economy, etc., etc."

Tommy was still not convinced. Either Charles was lying and holding something back or Sventloski was far more devious than he, Tommy, had thought. He chose to give Asprey the benefit of the doubt.

"I see," he said, "Let me think on it. In the meantime, what are you doing next with him?"

"Reporting to the Tunku – in the negative although I told our friend the opposite."

"Good, but be careful, he is dangerous."

This time Charles managed to keep his thought to himself – who isn't in this place – and said, "Thanks for the tip. Shall I see you tomorrow?"

"Yes, early evening, about 6.00. I will call on you. Bye."

Having reminded himself of his task for the night, Asprey poured himself a drink from the mini-bar, found pen and paper and began to draft his report to the Tunku. Like Tommy, he found it difficult to reconcile Sventloski's approach with their suspicions of his true intent. It had to be the U-134 yet that was quite inconsistent with everything that he had said and suggested. As Charles put together his report a new picture began to emerge. It would appear that Brash and Sventloski were in competition as far as C.I.H. was concerned. So whilst they might have a common objective, their aim could be quite different. Suppose Brash wanted it – up – and Sventloski also wanted it, but – down? If Sventloski could offer the Malaysians a vast increase in the potential of their new indigenous industries then he might well have their ear and influence. Could he then bargain? The more Charles thought about it, the more feasible it seemed.

He pushed back his chair and wandered across to the mini-bar for another drink. Sventloski might be gambling, but what had he to lose? If the Tunku said yes then he had an immediate audience and opportunity for persuasion. If the Tunku said no, then he would have lost very little even in terms of time. He could also have spread quite a useful smoke-screen and confusion. Asprey never under-estimated people, but he was certainly finding it difficult to over-estimate those being drawn together by the secrets of U-134.

The pot of honey had attracted more than the flies and bees.

Chapter Eight

The Deal

Rossi had not stayed at the Marco Polo before. In fact, he had never had occasion to use a hotel in Singapore during his visits to that city. Kuala Lumpur was only one hour's flying time away and he could comfortably complete his business within the twelve hours available to him between the early morning and evening flights.

In view of the relative importance of his mission, however, Asprey and he had agreed that he would stay overnight, thereby having the advantage of two days. They had put together a programme wherein they would spend the first morning together to ensure that they were fully prepared for their subsequent meetings. The first would be with Brash, inevitably over lunch, then the evening probably over dinner with Tommy. They would undoubtedly need a further meeting with Brash the following morning which in turn might require further sessions with persons at present unknown.

The morning discussion centred on the question – how much should they tell Brash? Charles was of the opinion that they should tell him everything that they knew which included that which they based upon other people's guesses.

"I feel that we have nothing to lose if we pass on everything that we know, but if we hold back something that is important, we take a hell of a risk. He's a pretty important guy. He may have sources of information quite unknown to us and they may be very effective. If we happen to keep back a critical fact of which he is already aware then he might well assume that we know other facts which we are also holding back and the result could be catastrophic. On the other hand if we tell all we know then not only will we have his confidence but he might even be able to add to the mutual fund of knowledge."

Rossi demurred. "Possibly, but I am unhappy that we should tell him what we learnt from Muller, that is what the cargo is. The risks involved might put him off. He may not want to be associated with a venture that could be transformed into a time bomb. He's obviously wealthy enough as it is. He might even be worth now more than his proporton of the final payout if we succeed. We've got nothing to gamble in comparison."

Asprey nodded. "True. All I'm saying is that if we hold back and he has already guessed the probability, he will have already decided to take the risk, so our fears on that score would be groundless, but in addition he will be suspicious as to our motives. If we don't tell him and he doesn't know now, he may well find out before the U-Boat is lifted and then we shall have a double problem. No I believe that he will go ahead even if it is news to him, but he may not, at least with us, if he knows and we don't tell him."

Rossi frowned. "How could he go ahead without us?"

"Just by playing the waiting game. He could probably obstruct any financing plans we might have to develop elsewhere, or drag his feet when in association with us. Either way, the Malaysian Government could lose its patience and be susceptible to a new approach from Brash or his contacts full of promises – and a lot of money!"

The dialogue ceased. Charles stood up and went over to the window. Rossi leaned back in his chair and stared unseeingly at the brightly papered wall.

"O.K.," he said finally. "I'll go along with that. If we're wrong, we're wrong. If we're right then we should get some action and that we need."

Asprey turned towards him. "Good, now let's have a look at the papers. Brash will not only want to see them all but he will want copies or even originals. The hotel offers a very good copying and typing service and if we have to use it, the sooner we know what we want the better."

Rossi grunted his agreement and reached for his brief case.

131

Some three hours later, Asprey glanced at his watch. "We'd better make our way down to the foyer. He's usually punctual and never averse to a drink. Have you got everything ready?"

Rossi looked at the neat piles of paper in front of him. "As ready as I will ever be. If there's something missing, I don't know what it is."

He placed the documents carefully in his brief case. "Better use the bathroom first," he said. Charles half smiled. Despite their friendship, the Australian automatically took his bundle with him. Perhaps he slept with them as well!

They had no problem in finding a circle of empty chairs which they immediately appropriated by filling two with their cases and seating themselves in the others. Asprey looked around at the now familiar scene. The young ladies were as perfect as ever, both in appearance and attentiveness. Two were already bearing down on them. One was obviously the supervisor. Her dress was a darker shade of brown when compared with the others, but it was her walk that promoted her. It was a graceful glide with purpose and authority. She gave the impression of a champion ice-skater who despite the most intricate steps and gravity defying twirls displayed not the slightest suggestion of other than a smooth and exultant finish to a very complete performance. Her skirt was as long as those of her subordinates and the slit no wider. Yet without the trace of any haste she overcame the disadvantage of having to walk the length of the lobby as compared with the breadth covered by the serving girl, and still arrived first, albeit just.

"Good afternoon, gentlemen," she greeted them with punctilious timing – it was five minutes after noon. "How pleased we are to see you again, Mr. Asprey. What can we offer you and your guest."

"The price of fame," laughed Rossi. "It now has to be your treat."

"Fair enough," responded Asprey, "we will have two whiskies and water, please – with ice." The supervisor repeated the order to the girl, then smiled at the two men again. "Certainly, I do hope you will enjoy your stay with us again." She bowed slightly and glided away towards the bar area at the rear of the lobby.

"Note the 'again' Charles," said Rossi. "Does she mean the stay again or the enjoyment again?"

"Both, I hope," replied Asprey. He saw no point in enlightening Rossi and in any event they had little time left before Brash was due. As this thought crossed his mind, he looked towards the entrance and, as if materialised by anticipation, the Brash bow wave swept into the lobby, followed immediately by its creator. Those preceeding him scattered as he changed course and headed directly towards Asprey and Rossi.

Brash made no effort to shake hands even on his introduction to Rossi. He just inclined his head and surveyed the Australian from under his eyebrows. The three men dwarfed those in their vicinity. Although almost identical in height, they graduated in width from the massive Brash through the broad Rossi to the slim outline of Asprey. Yet there was no suggestion of the "before" and "after". It would have been equally misleading to attempt to relate their mental ability to their physical appearance. The three were of like mind and intellect.

Brash appeared to have arrived at a conclusion. He completed his appraisal with a smile of greeting.

"How nice to meet you. Asprey's told me quite a lot about you and your efforts in establishing original business in Malaysia. I understand that you have been able to create a small public company that controls that venture?"

Rossi nodded in confirmation. "Yes, it's called Consolidated Industrial Holdings, an impressive name for a pretty small operation. However, we believe that from small beginnings we can get some useful growth."

"Particularly with its salvage rights?" Brash lost no time in coming to the point of their meeting. That's not in character, thought Charles, he's in a hurry. I wonder why?

And so it transpired. Although there was a slight interruption when they made their way to the restaurant, by the time the main course had been delivered Brash had not only re-

133

confirmed with Rossi all that Asprey had first told him, but had had sight of the relevant documents. He sat back and stared at his plate, his fingers completing a tower over his stomach.

"Not at all bad – and the food's quite good as well." Brash smiled at his two companions.

"Now we can get down to business, in more ways than one." He picked up his knife and fork. "I've brought with me the leasing loan contract and a draft salvage contract. If you agree with their terms then I shall want you to take them away with you for signing and sealing. I shall need a copy of your Board minutes approving the contracts and an irrevocable assignment of the salvage licence as security."

Further speech was rendered impossible by the simple expedient of stuffing his mouth full of rare beef. The mastication left his eyes free to judge Rossi's reaction to his last statement. He was not disappointed.

"Wait a minute," Rossi said angrily as he digested the words, his own considerably distorted by a lump of veal. He gulped to clear the way for the onslaught. "We can't give you that. First it's unlikely that the Malaysian Government would let us assign our rights under the contract to anyone. Secondly, even if we could we certainly wouldn't hand you our birth-right."

Brash continued to chew and look amused.

Asprey felt obliged to add his piece. "It might well be practicable for us to agree to use our best endeavours to achieve such an assignment if we fail to complete our side of the bargain."

Brash looked at him sorrowfully. "You forget, Mr. Asprey, that I am a Q.C. I was a lawyer before you were a twinkle in anyone's eye. Please don't waste my time with such, er, generalities." Brash almost said "banalities" but he realised that that might be too offensive.

Rossi had now recovered his equilibrium. "If we fail to keep our side of the bargain, then it would be fair for you to take it on. But I just don't see the Malays agreeing to that. They're almost regretting the present contract as it is. To suggest that it might be handed over to someone else even as a faint possibility could well encourage them to withdraw the rights." Brash swallowed. He had the opening he wanted. "I already have their unofficial consent. When we come to agreement between us, permission to assign will be granted."

Asprey could not prevent himself looking at Rossi, whose face said it all. If they had had doubts as to Brash's influence in that part of the world, the last remnants had quickly evaporated.

"Alright," said Rossi, "if that is the case I can see no harm in agreeing that if we fail to complete our side of the bargain we will agree to assign, but not before."

Asprey felt that he should attempt to summarise what had in fact been agreed and where they were. Brash was definitely in an almighty hurry.

"O.K. What we have agreed is that you or your company, Mr. Brash, will provide the finance necessary to hire a large salvage vessel and make it available for long enough to raise the submarine, complete with experienced crew and fully equipped. We have reckoned that that will cost about one million pounds Sterling. In return, we will pay you the one million and twenty per cent of the net proceeds or twenty million pounds whichever is the greater. If we fail to deliver we will assign the salvage licence to you or your company. That will give you our rights not only to the outcome of the submarine venture but also to any other vessels sunk in Malaysian waters."

Brash chewed contentedly and smiled his acquiescence.

"Good," said Asprey, meaning exactly the opposite, "that will give each of us a direct motivation to get on with the job."

The three men gave their undivided attention to the meal which lived up to their expectations.

Over coffee, Brash produced his papers. "These are the relevant draft contracts. Take 'em away with you. We can then meet again if you so wish, but if they're acceptable you can take them back to K.L. for sealing and minuting. Better it should be done formally, there's quite a lot of money at stake.

If you can have them in my hands by the end of this week, you can order your salvage vessel on Monday next. Then we shall soon see what we have for our money."

Rossi took the documents and glanced at them. "No reason why we shouldn't get them back to you by the end of the week provided there's no fine print and we don't have any trouble with the assignment clause. I'll make sure that all the company formalities are completed. Now, you'd better have your copies of our papers."

The exchange was quickly made, then Brash looked at the two very deliberately. "In addition to obtaining agreement to a possible assignment of the licence, I have also been doing a bit of digging. You were quite right to emphasise the sensitivity of the project. My first contact left me with no doubt that the Malaysians not only regretted the original issue of the salvage licence, but were in fact determined to cancel it at the first opportunity. But, when I visited them a second time, within a matter of days, their attitude had completely changed. I could find no apparent reason for this volte face other than that in some way their new assurance arose from some intervention by the Germans. Whereas previously they had complained about the lack of co-operation or even interest shown by the Germans, that was no longer even hinted at. So I must ask you, to what extent will the Germans be involved in the lift and the split of the spoils?"

There was a distinct pause. Asprey left the answer to Rossi, who appeared equally hesitant to committing himself. "We had to agree to divide the spoils as you put it equally with the German Admiralty, but that still leaves us with more than enough to pay you your twenty per cent." Brash nodded and waited.

"We have also had to agree to them having an observer during the whole of the lift including its preparations and he will have the sole right of first entry into the U-Boat as soon as it breaks surface. No-one else will venture in until he says so."

Asprey noted that Rossi had omitted to mention that the observer also had the right to suspend salvage operations if he wished. It was fair comment that that authority would not find favour with Brash, although it could hardly bind him in the event that the licence was assigned. So Charles kept silent.

Brash sipped his coffee and made no comment. His face had acquired its inscrutable facade. He put his cup down.

"Very well, that's reasonable if that's all it is. Does that mean the Germans rather than ignoring or even resisting the operation are now actively promoting it?"

"It would appear so," responded Asprey. "Certainly they have given us the green light."

The last statement was an outright lie. He had not heard from Eisendorf, although the latter had promised to contact him immediately upon his arrival at the Marco Polo.

Still, it seemed worth the risk. Until they had signed the contracts with Brash there could be no formal commitment. If Eisendorf did say no, then they would simply find fault with the papers and withdraw, more or less gracefully. Should Eisendorf agree then they would have saved considerable time. So, all in all, it was hardly a gamble.

Anyway Brash appeared satisfied with the answer. "Well, I must get back to work. Let's hope we can start together next Monday. The ball's in your court now. It's your return of service."

Asprey was tempted to follow up the allusion to tennis, but with an effort he resisted the temptation. There were too many opportunities for his customary faux-pas – serving aces, out of court, backhanders, etc., etc. The more he thought of the possibilities the more he mentally squirmed.

Brash looked at him with mild disappointment. He had obviously expected some inane response so that he could take his leave with the slight advantage of leaving Asprey in his usual discomfort caused by misplaced comment. But if he had learned his lesson, then it was not to be. Brash gathered himself together preparatory to levering himself up and out of the restaurant. There was no point in adding to his cavalcade, so Asprey and Rossi contented themselves with standing up to bid their guest bon voyage as he slipped his attachment to the table and steamed towards the exit.

137

"What a man," breathed Rossi, "formidable in any language."

"Indeed," said Asprey thoughtfully, "not in any circumstances to be underestimated. He's obviously got on with it whilst I've been away."

"And he's losing no time now," agreed Rossi. "We shall have to put our skates on to keep up with him. Perhaps I should go back to K.L. tonight?"

"No I think not," replied Charles, "you must meet Tommy this afternoon. But perhaps you should fly back earlier tomorrow than we had planned. Let's see how it goes." He looked at his watch. "Now, I could do with a shower. Shall we break off for a couple of hours and meet down here in the bar at 4.30?"

"Good thinking, bat-man," Rossi smiled. "I still have some jet-lag and if what I hear about Tommy is only half right, I shall need to stay awake this evening."

The two men walked through the lobby, into the lift and parted company in the corridor leading to their respective rooms. Both felt tired but reasonably content. Progress had been made and, provided they had no bad luck, it looked as though they would actually get under way within a week. The prospect started the adrenaline flowing. With the right vessel, equipment and expertise, they could have the U-Boat up in a matter of days. And then they would know some if not all of the answers to questions that had haunted others literally for years. But more important they would be in possession of a treasure trove of a value that was almost incomprehensible. Yet once again they had reckoned without the unforeseeable.

Chapter Nine

Intruders

Asprey opened the door of his suite and thought happily of satisfying his immediate desire – a shower followed by a glass of really cold white wine. His mental image and anticipation were rudely shattered and forgotten by the whiff of cigar smoke that greeted him. It was not stale. Someone already occupied the set of rooms which he had understood had been reserved exclusively for his personal and private use. Three strides into the sitting room were enough to provide him with an answer to the intrusion. Taking full advantage of the facilities offered sat a smartly dressed bird-like man calmly examining Asprey through steel rimmed specatacles. He had the courtesy to stand up on Charles's entry but did not offer his hand.

"My apologies, Herr Asprey, for waiting for you here unannounced, but I felt it would be mutually beneficial if we could meet as quietly as possible. I will not outstay my welcome."

Asprey raised his eyebrows. To an observer, the introduction and excuse might almost be an affront but to take exception would be to waste time and effort, as indeed would any attempt to seek clarification as to how the visitor had managed to gain entry to his suite and knew his time of arrival. So he contented himself by confining his reaction to facial signals which were blandly ignored.

"I don't believe we have met before, Mr. . . . ?" Asprey pointed a double-barrelled question at the intruder.

"My name is Weiss and in a manner of speaking, we have. I was with Herr Eisendorf when you and your Australian colleague called upon him."

"Ah," said Asprey, "the fifth man in the armchair."

139

"Precisely," smiled Weiss without any confirmatory indication of the slightest humour. "I must give up the filthy habit, particularly when I am the only one present who enjoys it."

Asprey could not prevent himself. He sniffed. "Couldn't agree more. I've been expecting you. Eisendorf promised to let me know his decision shortly after my arrival here. I hope it's positive."

Weiss looked carefully at Asprey. The German had very pale blue eyes, no eyebrows, with black hair greased to his head in strips from his forehead to the nape of his neck. Had he had a beaked nose, the illusion would have been complete. As it was, his nasal organ was short, fat and squashed. The contrast with the remainder of his facial features was as unpleasant as it was unexpected. He asked: "May we be seated? I promise not to stay too long but we have several things to discuss."

"Of course," replied Asprey. "May I offer you something?"

Weiss shook his head. "No thank you, but if I may continue my cigar?"

"Of course, " repeated Asprey. "Now what have you to tell me?"

Weiss leaned back again in his armchair, crossed his legs, drew on his cigar and casually waved his right hand.

"First I need some information. How well do you know Rossi, what is his background and what kind of person is he?"

Asprey emulated Weiss and settled himself comfortably. This might well take more than a little time.

He began by explaining how he had first met Rossi, what had transpired and the various steps that had been taken. When he came to a description of the man, he did his best to present him warts and all. Weiss nodded from time to time but never interrupted. Asprey concluded his chronicle of history and characteristics. Weiss then adopted the mantle of interrogator.

"Would you say that Rossi's strengths are his determination, his obstinacy and his will to achieve his objectives, regardless of cost?"

"Not regardless of cost."

"Could he therefore be bought?"

"Not at all," replied Asprey. "You miss my point. Rossi would not pursue his plans irrespective of the damage they might inflict on others, that is the cost to others. At the same time, he would ignore the costs to himself, they would be secondary. Once having nailed his colour to a mast, there would be no way in which he might be induced to unhook them, for sure not by offers of money or wealth."

"So," a sibbulant comment from Weiss, "he is wholly and entirely committed to C.I.H. – to make it a success and to fulfill all of the promises he has made to many people – almost regardless of the cost to himself?"

"Broadly, yes," agreed Asprey. "If what you are saying is that even if you withhold your co-operation and Brash fails to provide the salvage facilities, Rossi will still sooner or later find a way to raise the U-134 and thereby assure absolutely the success of C.I.H. which without that bonanza may one day sink despite all his efforts and endeavour, then the answer must be yes. Of that I have not the slightest doubt."

There was a long pause. Weiss looked steadily at Asprey, for once ignoring his cigar. Asprey returned the stare equally without emotion.

"Thank you for making it so clear," eventually Weiss responded. "I will convey your conclusions to my superiors. If you are right, and I am sure that you are, we will have to be equally determined in our approach and certain as to the outcome. In the meantime, however, I am able to confirm that the Admiralty will assist in the salvage of U-134 on the terms agreed in Frankfurt. We shall, of course, put nothing in writing, but you can rely on my word."

Asprey rose as Weiss completed his message. "Very good. That is understood. I hold a firm opinion on the questions you have asked and I hope you will convey it to your colleagues. If I can be of any further help, please do not hesitate to let me know."

The last sentence was as useless as it was superfluous. Weiss had no need of and did not offer any response. He simply stood up, walked briskly towards the door held open by

Asprey, paused on the threshhold, bowed stiffly and said: "Aufwiedershauen". His disappearance towards the lifts was as abrupt and economic as his entry. The only indication of any human weakness or frailty was the dying aroma of cigar smoke left like a calling card above the mantlepiece in the sitting room. Asprey changed his mind. First he would have a cup of coffee with a brandy, then he would take his bath. The implications of Weiss's cross-examination were far from pleasant, but it was the man's intervention that troubled him. If he was right in his assessment of Weiss and his occupation, certainty of outcome implied more than insurance. It had a distinct suggestion of finality – for someone.

In a matter of minutes, room service had satisfied Asprey's immediate needs for coffee and brandy. As he sipped the latter, the thought of a shower re-surfaced. If nothing else, it would help to relax him, physically and mentally.

Charles was by nature a tidy chap. As he undressed in his bedroom he stuffed his clothes into the two plastic bags provided by the hotel, one for the valet and one for the laundry. A major advantage to the seasoned traveller of staying more than one night in a first class hotel was that he could pack his suitcase upon departure with clean and pressed clothes instead of throwing into it an evergrowing tangled mess of soiled garments. Charles checked the contents of each bag against its list that he had completed and then telephoned the internal laundry to ask for their collection. He left the two plastic bundles lying on the floor of the lounge near the door, well knowing that the collector would undoubtedly carry a passkey. It did not occur to him that to encourage independent access might lead to a second unexpected vistor.

The bathroom was spacious and ideally appointed for gracious living. There were touches of comfort everywhere including herbal bath salts, bathing caps, bath-robes and even a soldier's friend. The bath itself was deeper but considerably shorter than its European counterpart. By far the most attractive feature, however, was the shower cubicle, enclosed on three sides by frosted glass and fitted with multi-level nozzles that reached all parts of the body that other showers only condescended to embrace by secondary trickles, being entirely dependent upon the posture and physique of the showeree. This complicated arrangement required extreme caution and care in the adjustment of its master control, since the more delicate areas received the same attention as to force and temperature as those used to harsher treatment.

Asprey's approach was entirely self-taught and would have routed the most experienced "What's My Line" panel. Indeed with a little practice and polish, it could well have been developed into a highly entertaining turn for television or cabaret. The first image to establish was that he was quite starkers, without a stitch. The second was that he intended to keep as much of his body as he could outside the cubicle until he was quite satisfied that everything within it was absolutely comfortable. Errors in the past, either of execution or judgment, had proven painful. This gave rise to the third point to be borne in mind. The door to the cubicle served both as a body shield and as a means of controlling the volume of water that might otherwise be directed before final adjustment into the bathroom generally. Charles was both tidy and cautious as well as sensitive.

The combination of intent and method resulted in a series of writhings and contortions which, from a slow sedate start gradually accelerated to a crescendo of movements that would have generated envy even in the breast of Nureyev and pop-eyed amazement on the faces of those normally excited by that ballet star's stage gambols. Whilst his leaps, twists and turns were limited by his desire to retain his grip on the door, they were comparable in every degree with those of the master, the difference being simply a matter of dimension. In that, Charles had more than ample compensation. Nureyev's cod-piece, whilst impressive, still left a lot to the imagination and has been said by those who are disposed to be unfriendly to be filled likewise. But Charles's state of undress eliminated any camouflage, imagination or disguise. By the time he had everything adjusted to his satisfaction, his performance would have turned on the most obdurate female tap. Sadly it re-mained wasted and misdirected effort, an opportunity squandered by its unconscious performer.

Another problem presented by an efficient shower is that of keeping the soap suds alive and flowing. As fast as Charles lathered his body, the cascades of water removed all vestige of the cleanser. He was busy contemplating possible solutions when he felt a cool draught on his left shoulder. Someone was opening the door of the cubicle. For a fleeting moment, Asprey had visions of Hitchcock's "Psycho" and raised his left hand in the chop position. The lack of clothes, utter saturation and blurred eyes seemed to make the gesture quite meaningless. He felt hopeless and helples. He imagined his face, contorted by pain, distorted by pressure against the glass door and creased with rivulets of bloody water with mouth open in shocked amazement.

The door continued to open and as he moved his head out of the line of fire from the top nozzle he could see his intruder. It was Marie, immaculately dressed and unstained by the jets of water that framed Charles. She smiled.

For a long moment they looked into each other's eyes, then she released him by dropping hers to look at his body. As he followed her example he realised that she had already unzipped the back of her dress and almost in unison with his eyes, it slipped to the floor. She was truly beautiful. He breathed in deeply. Her figure was near perfection both in colouring and shape. He wiped his forehead with the back of his hand to make sure that his vision would remain uninterrupted by water, whether from the shower or, as he now suspected from his own over-heated reaction. In fact, there was a distinct movement from below to confirm that his senses were beginning to respond to the situation without any reference to or agreement with his brain. The reaction erased the last remnants of his normal embarrassment and he stepped out into the bathroom.

Marie had already unhooked her bra and as she bent forward to remove her pants, he felt an uncontrollable urge to pull her towards him, head downwards. But he had reckoned without Marie and her understanding of men. She completed her manoeuvre and side-stepped him at the same time.

"No," she said, "let me first wash you in the shower." Without waiting for his reply, she took his hand and pulled him with her into the cubicle. He closed the door behind them and made to move across. Still she kept him away. "No, where is the soap?" Charles waved his hand in the general direction of the floor. The shower system had been carefully set for his personal benefit. Consequently the main jets of water were now acting as a barrier between them. His first reaction was that an adjustment was urgently needed. But commonsense prevailed. The arrangement could prove ideal. First they would soap each other and then unite in the middle. The prospects were exhilarating and any inhibitions that he might still have had were despatched with the water pouring into the grid in the floor of the cubicle.

Marie offered him the soap. His automatic reaction to the gesture was to indicate "ladies first". Not for the first time in his life, Asprey benefited from his natural good manners. He had had no idea as the pleasure that could be enjoyed from the simple application of soap and water by two small delicate and soft hands. It was an experience that as far as he was concerned could go on for ever and ever. But again he had reckoned without Marie. She was fully aware they they could spend the rest of the day in the cubicle unless she took avoiding action – which she did. Suddenly Charles became aware of a mounting excitement in his loins. The next moment he was completely lost in a frenetic climax. He stood there gasping and annoyed. For a brief moment he waited for the expected anti-climax, but it was missing. Perhaps he could . . . Before he could collect his thoughts, Marie had thrust the soap into his hands. "Now me," she said, "then we will lie down."

* * * * * * *

Charles was lying in the brilliant sun on a golden beach. A large crab scuttled across the sand. Charles was too relaxed, too lazy to do other than watch its progress. Then, without warning, the crab, beady eyes fixed on his angular feet, pinioned his big toe in its enormous claw and pinched hard.

145

"Ow," Charles sat up smartly. "What the devil . . ." He was lying on the bed in his suite and looking at a laughing Marie standing at its end. Obviously she had just bitten his throbbing member.

"What did you do that for?" he asked not a little angry. Marie pretended to look serious.

"I had to wake you. It's time for me to go. I could have bitten you anywhere I wanted but that might have affected our pleasure the next time. So I decided that your big toe was the most disposable part of you. I am sorry if it does really hurt, but I had to bite you twice, you were so deeply asleep. Of course I could just have easily walked out without waking you up, but I wanted to say good-bye."

Charles slid off the bed. "Probably my metabolic clock at work. I haven't felt so relaxed since I left England. Must you go?"

"Of course. If I hadn't, I wouldn't. I'd much rather stay with you. But I have an appointment I must keep and after all I am only a working girl."

Charles smiled rather bitterly. "Sorry for losing my cool and understanding. Anyway, I am due to meet Rossi this evening." He looked at his watch on the dressing table. "Good lord, I have to be down in the bar in twenty minutes."

Without looking round, he slid open the door of the fitted wardrobe and started to collect his clothes. "Can I give you a ring tomorrow morning?" he shouted. "I probably won't have to leave until later in the day. Perhaps we could meet here. Anyway, if we can't then, we can always fix up something for when I get back."

There was no rely. Asprey turned around, holding the pile of clothes in his arms. The room was empty.

"Marie," he called, "Marie, where the devil are you?"

He knew the answer before he had asked the question. She had departed as quickly and as quietly as she had arrived. Charles threw his clothes on to the bed. "Damn, damn, damn. I've got accustomed . . ." His voice was as tuneless as Rex Harrison's and equally passionate. "I've let her get under my skin. But why? There's no future, unless I regard her simply

146

as a . . ." The word was unacceptable and unsayable. Yet it was the only true interpretation of his intentions, that she should be available when he required her to satisfy his sexual needs.

"Damn, damn, damn." The words had become quite meaningless, merely punctuation marks as he quickly dressed. Any romantic view of their relationship, even if it could continue, had to be for the birds. He might have to deceive others but he could never afford to kid himself.

"Pity," he said out loud. But, really, was it? If he stood back and looked at it honestly, its pursuance or epitaph were both self-indulgent. There was little he could lose.

As he combed his hair he examined his face in the mirror. So far, time had been kind to him but there were already signs that its passage had left some marks. When he had been lying on the bed with Marie they had discussed her interest in reincarnation and whether they had met before in another time and place. That had led them into the question of fate and finally into a comparison between Chinese and European astrology. In particular the way in which the oriental regarded the year as more important in determining character than the western equivalent of the month of birth. Responding to Asprey's casual question, Marie had said that she believed that she must have been born on the day roughly equivalent to the middle of the Christian year. The comb was forgotten. If Marie had been born on or about July 1, then she was a Cancerian. His big toe throbbed.

Chapter Ten

The Fortune-teller

Tommy was far from his usual ebullient self although he greeted Rossi courteously and exchanged hellos quite amicably with Asprey. It was clear that his mind was elsewhere. Fortunately he had brought with him his friend and distant relation Johnny Chin. Johnny's contribution was the oriental equivalent of court jester. Whilst his mentor gazed morosely into the distance, Johnny worked at creating a conversation from monosyllabic crumbs of comment. There were no awkward pauses, pregnant silences to underline the absence of any worthwhile input from the host, which, as always, was the role automatically adopted by Tommy.

To give him due credit, Johnny did not have to descend to the depths normally plumbed by his western counterpart in such a situation. He could discourse on matters political, social or economic with gems of unique interest for his listeners, all gathered in his travels about Australasia. In particular, he knew how to activate and promote the contributions of others by deliberately posing provocative questions. Nevertheless, after about an hour of effort even Johnny was beginning to show the strain and inevitable gaps between discussion were emerging and lengthening.

Without warning, Tommy appeared to wake up. "Has everything been arranged with Murray Brash? Have you his firm promise of finance?"

Asprey deliberately allowed Rossi to answer. "Yes, subject to formal signature, everything is set up."

"Good," said Tommy, "but if you want a successful conclusion to your enterprise, you will need my help."

"How come?" asked Rossi. "What do we need in Singapore

148

beyond that which we already have?"

"Security." Tommy looked steadily at Rossi. "You are obviously on to something that must be attractive to a lot of people. I would guess for a number of different reasons. Some may even want to stop you getting it, but the majority will simply want to take it from you."

"That may be," said Rossi, "you may well be right, but how can you in Singapore help us in Malaysia?"

"Because your vulnerability is not confined to Malaysia. If what you are after is as valuable as it appears to be, there will always be somebody who won't worry about the price and such people could be anywhere in this part of the world – and most of them have their bases in Singapore."

"Again," persisted Rossi, "you could be right, but what in fact can you offer?"

Tommy did not answer directly but looked instead at Johnny. "Can you provide our friends with shadows even at mid-day?"

"No problem," laughed Tommy, "even when the sun has disappeared."

"Good enough," Tommy nodded at Rossi. "So we can help you here in Singapore or there in K.L. or wherever you go in the world. Any time, all the time any place and every place.

"If we need it," returned Rossi, "how much would such security cost?"

"Five per cent of the total profit from the venture," Tommy responded unhesitatingly.

Asprey did a bit of mental arithmatic. Tommy had set his sights unerringly. Either he knew from Brash the terms agreed or he knew enough of those involved to be able to guess the split. Either way, Tommy had arrived at the bulls-eye.

But Rossi was far from convinced. "We shall have our own guys during the lift. As soon as that has been completed there will be others who will have a part to play with us. I see no reason why we should cut you in, even if you are a friend of long standing, unless you are giving us the 'or else' treatment."

Tommy's face hardened. His eyes narrowed to the narrowest

of slits. "As you say, I am a friend of long standing and it is not a friendly act to threaten or to suggest that I might. I'm sure you didn't mean it that way." He paused long enough to make his point and allow Rossi to retreat behind a hurried nod of agreement and a muttered "Of course".

"Perhaps in view of the sums involved you are right to ask for proof of the value of my offer, especially as you and I have only met for the first time this evening."

Tommy turned to Charles. "Security ensures secrecy – at least that is the intention. You have been anxious to keep the whole story and facts to yourself, letting selected people know only that which you believe they need know – for your purposes. Whether you actually know the whole story, I doubt, but that's another matter. For the moment what you do know you want to keep. And that's where I and my colleagues come in. I can give you two examples. You remember our dinner in the Troika and that someone was listening very carefully to our conversation. That someone conveniently disappeared and will take no further interest in your venture. In addition your room at the Marco Polo had been searched by professionals who found nothing, because we searched first and that was the result of our endeavours. I have no doubt that you are both being tailed, not only in Singapore but wherever you go. We cannot stop that, indeed we wouldn't want to try for obvious reasons, but we can ensure that they keep a respectful distance and confine their interest to your perambulations. You chaps are the centre of attraction for a number of influential and powerful people and if some decide that they do not want you to succeed, then you will have your work cut out to conclude the venture. In fact, without our aid, or somebody like us, I would guess that your chances are pretty minimal – and you might find it difficult to find another "protector" whom you can trust. You have a tiger by the tail. Take your eye off him, and he has you. Yet if you cannot look over your shoulder you may be lost. Maybe you think I am being dramatic, but I am not. To some, life is of little value, even their own, as compared with what you may have almost within your grasp."

Although Tommy had addressed himself to Asprey, Rossi had followed his every word, gesture and expression. The combination had had a sobering effect.

"O.K.," said Rossi. "I don't understand the reference to the Troika but I do go along with the need to keep our eyes firmly fixed on where we are going and what we are doing. I also appreciate your help in this part of the world. In Europe, however, you can do little or nothing and anyway that's not where the danger, if there is any, will lie. So for half the service, half the fee. I would agree to two and a half per cent and cover in the East."

Tommy smiled, sucked his lips and rubbed his nose. "So be it. The West will be your problem, but while you are here or hereabouts, you will have no problem, Johnny will see to that."

"Agreements?" asked Asprey.

"Yes," replied Tommy, "we shall have to sign something. I will bring them across tomorrow morning if that's convenient. No reason why they should be complicated as between friends – even of long standing!"

There was no need for Tommy to explain why written agreements need only be superficial. It was more than clear to the four men that in any protection contract the means to obtain recompense for its breach were readily available simply by reversal of their original friendly role. Those that looked after, could, if circumstances arose do just that. There was no necessity to threaten, the promise was explicit. The irony of the arrangement was that the only way in which its effectiveness could be proved was by the consequences of its absence, like the man in Surbiton who prayed every night that his garden would not be overrun by elephants. If nothing happened who could deny that the action taken had worked? But to stop praying was an entirely different matter. In Surbiton, little risk, but for Rossi and his associates? The proof might be long in coming and when it did materialise it would be conclusive – in every sense of the word.

Tommy plainly had no intention of "doing the Town" that evening, so it was with mutual relief that the four parted

151

company with the expressed intention of "an early night".

After the Chinese had left, Asprey and Rossi adjourned to the lobby bar. As it would probably be his last day in Singapore before he returned to England, Asprey was determined to satiate his enjoyment of the hotel's famous Irish coffees.

Rossi pushed his glass of Black Label in small circles around the highly polished table top oblivious of the raised eye-brows of the young lady who would have the task of rubbing away the results of his artistic impressions.

Head on chest and concentrating on the glass, he spoke quietly. "Don't think much of your friend. Doesn't say much and certainly doesn't live up to his reputation with the girls. No doubt he is intelligent and obviously wealthy. And everybody cow-tows to him, but - - - " Rossi paused and looked directly at Asprey. "What's he up to? Why does he want in? It can't be the money. Even taking into account the amount involved, his proportion after expenses can't be much compared with what he's already got in the bank. So it can only be that he wants in. Why?"

Rossi's repetition of his question showed his anxiety. Direct of manner himself, he was quite relaxed with the Germans, the Malaysians, the English (including Brash) and his own kind in Australia and New Zealand, but the Western trained Chinese puzzled him and he did not like contradictions. He wanted to know where he was and where everyone connected with him stood. And he could not place Tommy.

Asprey was not clear himself. "I have no doubt that he can do as he says and provide us with protection. I cannot say whether he is a hundred per cent right when he says that we need it but I believe that he is. So we shall get value for money. But I still agree with you. He's not doing it out of friendship neither is he doing it for the money. Furthermore, if he is right, then he is taking some risk himself and that is out of character. So he must be determined to be in the game. Therefore he wants to know what is going on."

"Perhaps he's one of those who want to stop us or relieve us of the booty," Rossi said quietly, still concentrating on the patterns created by his glass.

"Perhaps," said Asprey equally softly, "but that he can do whether he is inside with us or outside waiting."

"True, in which case we have nothing to lose, except two and a half per cent and you feel that we shall get our money's worth for that?"

"Yes," nodded Asprey, "on balance, that's the easiest question to answer. Tommy will do a good job."

"O.K." Rossi drained his glass. Tommy was in, whether they liked it or not.

Rossi suddenly exploded with laughter. "Tonight, Charles, old chap," he said between gulps of merry thought, "we will spend a night on the booze. No food, just wine and women. What can you arrange?"

Asprey was not at all prepared for the suggestion. He had already arrived at the conclusion that the Brückenkeller fiasco had permanently persuaded Rossi that evening entertainment for them as a duo was an embarrassment ever to be avoided. But the idea did have its attractions. He might see Marie again, although how that could be arranged without Tommy knowing, he could not immediately perceive. Even if it could be done, it would be fraught with dangerous consequences if it leaked afterwards – and Singapore was as parochial as any large city when it came to sex and relationships. Still he could examine the possibility which Rossi's question allowed.

"O.K.," he agreed, "there's an excellent night club on the roof of the Intercontinental and if you are interested we would go to a fortune-teller's afterwards."

Rossi's eyes lit up. "That would be very interesting indeed. Perhaps we could get some guidance on whether we are going to be successful or not. It might save us a lot of time . . . " Rossi had obviously decided to relax and play. Asprey smiled in return. "Right, let's meet in the foyer bar at about 9.00 p.m. We can have a snack beforehand in our rooms" (both men smiled) "so an aperitif for the evening would give us a good drinking start. Then off to the nightclub, say about 10.00. Life starts early in the evening here – then on to the Mandarin for your cast into the future." Asprey looked at his watch. "If I get cracking now, I should be able to arrange that for us."

"Excellent, if I may say so. A well chosen, balanced and succulent recipe for a night's repast." Rossi had been unable to restrain himself. He just had to refer to Frankfurt. Asprey's smile broadened. So be it, he thought, well tonight I might recover some if not all of my reputation as a man about town.

"Glad you think so – nine o'clock it is. See you then in the foyer bar."

* * * * * * *

Both men were on time, so that although Rossi had actually arrived first, he had still to place his order. Asprey's prompt appearance enabled them to initiate the drinking with minimum delay and limitation. They started on the serious business of pacing their alcohol intake. Rossi had beer and Asprey had a glass of white wine. That should provide each with a gentle push start.

"What have you laid on, Charles?" The question was deliberately ambiguous.

"Nothing in particular. I had thought of introducing you to Marie, but she's a special friend of Tommy's, so I decided that discretion was the better part of temptation." In truth Asprey had arrived at that conclusion, but he had never had any intention of offering Marie as Rossi's partner for the evening, let alone the night. "So we will take pot luck, but I have some ideas which should put the odds distinctly in our favour."

The phrase "pot luck" was unfortunate. Rossi's suspicions re-emerged, Asprey was going to repeat history! This time Rossi would bail out if that became even a suggestion.

"Right, sport, I'll leave that entirely in your hands." Rossi's reversion to Australian slang was quite out of character and Asprey took the warning. He sipped his wine thoughtfully. Perhaps his knowledge of the over-all situation was making him too sensitive. Perhaps he was beginning to read more into words than was intended. However right or wrong he was in his interpretation, there was not the slightest doubt that he had to maintain a delicate balance on his tight-rope whatever gyrations others might perform.

154

He was now more than a little glad that he had decided against Marie joining him. That could only have been a step way out of line and a quite unnecessary complication.

The Intercontinental Hotel was not as attractive a building as many of its competitors in Singapore. Asprey recalled its origins when it had climbed into the skyline, supported by a desperately slippery wooden scaffolding, the death trap of a number of female coolies who clambered like ants carrying bricks up to their male counterparts. Every time it rained, and that was usually a daily occurrence although for a very short spell, the bindings holding the scaffolding together loosened, then, as the sun took its effect, clasped the pieces of wood tightly together. Why the structure did not collapse each day was a mystery. Yet it survived – even if some of those working on it did not. The interior of the hotel, although tasteful and luxurious in finish was far from unique in concept or execution. The lifts worked effortlessly and efficiently, transporting the two would be gentlemen on the prowl swiftly to their first destination, the roof-top night club.

Americans prefer to drink in the dark. Even during the day, their bars are like black holes in the galaxies of their internal illuminations. Whether it is to provide anonimity for those engaged in sampling their wares or to allow the barmen even greater opportunity for relieving customers of their thirst and wallets is impossible to discern. Even so, the night club itself provided a far less gloomy environment than that which Asprey had previously experienced with Tommy. He and Rossi had no difficulty in following their guide to a table located about three-quarters around the perimeter of the large circular room. This placed them conveniently near the small stage hidden behind dark velvet curtains. The noise level was surprisingly moderate.

A small live band was endeavouring to please a large number of middle aged caucasians who had no intention of doing other than drink and extend their eyeballs. Charles was able to place their first drinks order without resorting to the language of the deaf and dumb or even shouting.

The two men relaxed into very comfortable modern chairs

155

of stainless steel tube and nylon upholstery.

"What happens next?" asked Rossi.

"Patience, my friend. First our drinks, then the offer of company, finally the show, whatever that is."

"Well, let's get cracking. The night is still young but it's the only one we are likely to get in Singapore for some time to come, so the earlier we start the more we can enjoy."

Despite Rossi's impatience, the programme unfolded in its own time. The drinks arrived promptly but it was nearly half an hour before Asprey was able to discern where he might obtain the service of the quality he sought. The more sophisticated the Madame, the more delectable her protegées – as well as the more expensive. Seated at a table next to the stage was an oriental lady of indeterminate age but distinct and lasting beauty. She handled her long ebony cigarette holder like an experienced debutante of the thirties with the grace of a geisha girl communicating through her fan. It was her wand of authority and office. With it she literally conducted her business.

Watching her carefully Asprey discovered that at infrequent intervals the head waiter would approach her, offer some request at which the lady would nod or shake her head after a suitable pause for careful cansideration. The head waiter would then make his way to another table to speak with a male customer who clearly awaited his return with some eagerness and a considerable amount of anxiety.

Shortly afterwards, one or more young ladies would miraculously appear at the customer's table and the resulting party would immediately blossom into a self contained satellite of the evening's entertainment. Once or twice the head waiter's return had had the opposite effect – a demand for the bill and a bad natured exit.

Asprey made up his mind. In for a penny, etc., etc. He summoned the head waiter who arrived with grave alacrity.

"Sir"?

"My friend and I would like a little company. The best – new, intelligent and English speaking – beautiful of course."

Listening to himself Asprey could not conceive a cornier line,

156

yet it came off the tongue as smoothly as a good dessert wine – and as sickly.

"Of course, sir."

"I believe the lady seated next to the stage might be able to help us." As he spoke, Asprey pushed the silver salver upon which lay the incomplete check for the drinks already supplied across the table towards the head waiter. He inclined himself towards Asprey and picked up the piece of paper and those concealed beneath.

"No problem, sir. If you will bear with me for a few moments."

If Charles had closed his eyes, he might well have thought that he had been listening to a butler in an English stately home responding to a request to decant a second bottle of claret. It was uncanny. Perhaps the man had been trained at one of the special schools for that profession in Norfolk – or even worked for Trust Houses before they had been fortified? There was no doubt at all about his nationality. He had to be Irish.

Whatever his background and training, the head waiter was as good as his word.

"Ahem," even the deprecating cough of the well known Jeeves, "Madame will be only too happy to oblige, sir. The retainer will be five hundred dollars, but any expenses incurred here will of course be on your bill and should there be any costs after you leave the club these will be agreed with and reimbursed to the young ladies. I am sure you will understand, sir. They are the normal arrangements, but naturally the young ladies themselves are very special."

The head waiter had returned the check to the salver. Asprey took out his wallet and placed six one hundred dollar bills on top of the salver. The incongruity of the situation appealed to him. He felt obliged to enquire after the cucumber sandwiches but he had the uncomfortable feeling that the man would know exactly what he was talking about and quote Wilde back at him. From many points of view, silent acquiescence was to be prefered.

"Thank you very much sir, I am sure that you will have a

most pleasant evening and, er, night."

The purveyor of glad tidings glided back to Madame, who, having received his message and offering, described a casual arc of smoke in the general direction of Asprey and Rossi. The latter was finding it increasingly difficult to contain himself.

"What a performance," he breathed. "If I hadn't seen it with my own eyes I would have believed it only possible on the London stage. What timing – s'marvellous."

Asprey was a little peremptory. "We have four seats around the table so that we can choose whichever girl we like. If it so happens that we both prefer the same one, then we can decide by shooting fingers. I don't want any overt arguments, O.K.?"

Rossi refused to bridle. "If you say so."

Fortunately the problem did not arise. The two girls were as alike as sisters, which in fact they turned out to be. They expressed their individuality with their dress. One wore a white gown of almost classic design, simple and free flowing. The other a satin sheath dress with a high Victorian neck compensated by a thigh length split in the skirt which revealed a surprisingly slender leg – that is surprising for an oriental.

Whoever had trained them in their dress sense had skilfully enhanced their individual attributes. Fortuitously, and it could not have been otherwise, these coincided with the tastes of the two men. The table arrangement allowed each to choose his companions with no problems at all. There was no need to shoot fingers, which as far as Rossi was concerned was just as well as he did not have the faintest notion as to the meaning of the phrase and its implications.

Communication was relatively easy, although the girls' command of English was not as wide as the men would have wished for table talk. This deficiency was soon eliminated by a roll of drums signalling the beginning of the floor show. Conversation had become superfluous. The performance was dominated by one act – an erotic simulation by a princess full of eastern promise. Asprey and Rossi assumed that the young lady's wriggles and writhings on a sumptuous bed were intended to arouse certain sexual emotions – hence the description, erotic. Whilst her main interest appeared to be centred on a bottle, the extent of her excitement was limited to its examination against a spot-light and to stroking the undeniable smoothness of its shape. The combination of what she saw, or thought she saw and touched overcame her so much that she finally collapsed in a tremulous heap on her white eiderdown.

The thunderous ovation she received contradicted the opinions of the two venturers. Untouched though they were, their yellow and American brethren were quite frenetic. Perhaps for the former it was because the princess had shown a predeliction for a brandy bottle, the container of the liquid which they regarded as the conveyor of male virility. As for their American counterparts, the only explanation available was that throughout her entire performance "Cleopatra" was quite naked.

By the end of the show, Rossi and Asprey were not a little merry. Both had consumed more than an adequate measure of assorted alcohols. But Asprey had promised the services of a fortune-teller, so off to the Mandarin they went together with the girls whose delight at the next phase of the evening was squeakingly confirmed and obviously genuine. It was an unexpected pleasure for those who regarded visits to clairvoyants as privileged and highly welcomed occasions. Asprey could not, as far as they were concerned, have made a better choice. For this they needed no extra reimbursement.

The Mandarin was almost garish in comparison with the Marco Polo or Intercontinental. It was strategically placed on the Orchard Road and topped by a circular revolving restaurant. Inside, glittering glass (or plastic) chandeliers hung from gilded ceilings and the walls were covered by enormous mirrors. The dominant colours were gold and red. The effect was that of an over-indulgent Hollywood set for an "eastern" spectacular, lacking both taste and glamorous chorus line.

On a previous visit to Singapore, Asprey had been introduced to a fortune-teller of considerable reputation. Where she lived he knew not, so he followed the arrangements made on the first occasion. Hence the meeting in the Mandarin. Her

159

particular strength was in reading palms. Her interpretation of Asprey's had been disconcerting at the time, but it was the evolution of subsequent events that removed any doubts he might have had regarding her talent.

So much so that he had no intention of repeating the experience especially with Rossi present.

The lady awaited their arrival at a large table on the mezzanine floor. She wore evening dress and had placed in front of her a large black hand-bag. She showed no inclination to move as the four approached her, although she obviously recognised Asprey. Introductions were soon effected and places taken around the table. Rossi immediately thrust his hand, palm upwards for Madam Ching to inspect. It quivered, partially from the excitement of its owner and partially from his intoxication. It was ignored.

Asprey then pulled out his wallet, extracted a number of dollar bills and handed them to Madam Ching. "For the three," he said. The fortune teller stared at him.

"Not for you?" she asked. Asprey shook his head. "A pity – you I would do for nothing." Asprey murmured, "You're very kind, but not on this occasion."

She looked at him a little while longer then turned her impassive gaze on Rossi. Charles took the opportunity of ordering a round of drinks. Madam Ching gave a remarkably accurate summary of Rossi's life to date, including quite a lot of previous information previously unknown to Asprey. The Australian's reaction was one of great absorption. He hung on every word, nodding and saying "Yeah" at frequent intervals. He was sobering fast. His drink remained untouched. From time to time one of the girls would giggle and attempt a joke or lighthearted comment to be completely ignored by Rossi. His eyes were fixed on those of the fortune-teller's like a snake fascinated by a mongoose. He was quite hypnotised.

Finally, there came the crunch comment. "Fine – now what about the future? Will I – will we be successful? Will we achieve what we are after?"

The woman's expression remained completely devoid of emotion. "You will certainly achieve your destiny in life quite shortly. Even quicker than you think. Your contribution will be for the benefit of those round you – even your enemies, but especially for those who do not and will never know of you. No, you will not have long to wait. Since it is inevitable, I cannot advise. Your love of life is in doing things to help others. So the outcome of your work will be as you would wish although your path may be different to that which you presently see. You will continue to help others by accident or design. Yours is a worthy life."

So saying, she folded Rossi's fingers into his palm and pressed the fist that she made, "Go in peace".

Basil Rossi was now completely sober. He felt as if he had entered a place of worship without invitation or intention and had been quickly but quietly led outside again, sent on his way into the brilliant sunshine by a simple blessing. The glare of the bright light was as effective as the closing of a door. It was summarily locked by the earthiest of interruptions.

"Do me," squeeled the two young courtesans in unison.

"Me first, me first."

The spell was well and truly broken. Rossi reached for his drink and drained his glass in one long pull. The fortune teller turned her attention to her two new customers. She spoke in Chinese.

Taking advantage of the absorption in her words, Asprey leant across to Rossi. "I'm not going to be much good, tonight, I've had far too much to drink and I shall have trouble just getting into bed. I'll probably sleep on the floor."

Rossi laughed. "As you wish, old bean, but I'm all right. In fact I shall need re-lubricating. You can leave me with the two of 'em. I am quite capable of looking after them, financially and otherwise – and that's not boasting."

"Suits me. As soon as the soothsayer (Asprey had trouble with that word. In fact it came out in a quite unintelligible form) has finished, I will wend my way back to the Marco Polo. I shall see you in the morning." Rossi nodded, then summoned the inevitable waiter hovering near at hand for a further round of drinks. Asprey excluded himself from participation which in turn could only be sustained by his

161

retirement. He had intended to stay until Madam Ching had departed, but having made his case he could hardly sit there and continue to drink. So he arose, stepped away from the table, bowed in an exaggerated fashion and zig-zagged in the general direction of the exit. The fortune teller paused in her explanations and watched him depart with a troubled expression.

"Your friend is leaving us?" she asked Rossi.

"Yes, he's had a little too much. The English are not very good at holding their liquor."

"Ah, he is English and a friend of yours?"

Rossi smiled. "Right on both counts, but then you should be – it's your job."

The woman returned his smile. "The word 'should' is for those who set standards. Whether they keep them is quite a different matter. What we 'should' be is never what we will be and seldom what we are."

Rossi looked puzzled for a moment. Then he remembered his intentions for the night – distinctly dishonourable – and laughed aloud.

"Enough of philosophy and serious matters. We only live once so let's enjoy it while we can. Now if you girls have had your money's worth we can retire to the Marco Polo and see if I can enjoy the same value."

Madam Ching collected her bag, confirming Rossi's wish that that part of the evening's entertainment was concluded. The two girls were obviously disappointed but took care to conceal their reaction as best they could. After all they were not there to enjoy themselves. If they did it would be a matter of chance, a bonus to which they were not entitled. So they dutifully made preparations for departure. As they made their way out of the hotel they consoled themselves with the thought that one Australian between the two of them was a far less taxing prospect than that for which they had been paid and would expect to be paid.

The fortune teller stayed in the foyer. She had another appointment before her night was done. She watched Rossi flanked by the two young ladies stride across the carpet and out into the humid air. She had come to terms many years before with the limitations and damage inherent in her gift. She had no power to change the course of events. If she tried she would only be accused of ineffectual interference. She might also be blamed for the inevitable outcome.

People created their own destiny. It was an extension of their own unchangeable characteristics. To point out the dangers of their paths was to invite disbelief, fear and suspicion. Even when armed with such knowledge, their deviations were but temporary and they must sooner or later return to that in which they felt most comfortable, whatever the forecast. She could only defer the inevitable and that was the best that she could hope to achieve. And it was not good enough. Far, far better to conceal and forget. One she could, the other she could not.

Her thoughts were still confused. She knew that one of the men would make his mark by omission and that the other's impact would be significant and by intent. One would help his fellow humans avoid a catastrophy without ever knowing it. The other had an aura of power which disturbed and frightened her. But that which truly terrified her as she concentrated upon his destiny was the black void that confronted her mind. The impenetrable hole that sucked in her being and that of countless others. A horizon that was finite and an infinity that had an end. She had experienced that cause of her fear only once before – and it had arisen through the same man.

Suddenly she decided. She would not wait for her last appointment. There were certain matters which should have been attended to a long time ago, highly personal and of little import to anyone else.

Madame Ching swept out of the Mandarin, looking neither left nor right. The woman who described the destiny of others was off to tidy up her own.

163

Chapter Eleven

Disappearance and Intervention

The following morning, Rossi duly departed to Kuala Lumpur. Tommy had kept his word. The agreement between Consolidated Industrial Holdings and his own group was very simple, concise and confined to one sheet of paper. That accompanied in Rossi's brief case the drafts prepared by Brash for sealing and signature by the company secretary.

Asprey could see no further need for him to remain in Singapore, waiting simply to be around for the exchange of contracts between Brash, Tommy and Rossi.

The next significant stage would be the lifting of the U-Boat and that despite the mutual understanding as to urgency, could not take place for several weeks. So he took his leave of Tommy by telephone and left a message in Brash's office before catching the British Airways late evening flight to London.

Rossi appeared to come to the same conclusion since on the following Monday Asprey received a cable from him confirming exchange of all contracts, the issuing of instructions for a suitable salvage vessel and concluding that since nothing further could be done, he had decided to take a short break in Portugal at a friend's villa, which address he included for information.

Asprey was not surprised. Rossi had been under very considerable strain and the last thing that he could afford would be to break down once the lift had actually started. Rossi's presence during and immediately after the salvage operation was vital. Indeed, without him, it could not go ahead. The C.I.H. licence specifically required his personal involvement and supervision. Rossi had insisted on that to ensure his indispensability when the value of the licence was problematical and related to a large number of unknown wrecks.

At the time it had been reasonable enough and from Rossi's point of view highly desirable. But now it had become a two-edged sword. So a rest, however short, well away from the scene of action could only be beneficial and Portugal was as good as any place and a lot better than most.

The days passed. Asprey had put the project to the back of his mind. He had assumed in the absence of any firm advice to the contrary that the critical day when the U-Boat would break surface would be about one month after his return from Singapore. So he pencilled in his diary a visit to Kuala Lumpur covering some five/six days at the appropriate time in the following month. His constant dependence on his diary was the only conscious reminder of commitment to the venture. It had been this ability to compartmentalise his concentration and thought that enabled him to apply his various talents to his satisfaction and the frustration and dissatisfaction of his friends and colleagues. It also avoided the otherwise unbearable burden that would have been created through an accumulation of the responsibilities that each enterprise represented. It was a purely selfish attribute developed for personal benefit and a cause of much criticism. Yet without it, Asprey would have been unable to survive in the world which he enjoyed.

The telephone call from Tommy was therefore quite unexpected.

"Ah, Charles," Tommy's voice was as clear as if he had been in the same room and not thousands of miles away. "What has happened to Rossi? We have heard nothing from him and the vessel is due in Kuala Lumpur at the end of this week. Do you know where he is and can you contact him?"

"Yes and no," Asprey spoke quietly into the receiver. "I know he went to Portugal to stay with some friends for a short break. I take it he's not been in touch?"

"No, not with me, Brash or even his office in K.L. We are getting a little worried. Without him we are stymied."

Asprey opened his desk drawer with his right hand. "Let me read his cable again." He smoothed out the piece of paper and quickly re-read the words on it. "Yes, it's as I remembered it. He says for a few days, but not precisely how long. If I give you the address you can cable direct. I will see if I can contact him by phone. If you get no response telephone me again. On the other hand if I get through to him, either he or I will phone you. So if you hear nothing within 24 hours ring me again."

"Will do," replied Tommy. He had understood the last request. Some of the preceeding advice sounded somewhat confused, but at least he knew where Rossi was. "Cheerio for now."

Charles replaced the receiver, looked thoughtfully at the cable without seeing it and drummed his fingers on the desktop.

"I hope not," he said aloud, "I hope not."

Despite his most patient efforts, he was unable to discover Rossi's telephone number in Portugal, so he sent a cable. It might duplicate Tommy's effort, but that would not cause any harm. Rossi's response was short, sharp and unhelpful. He had needed the rest and no-one could deny him that, and a few more days would not jeopardise things although they would be highly beneficial for him. He had cabled Tommy on similar lines. There had been no need for Rossi to advise Asprey that he had done so since Tommy was on the phone within minutes of its receipt.

"What the devil does he think he's playing at?" he asked rhetorically. "I've told him to get the hell out here. Brash is hopping from one foot to the other."

Asprey forebore from commenting on the image that such a performance conjured in his mind. Brash would be as physically capable of dancing from one foot to the other as a hippopotamus would be of performing the dying swan in the ballet. The addition of a tutu to either did nothing to help the mental image or indeed a sensible and prompt response to Tommy's question.

"Are you there, Charles," Tommy's voice shattered the cartoons. "This could be very serious. I think you should go to the villa and put him on the next plane to K.L."

166

"You're probably right," Asprey agreed soberly, his equilibrium quickly restored. "Leave that to me. Meantime send him another cable emphasising the urgency. I will cable him that unless he confirms that he is catching the next plane out, I will be on the door-step pronto."

Asprey recalled the contract. If C.I.H. failed to perform its part, the salvage licence would be assigned to Brash. It had been assumed by C.I.H. that that unlikely contingency could only occur sometime, if at all, after the lift had been completed, that is that the value of the treasure had proven to be considerably less than expected. No-one had foreseen or even hinted at the possibility of frustration before the work had even started. To assign the licence at that early stage would simply be to hand over the U-Boat and all its contents on a plate to Brash – regardless of its ultimate value which could well be in excess of any liability to him.

Asprey spoke quickly into the telephone. "Tell Brash that I am sure that he is as anxious as we are to see Rossi on the job and that everyone is confident that he will be."

Tommy sounded a little puzzled. Perhaps he felt that the message was round the wrong way. "Sure, Charles, anything you say, but let's get on with getting Rossi back to K.L."

"Will do, Tommy, let's both of us get on with our cables. Will talk with you again."

Asprey put down the phone. The project was now very much in the forefront of his mind. Perhaps he had not given it the attention it had deserved. Perhaps he should have winkled Rossi out of Portugal before. Perhaps Rossi had been encouraged to languish in the sun – by whom? Brash? But that was speculation and took time and time he did not have to spare. Enough had been wasted. Now he had to move.

The villa Segara was just outside Corunna and Asprey had had no trouble in making the necessary arrangements for his visit even at such notice. He had not bothered to wait for a reply to his second cable to Rossi. If he afterwards discovered that he had wasted his time and money because Rossi had left for K.L. before he had found the villa, then it was a price willingly paid. If on the other hand, Rossi was still there lazing in the sun, it would be an investment well made. Whilst he could not remedy his past errors of omission, there would be no future mistakes of commission. The former had to be paid for, and the cost of an unnecessary journey to Portugal would be a minimal fine for taking his eye off the ball.

The taxi hauled itself up the winding road and shuddered gratefully to a halt outside the inevitable iron gates protecting a villa perched on a rocky garden which commanded a magnificent view of the surrounding hills and valleys. Charles could quite understand Rossi's reluctance to leave such an idyllic location in favour of the dank humidity of Kuala Lumpur.

As he climbed out of the cab, he indicated to the driver that he should wait, an instruction easily achieved by failing to pay him. The gates were locked but compensated with a bell push clearly marked on one of the stone pillars flanking the entrance. Asprey placed his thumb firmly on it and listened. He could just hear it ringing somewhere in the villa. He kept it ringing. It was still afternoon and the siesta might well extend into the evening, particularly for inhabitants on holiday. In addition, Rossi was unlikely to want to be disturbed if his cable was anything to go by.

Asprey's conclusions appeared to be justified. No-one came. The villa appeared to be deserted. Asprey examined the gate. It was locked and chained. He looked down at the ground beyond the gate. The sand seemed to be undisturbed. The more he saw, the more evidence pointed towards one conclusion. The villa had no occupants neither had it had any for quite some time. Yet he had sent a cable to this address, as indeed had Tommy, and they had both received replies. He turned towards the driver and indicated that he should be patient. The man shrugged and pointed to the palm of his hand. The inference was crystal clear. "Take as long as you like, provided I am paid for your indulgence." Asprey nodded and strode off round the perimeter of the villa. Perhaps there was another entrance. That might be open or openable, or at least show some signs of life. He completed the circuit with no success.

As he turned the corner and the taxi came back into his view, he could see that their arrival had not gone unnoticed. An untidily dressed individual was in deep conversation with his driver. His clothes gave no positive indication of nationality or occupation. His hair was yellow and long. The taxi-driver had obviously commented on Asprey's approach since the newcomer turned around to greet him with outstretched hand.

"Hello, you are looking for the owner of this villa?" His English was excellent but not his native tongue.

"Yes, I wonder if you can help me?"

"But of course. He is Senor Retsek, but we seldom see him here, only when he has guests. It is his holiday home, you understand."

Charles was beginning to feel even more depressed. "Does he have guests whilst he is away?" His informant looked a little bewildered. The question was almost a nonsense. Asprey re-phrased it. "Have there been any visitors over the last few days?" This obtained the desired but unwanted effect.

"Oh, no. We have seen no-one here for several months." Asprey tightened his jaw muscles and pulled his mouth in. He stared across the valley for several minutes. Then he became aware of the intent gaze of the untidy source of the confirmation of his worst fears. There was more than a sporting chance that that individual knew enough to be able to answer more than a few interesting questions, but knowledge was one thing and its extraction entirely another. Direct examination would not only be unfruitful but possibly helpful to "the other side" – if only he knew who "the other side" was! Someone wanted to delay or prevent Rossi's return to Kuala Lumpur. But who? The choice amongst the known was confusing enough, but if there were others as yet unidentified, the task of finding "who" was rapidly becoming impossible.

Standing there looking out into space was even less productive than asking unanswerable questions. He thanked his informant, climbed into the taxi and pointed back the way they had come. "Corunna". The driver started the engine, engaged the requisite gear and moved smartly away to generate a cooling draught to refresh the stale atmosphere and both occupants within his vehicle.

Asprey's air ticket was a return to London. He toyed with the idea of going on from Lisbon to Singapore but by the time he had returned to the Portuguese capital he had come to the conclusion that he should speak to both Tommy and Brash before making that long haul. In addition, he needed to think through very carefully the consequences of the present situation.

He was back in London before he had completed his analysis to his satisfaction. He booked into the Heathrow Hotel and checked local time against that in Singapore. He was too early to catch Tommy in his office and it was not a matter about which to talk to him at his home. Certainly Brash would not appreciate being disturbed in the middle of his slumbers. So he bathed and went to bed, if not to sleep, at least to rest.

When he did telephone Tommy, he had still not arrived at any conclusion as to the next step that should be taken. In a way, he had abdicated from the situation assessment. He had decided to react to the reaction of others. Whilst their total information may not be more than his, its substance could be quite different. By listening he might learn more than by offering recommendations. It was not in character, but it could be more productive than his normal assertive self.

"Ah. Tommy. I have some bad news. Rossi has disappeared at least as far as Portugal is concerned. I went out there to the address he gave in his cable. He was not there and there were no signs that he had ever been. Certainly not on this trip."

Charles paused for Tommy's response. He waited a long time. Listening intently, he could hear background noises which gave the aural effect of standing in the centre of a high-vaulted church, the third dimension of silence, pure yet impure. Tommy's voice, when it came, sounded like a verger standing at one end of the building complaining to a listener at the other about the thoughtlessness of visitors to a holy place.

"That's really not good enough. He must be there. He replied to my cable. He's certainly not here in K.L. He can't just disappear. He must be found. You must go back again to the villa and search properly. Someone must know where he is."

The "musts" were about as effective as the exhortations of the verger, but the comment "search properly" was more than interesting. If he referred to the fact that Asprey had relied upon the word of one neighbour, how did he know that to be so? That had to be explored.

"Calm down Tommy," replied Charles. "How would you suggest I conduct a search? I did all that I felt could be done in the circumstances."

Tommy avoided the trap, leaving Asprey suspicious but no wiser. "You're right, Charles. We must think calmly. What to do next? I feel I should meet Brash and tell him face to face. He may have some ideas. After all he can insist on assignment and carry on with the salvage even if we cannot find Rossi in time to start. I will cover us for our shares in the outcome."

Asprey saw no advantage in explaining to Tommy that assignment of the licence would be unproductive.

Brash would only have the ability to work under the same conditions and requirements that were in the licence and those included the personal involvement of Rossi. If Tommy was in any way involved in Rossi's absence then either his ignorance of the implications had caused him to make a very bad error of judgement which he would have to rectify or he had followed a course deliberately that could lead to a final frustration of the project. Asprey felt that it would be very unwise for Tommy to discover that he, Asprey, could be aware of either eventuality since the outcome could only be Tommy's loss of face and that he would not wish to be known to any man. If Tommy was one of those who wished the U-Boat to remain on the sea-bed then the end would justify almost any means and Asprey had no desire to join Rossi, however pleasant the latter's circumstances might be. So he merely responded to Tommy's suggestion.

"I would go along with that. Brash is the chap holding the cards. The German who helps Rossi in K.L. knows the location of the wreck and I think he is a seaman, so he can mastermind the actual lift. In fact, come to think of it, that's the arrangement with the German Admiralty. He is commanding the salvage operation including the first inspection when it is on the surface."

"So it's not so bad," breathed Tommy. "I'm sure that Brash will play the game and we will all share the cake as originally agreed. He may want some compensation for a more active part but that I think I can arrange it with him."

"O.K.," replied Charles. "Give me a ring as soon as you can. I will not come out until I can do something positive – that's probably at the final lift stage. I want to be there for that."

"Of course, Charles, we will let you know in good time so that we can both be there to see the treasure from the tomb. Be in touch."

As Asprey replaced the receiver he thought the reference to the spoils to be somewhat inappropriate – or hopefully so. Those who had ransacked the burial places of Egypt had not exactly enjoyed the fruits of their endeavours. The metaphor was uncomfortable and disturbing. But the immediate problem was hardly less. Brash had carefully read the licence. He had a copy if necessary to refresh his memory. He was a Q.C. He must know the implications of the conditions. It was unlikely therefore that he had had a hand in Rossi's disappearance, unless he also did not want the project to succeed. But his whole attitude and interest contradicted that motivation. So the probability was that Brash did not know of Rossi's disappearance and when he was told he would immediately construct the consequences. And then he would be really mad. His only chance would be to persuade the Malaysian Government to grant him a new licence or delete the reference to Rossi in the assignable licence. He might well have sufficient influence to achieve one or either. But if he couldn't? His reaction would be explosive. Asprey was glad he was well away from Singapore. If Brash was unsuccessful, it might be quite a while before he could venture into that part of the world again. That would be unfortunate but bearable. In the meantime, however, he had to think positively. Either Rossi would re-emerge in time for the lift or Brash would manage without him. His own contribution could be that which Tommy suggested, to make the fullest possible enquiries as to Rossi's whereabouts and enlist as much support as he could in his endeavours to find him.

Asprey's first move was to cable the C.I.H. office in K.L. requesting confirmation of Rossi's movements, addresses for contact and of friends and acquaintances in Europe. He then telephoned Rossi's office in Scotland where C.I.H. had a small subsidiary, but drew a complete blank there.

The Australian High Commission in London was friendly but unhelpful. No they had no knowledge of his wherebouts although they knew him well.

Asprey considered contacting the German Admiralty but he couldn't persuade himself that he could get any benefit from their involvement in the search. On the other hand, he could see problems that might arise if they were advised of Rossi's disappearance. They could also be aware of the conditions of the salvage licence and that might encourage them to make a direct approach to the Malaysian Government for a fresh licence in their favour – just for the U-Boat. No, they were probably the last to be told – if they did not already know!

As he had expected, Charles heard from Tommy before he heard from C.I.H. And Tommy was in quite a state.

"Charles, you'd better get out here quick. Brash is beside himself. He's threatening everyone with everything. Apparently Rossi's absence upsets everything. Even if the licence is assigned to Brash, we still need Rossi. Without him out here we are sunk. We have to persuade the Malaysians that we can do what Rossi promised to do and as that involves C.I.H. and its industrial activities we need your help. We can look after the salvage business but we must have someone with industrial knowledge and experience to replace Rossi in the rest of the business. And you are the only chap. You will gain both ways. If Rossi doesn't turn up you can have his share, or at least most of it."

Asprey had not expected that offer. Brash's anger had been anticipated but not the tactic of promising the Malaysians the continuity of Rossi's work on their original manufacturing companies that constituted the main business of C.I.H. Asprey could see the logic and attraction of that approach. The Malaysians might well buy it. But that would commit him irrevocably to an undertaking in a part of the world that he did not find particularly attractive.

There was no way he would be allowed to take his slice of the cake and run. The Malaysians would make certain that if they played ball, he would have the chain firmly attached. It needed careful thought.

"I take your point, Tommy. I have put in hand a number of enquiries. Obviously if we can find Rossi and get him back to K.L., that is the best and right answer to our problems. So let's exhaust that first. It may take a day or so but it would be worth trying if only to make sure, as you said yourself. If we can't find him and it's probable that he will not turn up in time, then I will ring you and we can plan from there. After all, Rossi did say in his cables to us that he intended to make the most of his break and he may just be doing that. Perhaps he sent us a false address to make certain he could not be disturbed before he was ready."

Tommy was not convinced, but the argument had considerable merit.

"O.K. Let's give it three days. If by then we haven't found him, wherever he is, you and I will agree a plan of action for you to come out here and meet with the authorities to persuade them to let us go ahead. If I hear nothing from you by then, I will ring you. Will you be at your usual number?"

Asprey responded immediately. "Yes, I will make sure that I am here in three day's time if I have had no news on Rossi or we haven't talked before then."

Tommy expressed himself satisfied, although the tone of his voice was anything but confirmatory. He really wanted Asprey in Kuala Lumpur as quickly as possible if only to satisfy Brash. There seemed little doubt that Tommy truly did not know where Rossi was, who had him under their wing and had been similarly in the dark as to the consequences of his disappearance. Furthermore, he seemed as dedicated as ever to the recovery of the U-Boat and its contents. The nigger in the wood pile – or mole according to more modern and less realistic thinking – had still to be identified.

Charles's hand was still poised above the replaced receiver when the telephone bell rang again. He jumped, the sound always jarred. This time the caller was Bobby Fitzpaine.

"Ah, there you are Charles," he drawled. "Tracked you down at last. Are you free tomorrow evening for a bite of dinner? Bit formal, black tie and all that, but should be interesting. No women but the best claret in London."

Asprey was somewhat taken aback. A social invitation at short notice was unusual, but for him from Fitzpaine, that had to be unique. It so happened that he did not have a commitment, only the possibility that Tommy might phone. But he could hardly be expected to wait in on the off chance. Anyway the request had to have an ulterior motive.

"S'matter of fact I am staying up tomorrow night. Delighted to join you in a glass of claret."

"Jolly good. Let me pick you up at say 7.30. See you then. Cheers."

The phone clicked. Asprey had had no opportunity of responding but it appeared that no acknowledgement was needed. He returned the instrument in its cradle and wondered. How had Fitzpaine "tracked him down" and why? Somebody was taking more than a passing interest in him.

*　*　*　*　*　*　*

As promised, Bobby duly arrived in his chauffeur-driven Daimler which swept the two penquin style men into St. James.

"Don't expect you've been to the Carlton. Pretty boring place but the cellar is not half bad."

No answer seemed expected. Apparently Bobby carried on conversations constructed entirely from rhetorical questions. It certainly helped to avoid any possible embarrassment in having to respond and admit that his assumption was indeed correct. Charles had never entered the Carlton Club and had always believed such a possibility to be extremely unlikely. He knew it to be exclusive and expensive and not a little related to politics – conservative of course. In fact, if there had to be a temple of the true blues then the imposing mansion in St. James must qualify.

The chauffer skilfully slid the large car like a flexible knife amongst the whipped-up mixture of eager London cabs, private and public passenger conveyances. They arrived smoothly and safely at the unidentifiable entrance of the Carlton.

Bobby led the way, immediately cornering the uniformed flunkey guarding the inner door. Asprey could not hear the conversation but its content though brief was obviously sufficient to obtain bowed agreement, a waved direction and a nod of approval. Neither man had a top-coat so that further assistance was unnecessary.

The recommended bearing took them to the foot of a most impressive staircase that wound around the walls of the large entrance hall which were endowed with a number of large oil-paintings of elderly men staring at all and sundry with un-focussed eyes secure with the knowledge of permanent sub-stance. The staircarpet was blue in colour and deep in pile. The whole was entirely as expected and without surprise. That is with the exception of a distinguished figure imperceptibly descending. It was the Right Honourable Harold Macmillan. The width of the stairs eliminated a difficult decision for those at their feet. To wait would have been far more discourteous than to pass the former Prime Minister which they duly did. He ignored the unwashed and unaccepted.

At the top, Bobby turned to his left passing the open entrance to a well populated bar and instead pushed open a large oaken door set between an Admiral and a Field Marshall.

By Carlton standards, it was a small room, about thirty feet square. At one end was a small table supporting an array of glass decanters and gleaming glasses. A small number of leather arm-chairs, occasional tables and a bookcase of con-siderable proportions were dominated by a continuation of the gallery of oil-paintings. Curiously enough, unlike Asprey had been led to expect, the eyes did not follow him about the room. Their owners were much too supercilious to note individuals. Yet there was no doubt that in that room the present was under the constant scrutiny and siege of the past.

"Ah, good to see you, Bobby." A tall, spare man detached himself from the small group of D.J.'d men standing in the middle of the room and advanced towards the newcomers. "Glad you could come."

Bobby nodded nervously, "Yah, this is Asprey."

"Good," said the apparent host, "what would you both like?"

"A malt would be fine, thanks." Charles decided that would do for him as well as anything. "The same for me, please."

A superior person resplendent in white tie and tails served their satisfaction. The size of the measures clearly indicated that his attendance would not be required again before dinner, which he duly confirmed by disappearing in a manner more consistent with a member of the magic circle than that of his obvious calling, although he was equally well dressed for either.

"Glad you could make it." This time the comment was aimed at Charles who could only think of the inane response of "Delighted I could come." Since that was hardly conducive to a brisk and lively conversation, his host turned back to Bobby. "How's the handicap?"

Charles almost expected "She's safely at home" but realised that that would be rightly regarded as puerile. He really had to improve his small talk!

Bobby was up to it. "Not at all bad – enables me to win the odd fiver without fear or favour, or even amendment." It was obvious that Bobby and his host had a subject of common interest and Asprey's contribution was neither expected or sought, so he looked around as discretely as circumstances permitted. Before he had time even to review the nearest portrait, his self indulgence was rudely shattered by a most unexpected turn of events. He suddenly realised that despite the quantity of malt liquer originally in his glass, Bobby was already draining the last few drops and glancing at his watch.

"Well, must be off," he said. "Thanks for the snifter. You must pop in one weekend." Just to avoid any ambiguity, Bobby turned towards Asprey. "Sorry can't stay. But I know that you will thoroughly enjoy the evening. Always handy to make new friends." Before Charles could think of an adequate response, Bobby had disappeared.

"Good," repeated the host – it was obviously his favourite word – "now, let me introduce you to your fellow guests." So saying he walked towards the half circle of men who re-formed as Bobby left the room and took up his position as "right-marker".

There was something unnerving about the grouping of four of the five men. They were standing in identical postures, each holding his glass in his right hand with the elbow tucked into the side. The goblets were merely objects of convenience, that which was to hand, and could easily have been side-arms or lances. They projected a calm aloof and timeless authority. It needed little effort to visualise them as four English noblemen partially accoutred before the fray, whether in mediaeval or modern times. They were met as they had met on innumerable occasions before and would so meet again.

Asprey and the fifth man were completely out of place. Each had a contribution to make but once – then and there. Their importance was transitory and only of temporary relevance. The other four represented a constant and consistent source of power set like an outcrop of rocks in an everchanging yet predictable sea.

Charles was rudely brought back to reality by the realisation that his blinking eyes and open mouth would not enhance his reputation or further his participation in the evening's programme, whatever that was to be. He struggled to return his senses and reaction to the present. His host was speaking.

"This is Harry." Harry was dark of hair, eye and brow, medium height and build, with a face almost devoid of expression. He raised his eyebrows and glass. Charles almost followed suit but recovered himself in time and inclined his head instead.

"This is George." George was considerably older than Harry. What remained of his hair was grey. His face was round, a little flushed and dominated by a large nose of an unpopular shape. He was over six feet tall, stiff-backed and lipped. In fact, Charles felt he should have sported a moustache. Curiously enough all four were clean shaven which somehow seemed rather odd.

"This is Edward." There was no mistaking Edward. Unlike Harry and George, Edward was a fairly familiar figure on the box and in the more fashionable parts of London. His profile was unmistakable, finely drawn and bronzed by many outdoor public engagements.

"And this is Michael." Michael's face was ridiculously familiar. As a politician whose star was undoubtedly in the ascendance his features had received much attention from photographer and cartoonist alike. It had long been mooted that at the appropriate time he would be given the key to number ten.

It was abundantly clear that Asprey was not required to recognise any of his fellow guests beyond the names given to them and the fact that they were Christian names was sufficiently out of place to endorse the unspoken instruction. Any suggestion of familiarity arising from their use was to be unthinkable.

At that moment and by remote control, the resplendent person re-appeared, this time in the conventional manner on the threshold, bowed and announced "Your Grace is served." The host enquired: "Shall we go in?" Any answer would have been superfluous, since the original statement had had the same effect as the green lights at the start of a Grand Prix. All moved forward smoothly towards the door, each retaining his precise position on the starting grid. Harry first, George second, Edward third, the host fourth and Michael and Charles bringing up the rear. Asprey felt like the official pace car in such a situation, completely out of character and place, making a passing contribution to the race through necessity and sufferance and then only for the warm-up lap. As soon as the race proper started, he would have to vacate the track as quickly as he could to avoid being shunted by vehicles which by then, in their terms, would still only be cruising. So what the hell was he doing there anyway?

The procession wound its way through silently opened doors and along deserted corridors into an even smaller room dominated by a magnificently laid mahogany dining table. There was no hesitation as to seating arrangements. Each knew his place and took it. Harry at the head, George to his right and Edward to Harry's left. The host sat next to George and Michael plumbed for tail-end Charley's chair. Asprey had no choice which pleased him. At least that was one decision avoided. He sat next to Edward.

The first course of melon was laid and wine glasses covered in condensation from the effect of their chilled contents. There were no flunkeys.

Michael did his best to bring Asprey into the centre of the conversation. "Tell us about yourself," he asked, "what do you do? I believe you're something of a financial wizzard."

Charles took a deep breath. He was going to sing for his supper but to what tune was as yet unclear. "Hardly a wizzard, but I have been known to make something out of very little."

"Good, good," obviously in the in-word of the day. "Ever thought about using your talents outside business – say, politics?"

Charles swallowed a lump of melon. Surely they had not gone to all this trouble, pomp and circumstance, not to mention circumspection, simply to get him to join the Party, however rarified the level of membership offered?

"Yes, but I feel that businessmen can be far more effective behind the scenes. They make for very bad politicians. To each his own."

"Couldn't agree more," said Michael, "and vice versa. But both have one thing in common, wouldn't you say, ambition?"

"Surely," responded Asprey, "it's just the means that differs."

The conversation, such as it was, then ceased completely as

the course was cleared and replaced by an excellent Beef Wellington by two servants, one of whom delivered two decanters of claret. The effect of the white Burgundy and the truly silk-like quality of the Bordeaux began to take its toll of Asprey's restraint so that he found the conversation easier to maintain and even extend.

By the time the choice of cheese and port had been made, the discussion had been raised into the realms of philosophy and Charles sought to bring the conversation around to an examination of the motivations of those to whom authority had been delegated, but it was a subject that was not of mutual interest. Harry cut across it with a direct question of Charles.

"Having admitted that you are ambitious, what exactly would you like to achieve – wealth, power, recognition or the praise of posterity – or any combination?"

Charles looked at his interrogator. He still had no idea who he was but the ring of authority in his voice was unmistakable. There was no trace of any regional accent or indeed any affectation at all. It might well have been the tones of a B.B.C. announcer under the close direction of Lord Reith – clear, cool and without emphasis.

George joined in: "A fair question. We all have our ambitions. If unspoken, they can be misinterpreted by others and that can so easily lead to unfortunate and unnecessary consequences."

George's voice was very similar to that of Harry except that it was pre-emptory. His authority was more impatient and asserted by consistency and certainty of purpose. He expected others to agree with him and had little time to spare for those who were doubly unwise not to do so.

Asprey took note and responded carefully.

"Today's wealth is tomorrow's power. Recognition can come about through envy and that can be destructive. As to posterity the good is oft interred so what is to be gained there? So I am after wealth today to form the foundation for power sometime in the future."

There was a long pause. Harry looked around the table.

181

Michael spoke. After all, he was a politician.

"That's all very well. A bird in the hand and all that. But if you are only after money you will simply sell to the highest bidder and that can be short-sighted in the extreme."

"Perhaps," said Asprey, "but I have a feeling that you other gentlemen appreciate what I am trying to say, however inadequately. I would guess, with respect, that your respective families several times in the distant past have chosen to accumulate considerable wealth in preference to other inducements. And that that hord, whether in land, gold or other valuables has enabled each of you to exercise power and influence through the centuries to an extent undreamed of by those who were unable to compete in those endeavours or simply made the wrong choice."

Asprey expanded. The claret was undoubtedly the best in London. "I would bet that the real power base in this country is and has been controlled by a mere handful of men. A base that is so deep rooted that its existence can be denied or ignored. It supports a visible growth of such magnitude and proportions that the trunk, branches and leaves are taken by all to be the total structure because it is so impressive and awe-inspiring of itself. After all, who wants to grub around in the dirt to uncover old, uninteresting and tangled roots."

He nearly added but mercifully restrained himself from voicing the answer "except pigs after truffles". He felt that he had said more than enough. The silence was oppressive, a burden to be lifted but none ventured.

Edward folded his napkin and looked at the ceiling. "I think we can leave that line of thought for another day. Perhaps we should now get down to specifics. We all know where we stand on generalities."

Harry nodded; "Agreed. So to the point of our invitation. You are intimately concerned with the possibility of bringing to light certain documents which we wish to leave where they are. We seek your co-operation to ensure that that is precisely what will happen. The papers will stay where they are, undisturbed and unread. We do not wish them destroyed, just to remain sealed. Quite correctly, you have assumed that there is a modicum of wealth and influence around this table. In return for your acquiescence, we would see that it would not go unnotied and unrewarded."

George intervened: "Of course there could be no promise or undertaking. You would simply have our word."

Harry frowned slightly; "That goes without saying. Neither will there be any threats."

Michael had to add his piece: "We need your undoubted talents in financial matters and given the opportunity I have no doubt that you would be extremely successful which in turn must lead to recognition in various interesting ways."

Asprey could really see no alternative to agreement, but he could at least find out as much as he could before he capitulated.

"The reason why I am here is the U-Boat in Malaysian waters?"

Harry nodded.

"But, with respect gentlemen, why you?"

George answered: "Because the matter is one of national security."

"National, not party or other classification?" Asprey persevered.

"Of course," the answer was very curt.

"Then why not the intelligence services – unless you are that body?"

Harry intervened: "We are not members of MI5, MI6 or any other MI so you can put that thought aside. If we had been you would have been asked to sign a piece of paper long before this – and I doubt whether you would have had any option put before you."

"So, if it is a question of national security, someone has seen fit not to involve the intelligence services. Instead..."

Asprey was not allowed to finish his thinking aloud. Edward, eyes still fixed on the ceiling, cut in: "You can work out your answers later if you like. As far as the facts are concerned, you are here at our invitation to respond to our, er, request that for the benefit of your country you will not complete the salvage of U-134."

183

Asprey decided to demur: "But I only have your word that it is a matter of national security. How do I know that in reality it is not solely for the benefit of you gentlemen and those whom you may represent."

Harry joined the attack: "If it is as you say solely for our benefit then you may take it that that is synonymous with national security. We are, if you like, custodians of the nation's reputation if not its conscience. This is a highly sensitive and potentially very damaging matter. Whoever may or may not be directly hurt by any disclosures of these documents, the consequences must be harmful to the country as a whole. It will provide our enemies with a totally unexpected ammunition dump which they will use to their great joy and our considerable discomfort. The repercussions may last many years and irreparably damage many deep relationships."

Asprey tried to assimilate the argument; "Then you gentlemen must already know what is in those documents?"

Harry agreed; "Yes, and if nothing else it confirms that we are custodians of secure capabilities." He laughed but it was not with humour and the atmosphere did not lighten.

George was becoming increasingly impatient: "Young man, you have little choice. If you have any ambition then you have a unique opportunity. You must appreciate the importance of what you have within your grasp as by now you will have realised who we are and what we represent. Whenever our country has faced a crisis it has turned to us and we have and never will let her down. Neither I think will you."

Charles almost asked as to the result of a refusal to co-operate but he realised that he would only receive confirmation that he was a fool even to enquire.

"O.K., so be it. I will do my bit for my country. On that you have my word."

"Good." The word rippled around the table. The tension eased. Chairs scraped backwards and it became immediately apparent that once again Charles was superfluous. The official pace car was invited to leave the track.

Harry stood up. "Nice to have met you, Asprey. We shall watch your progress with the greatest interest. You should do well."

The murmers of agreement reminded Charles of the noises recorded in the upper house for the radio programme "Today in Parliament". Insincere background noises vented automatically as indications of minds absorbed elsewhere but trained to make the right sounds if only for effect. The finger having writ, the chapter is closed and the custodians move on.

The final surprise of the evening was to find Bobby's chauffeur and Daimler waiting for him outside the Carlton. Since it was raining and Charles suddenly felt quite tired, he was grateful for the thought. As he relaxed in the rear of the low car, he shut his eyes and thought first of Bobby. Even he had not been privvy to the dinner. Perhaps he, Charles, might take advantage of that at some future date. Then he recalled his promise. It was quite ironic, but he had no doubts as to his capability in keeping it. Still, he did not know just how much was known to the custodians. They should never be underestimated. Suddenly he shivvered. He really was tired. A hot bath and then straight to bed.

But it was not to be, at least immediately. As he opened the door to his flat he heard the telephone ringing. Although he had no way of proving it, he felt that it had no intention of stopping. Wearily he picked up the receiver. "Hullo."

"Is that Mr. Charles Asprey?"

"Yes."

"Would you hold the line for a moment. I have a person to person call for you from Kuala Lumpur."

Charles forgot that he was tired and anxious to be between the sheets. Basil had turned up. He prepared the question: "Where the devil have you been?" with varying degrees of emphasis. The answer had better be good or else . . . His anticipations were rudely shattered by the soft voice in his ear.

"Ah, Mr. Asprey, thank you for your excellent report on Mr. Sventloski," it was the Tunku. "I agree with your recommendations and I will advise the gentleman in due course – probably after we have completed our project."

Charles had recovered most of his composure but not enough to remember the time lapse in speech during long

185

distance calls. He began to speak, then had to stop abruptly as he realised that the Tunku was continuing.

"I understand that Basil has extended his leave and you have been unable to contact him?"

This time Charles got it right. "Yes."

"A problem but not insurmountable with your help. I understand that you would be prepared to stand in for him if necessary?"

"Yes."

"Good, then may I suggest that you join us here as soon as you can. I have taken the liberty of having you booked on the B.A. flight tomorrow although you may have planned a later arrival. I hope the acceleration is acceptable. Mr. Chua will meet you at the airport. Good luck."

Charles could only say, "Thank you." The balance of the conversation reflected the relationship between the two men. Whatever wealth or influence Charles might have had in his personal capacity, as soon as he had accepted the patronage of the potentate his independence had been discarded. The best that he could hope for was the accolade of a Machiavelli – and he had had something to say about putting one's trust in princes.

Chapter Twelve

Bribes

Tommy and his ubiquitous Mercedes were waiting for Asprey at Kuala Lumpur airport. His greeting was almost frenetic.

"We must get cracking, Charles," he said, practically wrenching Asprey's case out of his hand in his eagerness to lead the way towards the car. "Time is short, we have much to do."

Yet despite these injunctions and his obviously disturbed state of mind, when the two men were comfortably seated in the limousine Tommy made no attempt to take advantage of either the time or the privacy. He sat slumped in his corner, his attention focussed on cleaning his glasses and mopping his brow. Asprey decided to wait. Whatever Tommy had in mind would eventually surface. To attempt its acceleration would only serve to add fuel to a state of internal combustion. The result could be explosive.

The Mercedes turned into a multi-storey car-park and climbed the internal ramp up to the top floor. As far as parking was concerned, it was an unnecessary journey as there were many places on the lower floors that they passed en route. It was obvious that their destination had a purpose other than the storage of a motor. Having set the hand-brake the driver turned towards Tommy who spoke quickly in Chinese. The man nodded, handed over his keys and left the car.

Tommy relaxed. "Good, now we can talk. Let me first fill you in. I understand Brash has persuaded the Tunku and the Malaysians that you can run C.I.H. until a permanent successor to Rossi can be found. Therefore he now has an effective assignment of the salvage licence. The lifting gear arrived

187

three days ago. They started work immediately so that by the end of this week the U-Boat could be on the surface.

Tommy paused and changed course abruptly. "We've known each other for a long time, Charles. I have always admired your business acumen and flexibility."

"You have the ability to respond to changing conditions which is quite unique. I believe that you are very resourceful and that is the main reason for your success."

Asprey felt obliged to respond. "Well, that's very kind of you to say so, Tommy, but there have been times when I have been guilty of the gravest entrepreneurial sin, the omission of an opportunity."

Tommy jumped straight in. "Precisely, and that admission brings me nicely to the point I was about to make. You will receive a large sum of money from the division of the salvage. How would you like to have half as much again?"

"Obviously I would not say no."

"Good," Tommy sucked his teeth, "then I will tell you how you can achieve that delightful result. All you have to do is find out exactly what Strauss discovers when he enters the U-Boat and pass on all that knowledge and information directly to me. In return for that I will pay you my share of the proceeds."

Asprey looked thoughtfully at Tommy. "The offer seems generous enough, but how am I going to persuade Strauss to part with such valuable knowledge? It must be worth a lot if only because of your offer."

"That's your problem," replied Tommy. "That's what I'm paying you for. If I knew the answer then I wouldn't need your help. How you do it is entirely your business. Whether you think Strauss can be bought, or persuaded or whatever, is entirely up to you. The end justifies the means and the end is a very large sum of money indeed."

"I don't think he can be bought and I doubt very much whether he can be persuaded, but there may be other ways of getting what you want and I would assume that you would be happy to leave the method with me?"

Tommy nodded. "Certainly, as long as I can be certain that

what you tell me is accurate and complete. You will have to satisfy me as to its veracity if it cannot be confirmed by Strauss."

"Understood. Now let me think about it. It may be possible that I can find a solution. For the time being however, let us agree that if I can come to you with that information the deal is on the terms you offer. There is one question which I must ask now. The answer will help me satisfy you. What are we looking for and why?"

Tommy furrowed his brow. "Those are difficult and dangerous questions. Still I can see what you are after. Strauss may not pass on what we really want although he could still give you a lot of interesting information. I will tell you what you need to know, but that will be more than you should know on your assurance that you will never pass on what I am going to tell you to anyone else and as soon as the job is done you will forget it completely."

Asprey looked casually at the concrete expanse surrounding the car. "You've no need to worry on that score. As soon as I have done my part, I shall be off to a nice quiet corner of the world where I can enjoy the fruits of my labour in peace. I shall be living in the present and the future. There will be no place for the past. That will undoubtedly be left in K.L."

"Fair enough," said Tommy. "Now, what am I looking for and why? My prime target is the intended destination of the U-134. My secondary objective is the identity of its passengers."

"I want to know where it was going as that would tell us the proposed nerve centre of the new right wing Germany. It would also lead us to the welcoming committee and probably those who were previously successful in getting through to their new home. We are confident that U-134 had no intention of going to the obvious places, such as South America. We are also sure that it was the most important member of the escape fleet so that it must head for the centre of the spider's web. It is also probable that it contained the spider. It certainly carried wealth, personalities and possibly holy relics. In all a terrifying combination of seeds for controlled germ-

189

ination – if that's not too terrible a pun."

"That's all very well, Tommy," said Asprey, "although it ties in with what we know, it still doesn't answer the question 'Why?', or specifically for what purpose."

Tommy looked thoughtfully at him. "Alright, I'll tell you – but if at some later date you even hint at what you are about to hear, then the consequences could be much more than painful."

Asprey nodded and deliberately avoided interrupting with any comment – he was learning.

"I have friends who want to complete a jigsaw. They have most of the pieces showing the sources and strengths of various political influences and control in this part of the world. Appearances can be deceptive. Allegiances may be temporary, matters of convenience, superficial or deep-rooted. The most difficult to define accurately are the last. Yet it is the most valuable identification because in periods of international stress and strain they are the ones that will hold firm."

"U-134 expected a welcome. If, in addition to its rich cargo it contained the caucus of the new Germany then those who organised and arranged its departure must have been supremely confident that it was going to the right place. Somewhere had already been chosen as the nerve centre for a fascist state and that somewhere was receptive to both the ideology and the people. Even though 134 did not make it, perhaps others did. Yet even if none succeeded, somewhere in this part of the globe there are those who were more than prepared to partici-pate in the regeneration of the Third Reich."

Tommy paused. This time, Asprey felt he could say some-thing that would help continuity of such a fascinating exposure. "So, if you find out who and where, will you or your masters try to establish a relationship, merely note, or expose and destroy?"

Tommy smiled. "One or the other, yes."

"Very helpful," said Asprey drily. "Let's see if you can answer me more directly on one question. Why do you want to find out what Strauss discovers?"

"We want to know more than that. By the way, I have no masters as you put it, I have only associates. I am, as you know, a man of independant means and I can work with whomsoever I like. It so happens that I believe in what I am doing and my belief happens to be that of my friends. But to your question. Strauss may well know more than we do. Even if what he finds is a mixture of confirmation and new revelations, his orders could be to memorise and destroy rather than risk retaining documents or momentos that might be stolen or copied. Therefore we may never know. To be candid, I would not like Herr Strauss's job, since if we are correct he would be the only one to have the complete story and his masters are only interested in silence!"

"But," Asprey could not refrain from completing the logic, "if I share Strauss's secret I share his risk."

"Ah," smiled Tommy, "but a risk shared is a risk halved. Anyway as you will also have told me, you are for all practical purposes insured since it will no longer be a secret. Of course if you tried to keep it to yourself . . . "

Asprey digested Tommy's soliloquy. With whom, as he put it, was Tommy working? Did it make any difference if he found out? He looked at his friend with some surprise and not a little respect. "If I put that little lot together and if I have you right, then one of the answers would appear to be that you are working with the C.I.A. Now that calls something else to mind."

"A few years ago I was involved in a documentary about a Mr. Thompson who lived in a house beside a klong in Thailand. He was reputed to be a former head of the C.I.A. who had retired and then concentrated upon the successful resuscitation of the Thai silk industry. Then he disappeared and has never been seen or heard of since."

Charles's brow gathered into a knot as he did his utmost to recall the details. Tommy made no effort to help him, neither did he attempt to deny or confirm Asprey's assumption. "You must work it out for yourself, Charles," he said, "I have told you all I can and probably more than I should. Suffice it to say that you know enough to understand what we seek, so that your task is now that much easier."

"In that respect, yes, but I still have to work out the modus operandi and that will certainly not be easy."

"But it's a worthwhile challenge, Charles, and you like challenges. Succeed and you and your descendants need never worry again about money."

Asprey laughed out aloud. "I am glad you mentioned my descendants, Tommy."

Tommy returned the laugh. "No threats, Charles," he said, "only promises. I know you will do your best and that's good enough for me. If you don't succeed it will not be for the want of trying. If you do, then we will keep our side of the bargain. Now let us get into the front of the car. I will drive us down to my launch. You will be dining with me tonight and there will be three of us. I have invited Herr Strauss. That will give you a start."

The two men slid out into the heat of the afternoon sun. Asprey paused and quickly looked at Kuala Lumpur spread out in front of him. Man's concept of architectural improvement could only be explained as the competitive construction of egotistical monuments vying with each other as to the largest and ugliest tombestone in his graveyard. The thought did nothing to improve his already sombre mood. Life was becoming exceedingly unpleasant and the inevitable outcome increasingly distasteful.

*   *   *   *   *   *   *

Prompt though Asprey was, Tommy was waiting for him in the main cabin of his launch. "Come in, Charles," he said, "what will you have?"

"A little whisky and water, please. Has Herr Strauss arrived?"

"Not yet," replied Tommy, "I have just sent the dinghy across to the "Jean" where he has his berth. In fact you can hear it coming alongside. Germans are always punctual."

Strauss ducked through the door. He was coolly dressed in a white suit, open neck shirt and sandals. He still sported a full set of whiskers, neatly and methodically trimmed. He advanced towards Tommy with outstretched hand.

"Good evening Mr. Chua, I hope I find you well." His English held virtually no trace of accent. He turned towards Asprey without waiting for Tommy's reply.

"Ah, Mr. Asprey, how nice to meet you again. You have arrived for the last act. The denouement?" Charles took his hand. It was warm but dry. A firm handshake with a tingle for which there seemed no rhyme or reason.

"I hope so. As you know I have had an interest in this venture spread over a number of years. My only regret is that the chap started it all, Basil Rossi, will not be here to share the excitement with us. I suppose you have no idea where he is or where we shall be able to find him?"

Strauss shook his head and looked grave. "No, I wish I could help. The best I can suggest is that as soon as the salvage has been completed we pool our knowledge and concentrate on finding him."

"First things, first," Tommy said, "which reminds me, what can I offer you, Herr Strauss, before we eat?"

The meal was thoroughly enjoyed by the three, who relaxed and exchanged experiences and views concentrated upon the Orient. Some mention was made of the West Coast of the United States, but Tommy soon brought the evening back on his course by terminating the three-sided discussion.

"As a matter of fact," he said, "I have promised to ring a friend in Hong Kong this evening. It may take some little time. If you will excuse me, I will go back to my cabin. It will probably take upwards of an hour. Please don't wait up for me Charles, and if you, Herr Strauss, wish at any time to return to your ship, you have only to ask the steward to run you across in our outboard. Sorry about appearing to be a poor host but I really have no alternative. It's an important call. Please make yourselves completely at home. Whatever you want, just ask the steward – no matter what it is. I won't wish you both good night as I am sure you will be made so comfortable that you will be here when I get back."

Strauss and Asprey did their best to convey their understanding and appreciation as Tommy made his somewhat rushed exit, then settled back to contemplate their liqueur coffees.

"Reminds me of the Marco Polo. The girls there make the best Irish coffees in the world. Have you ever stayed there," asked Asprey.

"No, I can't say I have," replied Strauss, "where is it?"

"Singapore. Very comfortable and relaxing. Which brings me to a suggestion. Shall we go up on deck and relax with our drinks in the stern. It may be a little cool but I would enjoy the sea air even if only for ten minutes."

"Surely," said Strauss. "Lead the way."

As the two walked along the passage, Asprey wondered whether Strauss knew or suspected that the cabins might be bugged. Perhaps they should sit at the stern and not lean over its rail where there could be another little insect!

Asprey re-arranged the chairs set out on the rear deck putting two close together and off centre. Strauss looked on with an expression of amusement.

"Trying to keep out the draught," explained Asprey, puffing slightly from the exertion. The chairs were heavy and very solid, designed to stay in one position regardless of swell and sway. "Let's sit here."

Having seated themselves, they looked around ostensibly at the night view. Asprey's concern was as to the proximity of other vessels, people and devices. Whether they could be overheard by accident or design. The answer appeared to be in the negative. A better location would be hard to find. The risk, such as it was, appeared to be minimal.

"It's not particularly warm, but it's quiet," he said in a low voice.

"I will therefore be brief and to the point. I have been asked to find out whether you can be persuaded to let me know what you find when you enter the U-134. The terms of persuasion have been left entirely to me. The price is whatever you ask, within of course certain obvious limits. My reaction was that it was a hopeless task. Nevertheless I was still asked to try."

Strauss looked ahead. If he showed any emotion, then the darkness concealed it and his voice gave no clue. "You were right, of course. I am not open to persuasion and you or anyone else would be wasting effort and energy in attempting it. But why tell me if you knew the outcome?"

"One never knows for certain, and I could have been wrong. All things are possible. You might have liked the idea of taking a large lump of wealth and disappearing. You might have become cynical about those whose motives seem to be similar to your own but in fact are quite different."

Strauss sounded surprised. "You meant, I might have wanted out even at this stage?"

"Yes, why not? The later the stage the more likely that the realities begin to emerge as what they are and not what they have been too long portrayed. As we get older we not only become more cynical but those about us get careless and drop their masks."

There was a silence, broken only by the throb of diesels powering the moored vessels.

"I am still curious, Herr Asprey, why you should think I would want out now?"

Asprey stretched his arms and shoulders. "But that is not important. The main thing is that you have confirmed that you do not, and that is right, is it not?"

"Absolutely," said Strauss, quietly but firmly. "So now what happens?"

"I suggest we go back to the state-room and enjoy ourselves."

For once, the warm air below deck was welcoming and both men were glad to take advantage of the easy chairs in the cabin. Their re-entry had alerted the steward who responded to their requests for brandies.

"I have a feeling," said Asprey, "that you are a naval man?"

Strauss's moustache and beard parted to reveal a white line of teeth. "May I say, elementary, my dear Watson."

Despite the German's friendliness and lack of malice in his comment, Charles felt a sudden deep unease – almost a deja vu – and just managed to control a physical shiver. "I suppose it was. Which branch?"

"In the German Navy we have many branches but no trees. We learn skills in theory but have the greatest difficulty in putting them into practice."

"Rather like the Royal Navy, I hear," rejoined Asprey. "Apparently they have one and half Admirals for every warship, and that includes the Victory and the Belfast!"

"At least you have some ships in which to practice!!"

"I suppose you can get some experience in other countries. Have you been to the States?" asked Asprey.

Strauss paused. "Yes, you can probably tell from my accent that I have spent some time there. I did a degree at Boston and was fortunate to be seconded for a little while to the U.S. Navy. I also served in the Philippines."

For a moment the brandy and the warm room took effect. "I very much enjoyed that experience. Whatever their weakness, and they have many, the Americans are simple to understand and live with. They are not complicated by historical hang-ups. Their power bases are relatively new and built on finance accumulated for all to see. They are not servants of unscrupulous and ambitious men who died centuries ago. They are not confused by a tangled mass of motives and desires, half throttled by their thwarted half-forgotten purposes."

Suddenly Strauss stopped, aware that he had given voice to unspeakable thoughts.

Asprey decided to prevent any embarrassing silence and responded in an equally philosophical manner. "Whilst there are indeed many things to their credit that the Americans are not, they are singularly short sighted, almost myopic. They tend to regard anything that moves outside of their continent as belonging to another planet. If they had a choice they would be quite happy to stay at home, live in peace and ignore the rest of the world. For a while that might well work for them, but if they succeeded in their endeavours, they would prosper. If they prospered, the world would become envious. Add to that the ingredient of fear stirred in by politicians and you have all the makings of a self destructive cake. America could never be allowed to prosper in peace. Therefore she is obliged to mix and work with us – which is probably mutually beneficial in the long run."

Strauss had long since recovered his composure. "True, but they are still nice people to be with. I hope to be able to live there again, sometime.

"When you retire," It was not a question but rather a statement. Strauss took it as such, since he made no effort to reply.

Intead he rose to his feet and pressed one of the service buttons in the cabin.

"I really must away. I have my usual early start tomorrow and, if everything goes according to plan, we shall have two very full days on the trot. It's been nice talking with you and I did much appreciate your offer. I hope we will have many opportunities of continuing our discussions. Good-bye."

Asprey took his hand. "Good-bye and good luck." Somehow the words had taken a hypocritcal meaning and Asprey wished them unspoken. But it was too late – as it was on many counts. The die was cast. Each would do his job and like the Americans neither could afford to live according to his own inclination and desires. The world was far too small and there was nowhere to go even if one wanted to opt out. The price of membership of humanity was the loss of the unilateral ability to resign.

Asprey remained in the state-room after Strauss had left. He had no urgent need to get up early the following morning. He also wanted to talk with Tommy before they both retired.

He did not have long to wait. Tommy was eager to discover the outcome of his conversation with the German.

"How did you get on, Charles," he asked, "did you manage to persuade him to co-operate with you?"

"I think so," replied Asprey. "It may well be that we have caught him just at the right moment when he is disillusioned with his lot and the opportunity to get away from it all in peace and comfort may not come amiss. However, I am not certain."

"But at least he didn't say no," said Tommy. "Where there's life there's hope!"

"Precisely," Asprey could not prevent the one word. It was out before he had thought. Still Tommy could make of it what he wanted. He would not enlarge on it. The fact that he had deliberately misled Tommy did not trouble him.

It might be advantageous that in future Tommy construed events on that assumption. To tell him the truth could complicate matters, and the situation was complex enough as it was.

"Must have some shut-eye. Thank you Tommy for an excellent dinner. By the way Strauss asked me to give you his thanks as well."

The last was a lie and Tommy would know it was if, as Asprey suspected, the cabin was bugged. But it would hopefully be construed as a social lie and therefore not cast general doubt on his integrity in reporting. Tommy appeared to accept it at face value and made no comment. They wished each other goodnight and retired to their respective cabins. To his surprise Charles had no difficulty in getting to sleep. Strauss had been offered an out. He had turned it down. To some extent Asprey's conscience was satisfied. He had taken a dangerous course and a word or gesture too many might have led to his own undoing. So he had tried even though he had failed.

Chapter Thirteen

Now we have it!

The following morning, Asprey took his time in rising. A buffet-breakfast was laid in the main cabin and he enjoyed ample choice from fruit, cereal, fish and coffee. There was no sign of Tommy. It did not seem appropriate to enquire of the steward as to his host's whereabouts, so, having completed his satisfaction of the inner man, Asprey asked for transportation to the salvage ship. After a translation of the phrase "run-over", he obtained the man's eager agreement.

The "Jean" was a large example of her type. She could have been a converted whaling ship. Forward of the bridge, she displayed nothing out of the ordinary. Sturdy, well maintained and free of any clutter, she could obviously cope with anything that might be thrown at her in the way of storm and tempest. Aft of the bridge was an entirely different affair. Her stern was split in two like a tuning fork. Straddling the gap was a cluster of cranes, a few large and many small. This complicated web of chains, wire-ropes, pulleys and levers was controlled from a secondary bridge set well above the stern. Winches were already whirring and preparations for the lift well underway.

A few yards astern of the "Jean" lay a long open Malaysian fishing smack. Its gentle bobbing movement owed more to the bodies clambering on and diving off than to the ocean swell. The bodies were lithe, golden and bejewelled female forms glistening in the early morning sun. Asprey pointed towards the fishing smack. "Let's go there." The steersman waved his free hand and immediately altered course. He needed no second bidding.

Charles viewed the approaching cabaret with interest. He

199

had heard from Rossi about the girls that were trained mainly in Japan in the skills and endurance of pearl diving. Theirs was a prostitution with the sea. They had been committed without choice to a career that was as self destructive as glass-blowing in the early days of the industrial revolution in Europe. That the girls had the advantage of working in surroundings as idyllic as the European were satanic, was only a temporary consolation. They would not make 30 years of age even if they were lucky and luck meant the exchange of one prostitution for another.

They could catch the boss's eye, but it would not necessarily mean the substitution of one bed for another. It was more likely that compensation for a reduction in the number of daily dives would be participation in equally exhausting pasttimes. Either way, the prospects facing a girl skin diver were enough to daunt the liveliest personality.

Yet the sounds coming across the water were those of merriment and enjoyment. Girlish giggles punctuated the chatter and laughter of many voices. Perhaps because it was the beginning of the day and everyone and everything was fresh.

The first impression was of a party where the anonymity of dinner jackets was replaced by the uniformity of raven hair, gleaming white smiles, almond eyes and light brown skin. Close examination would undoubtedly destroy the age old myth that all Eastern girls looked alike, but their absence of clothing other than the flimsiest of bikini bottom halves discouraged the Englishman from other than the most casual glances. They, for their part, had no such inhibitions. Their impediment to an exchange of concentrated visual examination was simply they were at work and they had no time for anything else, regardless of inclination.

Asprey jumped from the dinghy, grabbed the rail of the fishing smack and hauled himself aboard. He turned to his boatman. "Would you mind waiting a little while?" Having satisfied himself that the man had understood and would in fact do as he had been bid, Asprey decided to seek out whoever was in charge of the bedlam into which he had thrust

200

himself. Since most of the activity was on the starboard side towards the "Jean" he made his way as close to that rail as he could, aiming for the bow. He had gone but a few paces when he saw the figure he expected. Herr Strauss was completely immersed in shouting instructions to a group of girls swimming in the water immediately beneath him as he leant over the rail. As Asprey got closer he could see that lines stretched out from the stern of the "Jean" and disappeared into the water a few yards from the bow of the fishing smack.

Strauss was passing over the side of his vessel additional lines one by one to girls who upon their receipt would up-end and dive. For a moment Asprey was diverted by the comparison between the antics of the skin-divers and those of the porpoises that have long entertained sailors at sea. The element of sex was as much apparent in one as the absence in the other. One would need the enforced absence of female companionship, the common lot of the sailor in times gone by, to confuse one with the other.

Charles decided he was superfluous. Strauss was clearly heavily engaged and would far from welcome any interruption. The girls might, but that would be to incur the displeasure of their master, whoever he was. Everyone aboard had a job to do and his intervention could only be a hindrance. Having failed to catch Strauss's eye and thereby further confirmed his conclusion that he was not wanted, he walked back along the deck and clambered into the waiting dinghy. He indicated the salvage vessel to the grinning steersman. As they moved away, he glanced back at the fishing smack and marvelled again at the superficial picture of fun and games. Its purpose was anything but lighthearted and those taking part were not playing. Their work was both serious and unpleasant. Yet they transformed it into an impression of enjoyment. Perhaps it was no mirage. Perhaps they had reconciled themselves with the philosophy that their god had at least given them their health and faculties which could and should be enjoyed in the beautiful environment in which he had also placed them. Perhaps.

Asprey's philosophy was rudely interrupted by the dinghy's

arrival alongside the Jean. The shock was physical as well as mental. He had been facing the way they had come and had been "miles away". Having collected himself, he swung up the ladder hung over the side of the salvage ship and pulled himself on to its deck. The noises emanating from this hive of activity contrasted almost rudely with those he had just left on the fishing smack. Grinding, creaking and clattering combined in a caucophony of a metallic symphony. Inhuman, robotic and of the workshop. It was like stepping from the Renaissance into the nineteenth century of Great Britain.

Here, despite good housekeeping, were grime, grease and oil. The smell of industry, the vapour of diesel swamping the salted air and diverting the fresh breeze around the vessel. The epitomy of "where there's muck, there's brass", the wreck recovery business of the sea.

The main bridge appeared to be the right destination for unheralded visitors. It was easily located and far from the madding bustle around the stern. Asprey made towards it and had almost accomplished his intention when he found his progress blocked by the formidable structure of Murray Brash.

"Ah, good morning, Mr. Asprey, how are we today. Did you sleep well? Is Tommy looking after you?" The verbal machine gun achieved its purpose. Charles stopped in his tracks, with his mouth open and unfocussed eyes. The second belt was let off. "You must come and dine with me on my launch. A good time would be this evening. Do hope you can come. We can have an excellent meal even out here. Shall we say seven o'clock. Not too early I hope? Good. I will send my cockle shell across for you at that time. Look forward to an interesting evening. Excuse me, must rush. See you then at seven. Bye."

The last words were aimed away from Asprey as by then Brash had continued his course which would have been directly through Charles but for the fact that the latter had stood aside at the critical point in the one-sided conversation. Verbal response had been made impossible. Physical obstruction would have been foolhardy. As Asprey looked with some amusement at the rear of the departing amorphous mass of humanity, he suddenly called to mind the standard law case of Baron versus Potter. In that renowned piece of legalistic morality for students, Mr. Potter had used his ample bulk to pin his co-director Mr. Baron, a gentleman of far lesser proportions, to the wall of a London railway terminus whilst he convened and held a board meeting, the business of which was advantageous for himself and not at all for the benefit of his unwilling partner. Now he understood perfectly how Mr. Baron must have felt, though to be honest the possibility of dining with one Brash was not entirely unwelcome. Nevertheless, it had an uncomfortable similarity to the position of the young skin-divers. They enjoyed the trappings of the sun, sea and breeze as temporary recompense yet knowing that at some not too distant time they would have to pay a price which would more than outweigh the initial benefits.

With Brash, the food and wine and indeed the conversation would all be thoroughly enjoyable. But inevitably there would be a sting in the tail. Brash was not a Yorkshireman, but he never did owt for nowt. Asprey wondered what it would be. What he did not expect and therefore should have anticipated was that he was going to be propositioned for the second time, but on this occasion the implications would indeed be comparable with those of the young ladies' activities. His agreement would be a death warrant certainly for someone else and possibly even for himself.

*   *   *   *   *   *   *

Brash busied himself pouring two large whiskies from a flat bottomed decanter. He placed the very full glasses on the table in the centre of the cabin and sat himself facing Asprey.

"Your very good health." "And yours." The preliminaries completed as swiftly as good manners allowed, the two men inclined their drinks towards each other and then sipped carefully.

Brash spoke first. "I would like you to do something that would benefit both of us. I want you to take Strauss's place when the U-Boat breaks the surface. To be the first into the submarine and to arrange for everything other than the so-

203

called treasure to be transferred to this launch. You will be well rewarded. You can have my share of the spoils after payment of my expenses. It will be an unpleasant job but the compensation should make it more than worthwhile."

It was physically impossible for Brash to lean back as his bulk more than adequately filled the space between the edge of the table and the padded bench upon which he sat. His verbal pause, however, gave precisely that effect. He now awaited Asprey's response.

"It seems a generous offer. But won't Strauss object?"

"I have made arrangements. He will not be in any position to make any comment, either for or against. He will also be well looked after."

Asprey forebore to enquire as to the terms of Strauss's compensation as he had a feeling that it would be in an entirely different coin to that of his own.

"What about Tommy and the rest? Won't they complain as soon as they find out?"

"There is no reason why they should. Strauss has special gear for the job which is fully protective and at the same time a comprehensive disguise. You will be literally covered from head to toe. Even the face mask is one way!"

Charles scratched his nose, an indication to those who knew him well that he thought he had a real problem.

"So, you make sure that Strauss is not around. I take his place suitably garbed. I make sure that everything that is moveable other than the glass containers holding the mercury is moved across to your launch. Does that include the bodies?"

"Yes, those as well. We have brought some plastic bags for those. There should not be many, say about a dozen and it will depend upon whether they have been submerged in water as to their condition. I accept that that is by far the worst part of the job. Since the rest is a piece of cake, I am sure you will agree that you have to earn such a large sack of corn."

The two men sat for a while in silence, each using his tumbler of whisky to avoid continuing the conversation. Asprey held his glass up to the light and, staring at its contents, announced his decision.

"O.K., you do your part and I will do mine. We can't put it in writing so that we shall have to trust each other."

Brash raised his tumbler in mock salute. "Good, I am glad we are agreed. I suggest that you sleep here tonight. I will get a message across to Tommy saying that you have dined rather well and are staying to sleep it off. He may wonder but I don't think he will do anything about it. At first light I will have Strauss's gear delivered to your cabin. As he will also have been my guest for dinner this evening, no-one will think it odd when 'he' emerges from this launch to return to the salvage ship."

"So," said Asprey, "we shall have Strauss with us tonight?"

"Yes, but he will not dine with us. He will be, er, eating with someone else. I would suggest that it could be mutually embarrassing if you bumped into each other while you're both aboard. That should not arise because of the timing of the arrangements, but one never knows." Brash shrugged, adding further ambiguity to his comments. His face was as inscrutable as ever. Charles could conjure as many scenarios as he might wish to forecast the large man's play for the evening.

For certain he would obtain no advice or clue as to their respective accuracy. But ignorance of the piece was acceptable as long as he knew the denouement and that could be in his hands.

Brash was still the consummate host. "Would you prefer to stay with the black label or would you like a somewhat lighter aperitif?"

"I'm more than happy to continue with the whisky. In fact," continued Asprey, "as I have no desire to change my alibi into reality, may I stay with it through the meal, despite the temptation of the excellent wine that I am sure you will have arranged for dinner?"

Brash nodded. "I quite undertand. It will be no hardship for me to drink full bottles."

Asprey noted the plural and wondered whether he could relax a little and sample just a small taste of the wine that would be served. As it transpired, however, commonsense for once prevailed. He resisted the temptation by concentration on the enjoyment of an excellent repast, supported by occasional sips of Highland water. Brash helped not a little by avoiding any comment on the wines delivered to his table, although he could not refrain from a few lip smacks of pleasure, for which he apologised with eyes and hands in gestures of helplessness.

As coffee arrived, Brash looked at his watch. "Whilst it is only 9.30, I think we should both call it a day very shortly. In addition to getting up at the crack of dawn, we have a very heavy day in front of us. By the time the sun goes down again, it must all be done."

"True," said Asprey, "which is my cabin?"

"The one nearest the stern. It's the last door on your left as you go down the passage way," advised Brash. "Strauss will be in the one adjoining yours and I shall be in the main cabin forward. I won't offer you a night-cap as I am sure you will sleep soundly."

Charles was unsure whether the last comment was a threat or a promise.

It was probably best interpreted as friendly advice. "Thank you, I am sure I will. Now, if you would excuse me," so saying Asprey finished his coffee and slid long the side of the table. He made his way to the cabin indicated by Brash and prepared for bed.

Charles did not sleep as soundly as either he or Brash had wished. He lay on top of his bunk, trying to decide on the best course of action. Should he intervene or let Brash follow his plan of campaign? After over an hour's speculation he had arrived at no clear resolution and it was almost a relief to have the interruption of noises heralding new arrivals on the launch. Charles moved swiftly across to the spy-hole through which he could look into the passage way. He heard a cabin door open and assumed that at least one person had already passed by. As he focussed his eye, he became aware of a female form sliding across his vision. It looked soft and lithe, but there was no way in which he could discern her features and therefore her identity. As for her companion(s), one at least should be Strauss if Brash had told him the truth earlier. He then heard a door click shut and all became silent again.

Asprey was still lying wide awake a considerable time later when an abrupt but soft sound catapulted him out of his bunk back to his spy-hole. Again he felt that he had missed one person, but his view this time left no doubt as to the identity of another. His focal path led him to the clearly defined figure of a young lady clad as nature intended. Even the absence of her usual bikini-bottom did not disguise the fact that she was the most nubile of the young Malaysian and Japanese divers the C.I.H. employed in their day-to-day salvage operations. They enjoyed living and it would appear that they helped others to apply the same philosophy. It seemed that a midnight swim had been organised for Herr Strauss.

As is often the case, procrastination had left Asprey with no further choice. Perhaps his subconscious accepted the inevitable. At any event, the next moment, or so it appeared to him, there was a decisive knocking at his door. This time his journey across the cabin was considerably slower, so that when he opened his door it was to find an impatient Brash trying to retain control of an armful of assorted clothing and equipment.

"Quick take this lot. Put it on. If you have any problems ring me on the bridge. If not, be up on deck as quickly as possible." Speaking in short gasps, Brash thrust the gear into Asprey's embrace and without waiting for any response steamed off towards the gangway. Asprey deposited the large untidy bundle smelling of rubber and disinfectant on to the cabin floor and surveyed it with distaste and foreboding. He felt he ought to have a quick shave if only to freshen himself up. Brash would have to wait for that.

The sun was already climbing steeply into the sky and a light mist and haze hung over the sea. The arrival of the police launch was as unheralded as it was unexpected.

"We are coming alongside," a disembodied voice floated across the water. "We wish to talk with the captain." Brash arrived on his deck at the end of the request and looked furiously for sight of the interloper. As soon as he had identified the voice's owner, he descended quickly into the bowels of his launch and rapped urgently on Asprey's door. "Strauss, I want you fully dressed and up aloft – NOW."

Having delivered his uncompromising and clear message, Brash spun on his heel and again with remarkable agility returned to the deck and then across the gangway which linked his launch with the salvage vessel. He arrived on the port side just as an inspector of police climbed over the starboard rail. The two made their independent ways to the bridge, climbed up their respective steps and were prevented from meeting in the precise middle of that structure by the ample form of the ship's captain. This personage gave every sign of disagreeable surprise at such an early and uninvited visitor.

Inspector Chung was a neat man, immaculately turned out in a lightweight uniform complete with Sam Brown belt and leather holstered revolver. At first sight his round baby face appeared to be inconsistent with the serious nature of his profession and the tools of his trade. Further examination soon dispelled any confusion. His was the toughness of a piece of smooth jade. A man not to be taken lightly.

The captain spoke softly. "To what do we owe this unexpected pleasure, Inspector?" Captain MacCleod's voice removed any necessity for him to indicate his country of origin, particularly when he was angry. "You are not going to tell us that we cannot complete our operations now?" It was almost a statement rather than a question.

The inspector's manners were as smooth as his face. His innocent brown eyes peered up at the captain. "Why should I," he asked. "Is not everything in order? It's just that in view of the importance of this project – and," – looking for the first time at Brash – "I am sure no-one would deny that it is important, I have been instructed to make absolutely certain that everything goes precisely as we have agreed."

Inspector Chung turned his attention to the stern of the vessel. "I see that the periscope has broken the surface so the conning tower should not be far below. That should mean that you will be completing your lift early this morning."

The captain looked quizzically at the policeman. "Aye, we

decided to hold our position late yesterday afternoon so that we would have a full day for the entry and initial inspection."

A slight frown creased the forehead of the policeman. "I don't see Herr Strauss. He must be present at all times during the operation and particularly he must be the first to enter the submarine. That is our undertaking as it is indeed yours. Unless it is observed, the salvage cannot continue."

"Herr Strauss is just getting ready," Brash quickly interposed. "You will appreciate he will have to wear special protective clothing in order that he may safely enter the U-Boat. If it is anything like the normal diving gear it will take him more than a few minutes to put it on."

Chung grunted and then waved towards his own launch. In response to an obviously pre-arranged signal, two men climbed up on to the deck of the salvage vessel.

In addition to side-arms, each carried a sub-machine gun slung across his back. The inspector pointed towards the stern of the ship where the crane and its supporting davits cradled the U-Boat some fifteen feet below the surface of the sea. Brash had his attention fixed upon his own launch. "Ah, here is Herr Strauss," he said. His two companions on the bridge swivelled their eyes and all three watched as the mis-shapen figure slouched its way along the connecting gang-way on to the deck of the ship. "You can start the morning's operations now, captain."

The policeman nodded agreement. The captain bellowed instructions to his first mate positioned below the bridge, and the rear of the ship started to vibrate with the movement of machinery and men.

In the meantime, Strauss or that which everyone other than Brash took to be Strauss, began to make his way towards the stern. "Good morning Herr Strauss, I wish you luck," the policeman called to him.

The figure below him made no response. "Of course," said the inspector, "he cannot hear me unless I speak to him through the intercom." He turned back towards the centre of the bridge and re-entered the covered portion. "May I use that?" he asked the captain, pointing towards a speaker

209

placed in the middle of the chart table. The captain shrugged and nodded at the same time, since there was no doubt that the request was no more than a courtesy. Chung was determined to speak with Herr Strauss.

"Good morning Herr Strauss," he repeated into the speaker, "may I wish you luck?" The reply was muffled and anonymous. "Thank you," the inspector stroked his chin then spoke again, this time quite firmly. "I wonder if it would be too much trouble for you to come up here on to the bridge. I know that your outfit is a little cumbersome, but it will be some time before you can get on with your part in the operation and I would appreciate your advice on a certain matter."

There was a pause during which the figure in the deck turned and looked directly up at the bridge. "Very well, I will join you immediately."

Inspector Chung turned and beamed at Brash and the captain. "It looks as though we shall shortly have quite a party for, if I'm not mistaken, Mr. Chua is coming across as well."

He was quite right. Tommy had left his launch in a small dinghy and was shooting towards the mother ship, popped along by a tiny outboard motor. In terms of time and effort his journey was almost identical to that of the rubber suited diver slowly climbing towards the bridge. They arrived at their common destination virtually together, albeit from opposite directions. Tommy was breathless, but whether from exertion or emotion was an unanswerable question.

"Good morning," he said addressing all and sundry, "are we ready to go?"

"It would appear so," replied the inspector on behalf of all those now filling the narrow bridge. "I have just asked Herr Strauss to join us as there is some time yet before the final act and I wanted to be absolutely sure that all is in order."

"Of course it is," Brash had had difficulty in remaining his normal calm and unruffled self. His impatience was now getting the better of him. "At the rate he can move on dry land, Herr Strauss had better start returning to his post otherwise he might hold up our programme."

Chung ignored Brash and looked directly at "Strauss"

across the chart table so that he could talk to him through the speaker between them.

"Herr Strauss, are you certain that everything is in order, that everything is going according to your requirements and you are happy to take full responsibility from here on in for all that might happen – particularly that your masters will be totally happy with the outcome?"

The figure stood like an android silhouetted against the bright early morning sun, head on its chest implying an almost quizzical attitude. The silence was broken by a nervous cough from Tommy, half stifled into a bird-like stoccato. Then, still without a word, the automaton raised its right arm and un-clipped the face mask.

Brash exploded. "What the hell do you think you are doing?" It was left to Tommy to ask the obvious question: "Where is Strauss? Why are you in his suit? What is going on?"

"Yes, Mr. Asprey," said the policeman, "just precisely what is going on? Whatever it is, you can be certain that we all know what is not going on."

"What do you mean by that?" shouted Brash.

"You know what I mean," said Chung in quiet clipped words. "No Strauss, no entry. No entry, no lift. We shall find out where Strauss is and why Mr. Asprey is impersonating him, but in the meantime, I want the submarine returned to whence it came – now."

The captain was the first to erupt. "You can't do that. We have almost completed the job. From here on in it's a piece of cake."

"Probably so," replied the policeman, "but someone has opened the oven door too early and it's been completely spoiled. Still, why should you worry? You will get paid for your time and trouble."

"Exactly," breathed Brash, "we have to pay him, but who pays us if we re-sink the sub? We might just as well go the whole hog. You can have my word that Asprey will do only that which Strauss would have done, precisely as the German Admiralty wanted."

211

"But you do not know what Strauss was supposed to do, beyond supervising the lift and entering the submarine first – or do you?" Brash did not reply. Asprey could almost hear the inspector's voice continuing, "and anything further you may say may be taken down and used as evidence, etc., etc."

"Right, gentlemen," Chung commanded their attention. "Where is Herr Strauss and why is he not where he is supposed to be?"

The ensuing silence was broken by the Jean's captain. "Ask them. He didn't stay on board here last night. Let me know when you've made up your minds what you want me to do. I'm going to my cabin." With that he left the four men staring at his retreating back which eloquently expressed his opinion of the whole mess that they had brought upon themselves.

Brash took up the challenge. "We don't know. Yesterday evening he asked if he could have the use of a cabin in my launch to entertain a friend. It was not the first time. He had done it before. On previous occasions he had also gone for a night swim. He might had done that again last night. I understand he was very good in the water. When I found that he was missing this morning I asked Asprey to take his place as it seemed to me that the most important requirement was that the lift should be completed. It was not a question of deception. Asprey is quite as competent as Strauss for the last act. The difficult part had been done. The captain's just confirmed that. If we delayed it could cost us real money. There could always be a change in the weather and that would have been disastrous. So I thought it a reasonable step to take. Anyway, Asprey agreed, didn't you?"

Asprey nodded but was interrupted in his verbal confirmation by the Inspector.

"I am not conducting a trial or even a preliminary hearing, Mr. Brash, merely asking a question. In simple terms you are saying that you do not know why Herr Strauss is not here, neither where he is. Now, whilst I would like to know the answers – if not now then at some future date – the present position is unaffected by their absence, unlike that of Herr Strauss. I have no option but to return the U-Boat to whence

212

it came."

Up to that moment Tommy had kept his silence and taken no part in the proceedings. He had already come to the conclusion that the sooner he could declare a non-interest and vacate the scene, the better. He seized what he thought to be his best chance.

"Well if that's the case, I might as well go on my way. I'll put my losses down to experience. We'll settle up later, Charles. Now if you gentlemen will excuse me . . .

Without waiting for consent or contradiction, merely leaving his threat in the air, Tommy walked swiftly away. No-one moved to restrain him by word or deed.

The interruption has been long enough for Brash to build up a head of steam. "You can't possibly do that." Brash's voice was almost a falsetto. He sounded and looked like a highly distressed Wagnerian heroine.

"I appeal to you Inspector. We can finally put an end to the instigators of the Holocaust. This morning we can harvest the fruits of *all* our endeavours. We can at long last be constructive and put behind us vengeance and vendetta."

The policeman spoke slowly. "Who exactly are we? The only body that has consistently invested time and money with implacable determination has been and is the state of Israel." His speech accelerated, as his mind began to piece together half-forgotten incidents and scraps of information. "Now it might make sense if you were David, the Far East controller of I.I.S. That would certainly explain your interest and your part in this venture."

Brash had regained control of himself. His voice had returned to it's normal cadence. "Whether I am the one you call David or not is irrelevant. What is important is that you have almost literally within your grasp incontrovertible total proof of that which the world only knows in part, having to guess at the remainder."

The Inspector acknowledged that as a possibility. "So, why not tell me what you know and what you have guessed. Then perhaps I would be able to make a judgement."

"Very well, if anything will change your mind then this

213

should." Brash folded his arms and supported his stomach on the chart table. "We know that U-134 contains the corpses of two of the highest ranking Nazis. The first is Bormann – and that verification will stop the ever present hopeless search. The second is that of Hitler. Whether he was dead or alive when the U-Boat left Germany is not over-important. His body will not only prove that he is dead, but that there was an almighty conspiracy to produce evidence of his supposed death. We shall also be able to remove a potential holy relic or shrine of evil. The third body is that of the intended successor to Hitler and the most interesting aspect of his identification is that he was not German. His nationality could well give us the final clue to the last nest of vipers. But even if it does not, we know the U-134 also holds papers, documents and contracts. These list the people and organisations that subscribed one way or another to the embryonic Nazi Party and the rewards that they had been promised when that organisation attained its ultimate targets. They have one element in common."

"None of them were in Germany at the time and therefore may still exist in complete anonymity. This information had two functions for those in U-134. The first was security – there were no copies so they carried everything with them. The second was insurance – those named in them would not wish to see such documents published. You might call that intended blackmail. If it was, then that would be the least of their crimes. There are two or possibly three other people entombed in the U-Boat. For these we only have educated guesses, but even so corroboration would be very valuable."

"You will now, I hope, understand the importance of the contents of the U-134, not only for us – but also for the free world as a whole. We must do everything we can to prevent a repetition of the horrors compounded by the Nazis. We can now complete our task and our dead can sleep soundly and peacefully. For the sake of millions what is the disturbance of half a dozen corpses?"

The air was heavy with humidity. Brash was sweating profusely. Asprey watched the policeman through half-closed eyes. Whilst he and the Inspector were the only two that could have heard Brash's plea, everyone on the salvage ship seemed to be aware that a decision was being made. The silence was one of breathless anticipation.

Still no word was spoken, but there was none needed. Chung quickly and smoothly unbuttoned his holster and slid the revolver into the palm of his right hand. The action was enough to demonstrate his conclusion. He was anticipating unpopularity. He wished to pre-empt any folly.

"Very interesting and if I may say so, Mr. Brash, very eloquent. You have indeed persuaded me that U-134 is vitally important and for that reason alone I must honour the undertaking that my government has given to the German Government to the letter. If that cannot for any reason be done, then the salvage operation must immediately cease – and that means committing U-134 once more to the sea. Now that Mr. Brash has explained the relevance of its contents, we can all understand why those very precise conditions were stipulated."

"I cannot, I dare not attempt anything other than the strictest compliance. We already know more than is good for our health. That may not worry you gentlemen, but it scares the hell out of me."

The policeman slowly raised his revolver towards the end of his explanation so that whilst not pointing at anyone, the slightest movement of his wrist would achieve that end. "I believe I can understand how you must feel Mr. Brash, so may I ask you to do nothing that might cause me to feel that you are on the point of being foolish whilst I give the necessary order to slip chains."

Inspector Chung raised his left hand and shouted a series of commands in Chinese without taking his eyes off his two companions. His subordinates responded and almost immediately the vessel started to vibrate with the thud of unleashed diesels. The Inspector reverted to English.

"May I suggest, Mr. Brash, that you should return to your launch. We are as you know technically in Malaysian waters – just. If you delay your departure from them, you may find

your sojourn with us somewhat longer than you might wish."
Brash hesitated, looked at Asprey and then made as if to
comment. The policeman intercepted his intention. "I would
much prefer action to words, Mr. Brash."

The large man shrugged and swung himself around. He left
the bridge and the salvage ship without a backward glance.
The Inspector followed him all the way with his eyes and
waited until Brash's launch had slipped anchor before he
attempted to speak again. "Now, Mr. Asprey," he said,
slipping his revolver back into its holster which he left
unbuttoned, "we haven't much time and I'm not going to
waste it by asking you questions that I know you cannot or
will not answer. So forgetting the why, when and how, can I
take it that we will not be meeting Herr Strauss again?"

"Yes, I think that's a fair assumption," replied Asprey.

"You knew it was likely to happen but you took no steps to
help or even to warn him?"

"That was not my brief. He had his."

"Hmm," the policeman pursed his lips, "you're not a very
pleasant lot, but I suppose your job hardly encourages gentle-
manly behaviour. Even so what I cannot understand at all is
why you should go to all this trouble when it would appear to
me that your masters had already decided that the U-Boat
should keep its secrets. Why not say no to the salvage and stay
with that from the beginning, rather than change your minds
and then have to go to these lengths to arrive at the same
conclusion?"

Asprey made no effort to respond. Inspector Chung began
to lose a little of his cool. "Well, it was too much to hope that
you might help as I will have to report to my superiors. The
only rational explanation is that you wanted to be sure that
the U-Boat's contents were intact, that those who wanted
sight of them were discouraged and placed in such a position
that they could never again obtain the necessary permission.
By overtly helping those who might otherwise be encouraged
to attempt a clandestine approach, you've identified a number
of key opponents and established a close relationship with my
people. So perhaps the tactics were right, even though the

216

cost to colleagues was high – because there were more than one."

During the inspector's comments, Asprey had appeared totally disinterested until the last sentence. For a moment it looked as though he would ask the obvious question – who? but, with difficulty, he restrained himself and turned to look out over the sea.

"A dirty game, Mr. Asprey."

Charles welcomed the opportunity. "Not a game, Inspector, quite a serious occupation in fact."

"So you say," the policeman looked at the departing launches. "Our friends are making good time so that's two down and one to go."

"I have my orders to get you out of Malaysia as quickly as possible. Brash has doubtless taken all your belongings with him so you will have to be kitted out. That may not be a bad thing anyway as you will be less easily recognised. I am sure that there are those who will want to invite you to join them if you stay in K.L. My instructions are to put you in a plane to the destination of your choice – perhaps you would like Singapore? No, that would be wishful thinking."

Asprey decided not to rise to the bait. "I'll let you know when we get to the airport."

"Well, said the Inspector, "wherever you decide to go, you may be sure that Messrs. Brash and Chua are very patient men."

Asprey again ignored the comment. "I'd better get out of this fancy dress and see if I can find something more appropriate for flying."

The policeman nodded. "O.K., perhaps the captain can help. You'll find him in his cabin."

Charles stumbled across the bridge and disappeared painfully in search of the captain. The inspector moved to a position from where he could watch the activity in the stern of the salvage ship and became absorbed in its complexity. The re-appearance of Captain McLeod startled him, a fact that he attempted to disguise by a sudden fit of coughing which the captain duly ignored.

217

"I have asked the steward to kit Asprey out as best he can," he said. Chung spluttered his thanks, "His previous outfit might have caused us some problem at the airport."

"So you are deporting him. As a matter of interest, may I ask where to?"

"You may ask but I cannot enlighten you. He will undoubtedly leave the choice of destination until the last moment. I have a feeling that he will not wish it to be released generally."

The Captain smiled thinly. "I can quite understand that, but as you will undoubtedly know, perhaps you would be kind enough to pass it on to our people in Kuala Lumpur."

"By our people, captain, do you mean the British Consul?"

"Of course."

"Excuse my confusion, captain," Chung was speaking very deliberately, "but I understand from your lists that you are Royal Navy and not, as you would say, wavy navy. In fact that this is your first commission in a salvage vessel – and I have a feeling that it is your last? We know that you have served in this part of the world but usually attached to a mission. Had you been in your previous role, then I might have understood your interest in the future of Mr. Asprey, but as Captain of this boat?"

McLeod winced at "boat". He had had no liking at all for his original assignment and its development had only added fuel to his feelings. To make matters worse, he was still no wiser as to the intentions of his masters and whether the reinterrment of U-134 was going to be greeted with pleasure or anger. Of one matter, however, he was quite convinced. They would be vitally interested in the whereabouts of Mr. Asprey for some time to come. If he, McLeod lost that trail as well, then any counterbalance he might have had in such information as against the unknown reaction to the result of the salvage operation would have disappeared. He could only benefit if he knew. At worst it might alleviate some pain. At best it might compound his success. So he tried to obtain the co-operation of the little police inspector.

"You are quite right," he began, "I am still R.N. and I

218

have had a watching brief for Her Majesty's government. My job has been not to interfere but simply to observe. I have had to record everything that has happened and report every night by radio. My instructions so far have been to continue to do just that. I cannot come with you to K.L., even if you invited me. Hence my request that you should contact the British Consul when you feel able to do so."

The inspector was now in command of the situation and relishing it. "Thank you for your candour. Pity it wasn't offered earlier but it would not have affected the outcome, I suppose. Still, it might have been helpful."

Whether McLeod would have apologised at this point or whether the inspector would have scaled greater heights in his verbal condescension are questions that will never be answered, since both intentions, if they existed, were interrupted by the re-appearance of Asprey, clad in an ill-fitting light grey suit. He was clearly embarrassed by his sartorial inelegance and anxious to set in chain the events necessary for his ultimate transformation back into his normal attire. "Right, I'm ready," he said to both men. Then addressing the captain, "I am much obliged for your steward's help. Sorry I can't pay for the togs, but I will send some recognition when I can. I expect he would prefer that to the return of them." Even in such circumstances Asprey could not stop himself saying the wrong thing. His inference was quite clear. Whatever sum he sent it would be worth more than the clothes in which he stood. Indeed, they would hardly be worth the cost of sending them back. But neither Chung nor McLeod cared. They were upset by their inability to conclude their conversation. Each for quite different reasons, but both annoyed enough to show their feelings.

The captain snorted. "Return them when you can. Don't bother about the money."

The inspector added his piece. "Nice to know you are ready. At least we shan't have the problem of providing you with a low profile. In that outfit you could hardly be described as distinguished or distinguishable. Right, let's go. I will see what we can do for you captain. It will not be up to me."

"Fair enough," replied McLeod. "Thanks anyway."

Asprey looked at each of the two men. He could see that if he wished to make the next stage of his journey safely, the less he said from there on, the better. He shut his mouth and kept it thus until he was in the departure lunge at Kuala Lumpur airport.

Chapter Fourteen

Now we don't!

Ten years after the Second World War, Frankfurt had a vigorous undergraduate population. The students were no longer a mixture of mature ex-service personnel and war scarred young men and women. They were in the main youngsters who had had explained to them after the event why they had suffered, what they had lost and what could still be achieved. They were the root cause of the economic miracle which transformed their Fatherland from a rubble of despair to a gleaming pile of prosperity.

Dedicated, determined, single-minded and quite certain that they would rise, not like a Phoenix from the ashes but as the heirs by right to the throne of Europe. They knew only the glory of Germany's past. The present was an uncomfortable but temporary compromise. The future was inevitable – a single all-powerful country. The immediate disasters of the two world conflicts had been but battles, lost through economic weakness, treachery and impetuosity. The war had yet to be won.

To the casual observer, German students were assiduously preparing themselves for the task of re-building their nation. They had little time to spare for the foreigner. There was now no suggestion of ingratiating apologetic self effacement. Simply a concentration of effort day and night to the exclusion of all except the essential.

Asprey's initial involvement was superficial. In order to man his company's stand at the Frankfurt Spring Fair he had decided to use the services of a University student. The Fair coincided with the Easter vacation – so that it was not difficult to find a language undergraduate who was interested in the

221

opportunity of making some money and also improving his knowledge of English. Wolfgang proved ideal. He spoke several European languages quite fluently, was neat in appearance and took an immediate interest in the company's products.

The Fair lasted some ten days. By the third the young Englishman and the young German had developed a mutual liking, so that when they had closed the stand on that evening, it was no surprise to either that they should be in agreement that Wolfgang should show Charles some of the sights of Frankfurt-am-Main.

This was best achieved on foot, at least according to Wolfgang, so they set out for the centre of the city. As they walked, the German pointed out the all too obvious scars of war and the round the clock efforts being made to re-build a city almost totally destroyed by Allied bombers. The only sector that had survived relatively undamaged was the old town in which the University had originally been located. Frankfurt was no different to a score of German cities that had been virtually obliterated. Even so it still had some unique features which Wolfgang was determined to uncover.

As they paused at a main intersection, Wolfgang suddenly pointed to a white convertible. "That's the Kapitan," he said. "You mean the car," said Asprey. "Yes and no," replied the student. "Let me tell you the story."

As the two young men strolled past the main railway station, the tram centre and the world famous opera house, all casualties but scarred survivors of the Holocaust, Wolfgang relayed his tale.

Defeat had cost Germany dear. The immediate plan had had to be survival. For this the Germans relied upon their conquerors, particularly the Americans. So for about five years, whatever the Allies wanted they could have, first for nothing then gradually at a price. The Germans had little to offer, but they managed to achieve their first objective, they survived – just.

Those who did better than most replaced their conquerors in the economic pecking order and in their turn accepted the offerings of their countrymen and women who were still struggling to make their way up the political and economic ladders.

One of the more lucrative resources made available in this way was inevitably sex. The Allies did well in the early days of their occupation, but later as wealth and influence could be overtly displayed and applied by the indigenous heirarchy, the more attractive goods were kept for the enjoyment of the latter.

According to Wolfgang, the most sought after purveyor of sexual satisfaction in Frankfurt was the Kapitan, a young lady who derived her title from the make of car she drove and the essential element that it represented in the marketing of her wares.

Early in the evening, engagements permitting, she could be seen driving her automobile around the city. Those who wished to take advantage of her services would endeavour to attract her attention. This could only be achieved by using a similar means of transportation. If the lady felt that a particular supplicant warranted her response she would indicate that he should follow her in his own vehicle. Her first port of call would be a petrol filling station where she would generously top up her tank. Her admirer would then have the privilege of settling the bill, as it were, "key" money showing genuine intent and capability. That transaction completed, she would lead him, both still driving independently, to her flat where they could get down to the real business of the evening and night, assuming amicable agreement as to the terms and conditions. It appeared that every comfort would be available and value for money included an excellent breakfast.

Asprey was intrigued yet a little uncertain as to whether his leg was being pulled. Merely to have a car pointed out to him was no real confirmation. Some years later, however, he was to learn that he had been told nothing but the truth. The Kapitan was murdered by one of her lovers and an international scandal avoided only by the suppression by the German authorities of the identities of her numerous and highly placed regular clients. By coincidence the instigator of

223

that invaluable cover-up was Wolfgang.

Their ultimate destination was in the older part of the city. It was an unfriendly black building that adjoined a night club that rejoiced in the unlikely name of T. S. Elliot. This den of joy was famous for its bathing competitions in which customers would be invited to soap, sponge and generally cleanse an already glamorous young lady and awarded points according to their ingenuity.

The club was also renowned for its chorus girls who, when performing in formation would have cast fear into an All-Black rugger scrum. Germans often prefer their objects of affection to be well endowed. Despite its obvious attractions, however, the T. S. Elliot was not on Wolfgang's itinerary.

Instead, Charles was vouched entry through a heavily curtained door opposite the entry to the club and ushered into the crowded hall of a student's meeting and eating place. Unlike the expected bier-keller, there were no wooden tables and trestles, no buxom waitresses carrying foaming steins. The hall was large, the floor and chairs occupied by and overflowing with young men and women, all talking earnestly yet deliberately. Some were drinking mugs of coffee, others biting into bread rolls filled with frankfurters and mustard. A few were attempting both occupations despite an equal desire to contribute to the debates.

On one side of the hall, a plain wooden staircase led up to a landing some eighteen feet above the floor. The cigarette smoke that billowed and curled prevented more than occasional glimpses of the occupants other than those nearest to the entrance. Asprey had the uncomfortable feeling that he was being carefully scrutinised despite the fact that his entrance had been completely ignored except by the keeper of the door.

Wolfgang pushed his way pleasantly but firmly through the mass of young people. Charles followed as closely as the throng permitted. Without warning he collided with Wolfgang's back. He had stopped. Charles forced himself alongside his guide and discovered that he was already in deep conversation with a young blond girl. "May I introduce you to a very nice girl, Helga. She speaks a little of your language."

Asprey bowed slightly. He just avoided clicking his heels as he looked down into a pair of grey eyes that were staring disconcertingly into his. He followed Wolfgang's lead and spoke in English.

"How do you do. Are you studying languages?"

The girl looked thoughtfully at him. "No."

Pity – Charles did not say the word out loud. Whilst not exactly a beauty, the girl looked decidedly attractive. She had the self-confidence of her generation and self-sufficiency that belied her years. He felt that she could make it a very interesting evening – but it would be platonic.

Helga turned her attention to Wolfgang and continued her conversation with him – in German. "The meeting is tomorrow but we have the initiations tonight. Have we many candidates this time?"

Wolfgang deliberately ignored her question and instead posed one to Charles.

"Can I buy you a cup of coffee and a hot dog?" With the exception of the last two words, he had asked in German. Asprey replied "Yes, thanks very much." The language of his response was immaterial. The point had been made. Helga now understood that he was bi-lingual. It was clear that the message had registered. She thrust at him with a question in her own tongue.

"What other parts of Germany have you visited?"

"Only Bavaria – Passau and your equivalent of our Potteries."

"Are you English?"

"Yes, of course – don't I look English?"

There was a pause. "Perhaps, but you don't sound like one."

Asprey expressed surprise – he was not sure whether he should be annoyed or flattered. As Wolfgang moved away to get the coffees and hot dogs, Helga motioned to Charles to take the chair next to hers. He hesitated as it was already occupied by a young fellow who looked more than capable of defending his rights. But he had reckoned without Helga. She

225

turned her head towards her neighbour said a few words out of Asprey's aural reach and effected the required vacation as smoothly as a gear change in an automatic car.

As Charles seated himself, he reflected on the similar ease with which his generation underestimated the weaker sex. Germany had lost millions of its young men in two World Wars, and like so many of its European neighbours suffered the inevitable consequences. The two tragedies had provided young women with an incontravertible opportunity to expand their horizons into areas of leadership and power rather than persuasion. Those that had taken that initiative were formidable and he had a feeling that Helga was of that ilk.

Wolfgang had returned with the consumables. If he was surprised to find Asprey seated next to Helga, he gave no indication. He simply handed over some of his wares and left them to talk – which they did.

In fact, it was Helga who did most of the talking. Surrounded by those of like mind and inclination, she had no inhibitions in expressing her views, philosophy and objectives. That evening Asprey learned more of the attitude of the new Germany than he had in the years before and indeed in the years that were to follow.

Helga's attitude was simple and positive. In 1914 the industrialists who by then controlled Germany attempted to extend their empire by force. Their efforts failed disastrously. Their only achievement had been that they had thwarted for all time the carefully laid plans of Queen Victoria and her establishment to annex the continent of Europe to the British Empire. Less than twenty years later, the industrialists tried again, having used one Adolph Hitler as their willing tool. The second attempt would have succeeded but for two major political errors. The first, for which they had to accept responsibility, was the timing of the campaign against Russia. The second, which they should have foreseen, was the result of Japanese ambitious impetuosity. Pearl Harbour forced the Americans to join openly in the conflict. Such mistakes would not happen again, if only because in the future Germany would have no need of Allies.

In his early days the Führer had revived hope through pride, expounded a promise and finally extracted a dedication and commitment. He had served his masters well, so well that they gave him too much power, and that was another mistake. Hitler wielded that power with terrifying success. There was no way in which it could be recovered. Despite the fact that his masters still retained some of his strings, the puppet had become Pinochio and pull as they might, the Führer did it his way. The outcome was inevitable and the industrial establishment had relearnt an original truth. The means cannot be divorced from the end. Each is as important as the other.

As well as knowing what had happened and why, Helga also knew what had to be done. Germany had to be rebuilt but in such a way that it could not be interpreted as a threat to other nations. To do this, it had to attract support and sympathy. Its efforts should be construed by all as a natural reponse to a universal challenge. Just as it had been agreed in 1928 that a strong Germany could only be for the benefit of Europe, so must the same philosophy be expounded in the years after 1945. The solution had to be a Cause and such a Cause could be the reunification of the Fatherland, the merging of the two Germanies, East and West.

Active support could be anticipated from the original Western Allies. They already had a guilt complex over the partition having deliberately dragged their feet in their drive across Europe in order to allow Stalin to rape and pillage a substantial area of land owned by an already beaten adversary. They would certainly encourage revitalisation of a West Germany to provide it with the economic strength necessary to achieve such an understandable objective. And so it had proved to be. The continued growth of Germany's wealth unhindered by the politically unacceptable expenditure on defence was hailed by those outside the country and modestly acknowledged by those within as an economic miracle. In reality it was the simple combination of necessity imposed on the vanquished by the greed and sloth embraced by the victors. Reparations provided the manufacturing industries of the Allies with the latest 1939 German tools, dies and machinery, thus enabling them to produce without imagination and innovation products to satisfy an uncritical and overwhelming demand. The Germans, bereft of their assets either through destruction or abstraction, had no alternative but to apply themselves without inhibition to their task of re-building. In this they were helped financially by the Americans, conscience stricken by the devastation of their bombers. The outcome was therefore no miracle. It was the off-spring of need and greed, conceived in hate, nurtured in desperation and educated through clinical determination. But the child would one day become a man. Then Germany would be wealthy enough to offer the Russians a deal that they could not refuse, in return for that which was rightfully theirs – East Germany. The length of time before the coming of age was unimportant. In fact, the longer the wait, the greater the relative strength of West Germany and the more incentive to the East Germans, toughened by the denial of their Russian masters. The price would undoubtedly be high as the prize would not be relinquished lightly. But even that could be accommodated with the development of the atomic bomb.

What better offer to humanity could Germany make than itself as the nuclear arms free zone between West and East? A sacrifice that would outweigh and obscure any misgivings that might be voiced by the cynics with long memories. An offer that western politicians could present to their respective electorates as evidence of their earnest endeavours to protect them from the possible terrors of an atomic war. A suggestion that eastern politicians might accept as a means of extending their borders and reducing the menace for ever encircling them. To ensure the latter's acceptance it would be necessary to express overt allegiance to the U.S.S.R., but treaties cost nothing.

Such generosity deserved the support of all. If the Germans were prepared to risk everything "for the benefit of Europe" who would be churlish enough to deny them that privilege? Who could publicly doubt their motives? Who would want to, if the band-wagon served their own political ends? After all, it only needed silent acquiescence and that was simple enough.

Anyway it had happened before, so why not again?

But the grand strategy had a moment critique. When West Germany made its formal proposition for all to see, it would be in the same position as a butterfly emerging from its chrysalis – vulnerable. The beauty of its wealth would not dazzle the eyes of the careful observer. It would be static and open to close scrutiny. That moment needed a man – a man with the charisma of a leader, a man of integrity, purpose and principle – and a man who in no way recalled the ghost of Adolf Hitler. Yet he must attract the same fervour and support that his predesessor enjoyed in and from the Fatherland. Helga and her colleagues believed that they had resolved that apparently impossible proposition. They had cast that individual's role as that of a prophet, indeed a messiah. Who better to lead one nation to join with another, to return the promised land, to sacrifice himself and if need be his compatriots in the creation of a barrier between opposing forces that might enable the world forever to live in peace?

So the call would be made that would resound long and loud enough for all to hear and respond, each in his own way – and Germany would be well on its way before the final implications became obvious.

So Helga had no doubts. Her country had lost two battles. Its destiny was to win the war and that could be achieved by patient hard work and unity of purpose. Provided that Germany was economically successful and played the political game with care and caution, the day would come when they would be acclaimed for doing that which they most wanted to achieve – the reunification of East and West and their birthright. That attained, they would be well along their chosen path, the economic and political domination of Europe.

And why not?

Asprey was impressed. Germany was not unique in its ambitions. Practically every country in that continent had attempted that very end. Probably Britain under Victoria had come nearest to its achievement. The very deviousness of her plans that had almost led to their success had resulted in their remaining virtually hidden for all time from those whom she thought to benefit, namely the British. Only the history books of Europeans touched on the sensitive secrets of royal intrigue. But the German logic and approach appeared ideally suited to the potential problems and opportunities of the brave new world in general and the continent of Europe in particular. Asprey was also intrigued.

"Can I return tomorrow evening? I would like to learn more."

Helga frowned slightly. Charles pressed on. "It is extremely interesting and it may be that I could be of some help."

That had the desired result. Helga's brow cleared. She smiled. "Yes, that would be nice. Then we shall see whether you look English or German."

Asprey had no idea what she meant by her last remark. Still, he had what he wanted, an invitation to return, so he took his leave before there could be a change of mind, either by Helga herself or Wolfgang when he returned.

The following day when they met at the company's stand at the Messe, Charles thanked the German student for the tour of Frankfurt and said how much he had enjoyed the whole experience. "But I must admit that I do feel that you were pulling my leg over the Kapitan." Wolfgang smiled: "You will see one day. When we are both older and wealthier – if not wiser – we must meet again and then I shall be able to prove, as you would say, beyond all reasonable doubt that such a service does exist. And what a service."

The two men laughed together. Then Asprey said very casually, "Oh, by the way, I was invited to go back to the student's hall this evening. I hope that's alright?"

"But of course, Charles," replied Wolfgang, "unfortunately I will not be able to come with you this time as I have a prior engagement – but not with the Kapitan!! I fear you will have to find your own way."

Bearing in mind the ease of identifying the T. S. Elliot, Asprey did not find that prospect at all daunting. And so it proved to be. By taking a taxi and directing the grinning driver to the night club, Charles had no difficulty in keeping his date with Helga. Not that it had any overtones of sex, but somehow he could not think of it as entirely platonic. There was an excitement that was quite inconsistent with the emergence of a simple friendship.

His immediate impression upon entering the hall was that everything was precisely the same as on the evening before, yet somehow Charles knew that it was not so. Meeting a person for the second time was quite different to being introduced to a stranger. He had had time to think and re-examine. Now he had expectations, whereas previously he carried the careless feeling of ignorance. On his first visit there had been so much activity that his vision had been blurred. Since he had been completely unprepared, he had had no sense of direction or purpose. The second occasion was quite different. He knew generally what to expect, he was an invitee and he was meeting someone. With all these advantages, he had entered the hall, crossed the floor and seated himself beside Helga within seconds of jumping out of his cab.

Helga looked at him with some amusement. "Good evening," she greeted him in German. "That was a positive approach." Charles realised the impression that he must have given. He quickly stood up.

"Please forgive so abrupt an arrival. My apologies. Let me start again." He took two steps backwards, bowed and returned Helga's greeting. "Good evening Helga. How nice to see you again. May I sit with you?"

Helga laughed and inclined her head. "Of course, Charles, be my guest." She indicated the empty chair which Asprey had just vacated. He sat down and relaxed.

Helga turned to him. "I am so glad you could come. I've kept something for you." So saying, she picked up a folded newspaper. "This is our local rag although it is read nationally. I've marked a passage for you on page three. Could you read it to me?"

It as more than a request. She handed the paper to him. It was neatly folded and clearly marked. Asprey looked at her with some astonishment. The command seemed innocuous enough yet there was little doubt that she was deadly serious.

He began to read it loud enough for Helga to hear. He quickly became acutely aware that the proximity of others must also put them into ear-shot if they cared to listen. Whilst there had been no overt interest when he started to read he had an uncomfortable feeling as he progressed that his audience was expanding through the combination of a reduction in the noise level and a slight movement of people towards him. Either he or the piece he was reading was being thoroughly examined and considered.

The article itself was complicated, analysing the current German economic policy as to its immediate and medium term effects on Europe generally and East/West relations in particular. As he read the last few words he glanced up to find that he had become the centre of interest for a large number of students who were listening and watching quite intently.

"Did you find it interesting?" asked Helga. "Yes, very," replied Charles, "it's amazing how different things look through someone else's eyes. Before reading that piece I would have seen the impact as much less significant. But if one adds to it the long term view that we discussed last night, then the present path is indeed well illuminated."

Helga nodded, "Just so." She twisted her head and seemed to seek guidance from the circle of students. If there was any then it could only be through abstention. None spoke or gave any indication of comment but the absence seemed sufficient for Helga. "Now, I'd like you to go up those stairs and meet some friends of ours. You'll see a door directly in front of you at the top. Knock and go in. They are expecting you."

Asprey hesitated. "It's all right. Nothing painful." Helga laughed and gave him a push. "Go on. I'll wait here." Charles did as he was told. Despite the number of people in the hall, he had no difficulty in getting through the crowd to the foot of the stairs. Since these were completely free, in a matter of a few strides he reached the landing at the top. As he knocked on the door facing him he looked down at the throng, still chattering, laughing and gesticulating, but now a mass of white faces peered through the cigarette smoke, staring at him. He opened the door and walked in. In complete contrast, his re-emergence and descent were completely ignored. He had to fight his way through to Helga who hardly greeted him, being heavily engaged with a tall, flaxen haired man of indeterminate age. Asprey's mouth was arid.

"Can I get you coffee?" he asked Helga and her companion. "Yes, please," she answered for both.

The coffee was steaming. It did nothing for Asprey's thirst and its temperature eliminated any excuse that he might otherwise have made for an early exit. Suddenly he felt tired and anxious to get back to his room, yet he knew that he could not make too abrupt a departure. His inner conflict must have communicated itself to Helga. She looked at her watch, glanced at him and inclined her head towards the door. Asprey nodded with relief. She spoke quickly to the flaxen one, shook him by the hand, then taking Asprey by the arm guided the two of them out into the dark damp night.

As they stood on the street corner, Charles became aware of a small Volkswagen parked opposite them. Without visual confirmation, he knew that the driver had to be Wolfgang. The passenger door opened. Obviously the person for whom Wolfgang was waiting had arrived and her identify was quickly revealed.

Helga looked up into Asprey's eyes. "When you came down the stairs, you not only looked like one of us – you were . . ." As she spoke she squeezed his hand, hard. For a moment suspended in time, they stood on the black wet pavement petrified by a common realisation. Then she was away, running like a fawn across the street, her shoes clattering on the cobbles, apparently oblivious of the slippery treacherous surface. As long as emotions overwhelmed her rational thought, she would retain her balance. She jumped into the car, slammed its door shut and was gone. If she looked back, Charles did not know, but he cared.

Life is full of coincidences, some inevitable, others impossible. Asprey never saw Helga again. She disappeared whilst working in Singapore, being last seen in a Russian restaurant. If Charles had turned around, who knows what might have happened? On the other hand he and Wolfgang were to meet face to face on several occasions unbeknown to the former who knew the German only as Herr Strauss.

* * * * * * *

The Boeing 747 curtsied to a final stop on the airport apron at Bangkok International after its short flight from Kuala Lumpur. Asprey looked through the drenched plastic window at the usual scene that welcomed the arrival of every large jet liner. He had no luggage, not even a brief case, so other than the passage through passport control there should be no delay in clearing the formalities. It was unlikely that there would be any comment on the complete absence of any baggage. Inspector Chung had provided him with only the bare essentials for travelling about which he could hardly complain. The plane was almost empty and those disembarking had gathered themselves together long before the aircraft had come to a complete stop – heedless as ever of the routine warning of the stewardess.

Asprey sat in his seat and waited a few moments, then when it became apparent that he was the last passenger left in his section, he stood up and walked to the exit. The stewardess pointed out the slippery nature of the steps leading to the ground and wished Asprey an automatic "have a good day", a much devalued desire.

Charles's descent coincided with the arrival alongside the plane of a long black limousine which drew to a halt at the foot of the aircraft steps. The rear door opened and a tall slim man dressed in a formal dark suit, white shirt and blue tie stepped from the car and stood patiently waiting. Asprey made no attempt to hurry despite the fine rain and negotiated the remaining treads as carefully as he had the first. He then walked with equal precision towards the figure standing at attention. Neither man held out his hand. When about a yard apart, Asprey stopped and bowed slightly from the waist. The other emulated him, but added two further greetings, one by gesture, the other by word. He placed his right hand across his chest parallel to the ground so that his right fist was pressed against his left breast, almost as if he were presenting arms without a rifle. At the same time, quietly but clearly, he said: "We are ready, Mein Führer."

Epilogue

"There is a tide in the affairs of men that taken at the flood leads on . . ." The inexorable passage of the earth in its orbit around the sun coupled with its unchanging relationship with its moon induce the regular tidal pattern of ebb and flow. Long ago man learned to take advantage of its regularity rather than to attempt the impossibility of its change. There have been many moments in man's history when a combination of different factors and elements have created unique opportunities that he has grasped with outstanding success and worthwhile results. The occasions have been even more numerous when man has tried to create an acceptable environment for the achievement of his purposes and failed miserably. Power is timing and as in the case of the noble art timing inevitably vanquishes brute force. The trick, if trick it is, is to know what is wanted, what to look for, to wait patiently and then move very rapidly when the moment arrives. To walk from the deck of one ship on to that of another requires but a single step at the right instant, even in a rough sea. To get it wrong necessitates superhuman effort with the painful probability of missing the target altogether.

Herr Doktor Muller's theory was that the Nazis had missed their flood-tide and try as they might in the future the opportunity in the form suited to their purpose would never present itself again.

Young Germany's theory as expounded by Helga was that the next flood-tide would be the culmination of new circumstances, but when it arrived they would introduce their resources in a form compatible with the new situation and let the force of the tide sweep them on to their goal. There was nothing original in her thinking, the principles she sought to apply or her objective. But the forecast environment contained an element which for the first time made the ambition so often attempted before now attainable. The ability to destroy man's civilisation would start with a ground swell of recognition gradually building to an overwhelming fear of inevitability. At that point, mankind would be offered a

236

second crucifixion in the form of the willingness of a nation to sacrifice itself in shielding its neighbours from the terrible blast of atomic bombs.

Since there is no more powerful motivation than fear, the emergence of a man representing such a nation and holding aloft an insurance policy long before drafted would be welcomed without hesitation. The risks facing mankind would be such that no premium could too high.

As in all things human, however, the unforeseeble can wreck the most carefully laid plans, but if the instigators are determined and courageous enough, that possibility can sometimes be avoided by the sacrifice of individuals, starting first with their opponents, then their supporters and finally as the last resort themselves.

Of those who contributed to our story, Davis and Foster never reappeared and Basil Rossi is believed to have died from natural causes in Portugal. Helga and Wolfgang Strauss are no longer in the game and if their activities are on this earthly plane they will be under new identities and living quite different lives. Singapore is even more rich and powerful and its people still charming, cheerful and determined to succeed. Frankfurt remains its western counterpart in all except the attitude of its people to its self-imposed challenge. Theirs is the determination of the dedicated.

The results in Malaysia were equally negative. Consolidated Industrial Holdings Berhad was liquidated – in the legal sense, being wound up to the detriment of its staff and creditors. The salvage licence reverted to the Government. The Tunku died and the only epitaph for a conglomeration of praiseworthy intentions for the betterment of the Malaysian economy was a piece of land that, for the most obtuse reasons, actually realised some value – for others.

The voluptuous Marie did become a Madame in her own right. Her business was based in Kuala Lumpur and was another example of her long term planning. When she had accumulated sufficient wealth, she discontinued her operations and travelled to London to learn the art and craft of hairdressing. She could and did then return to Singapore to etablish her own shop in the knowledge that her original apprenticeship in that city had long since been forgotten. Of all the characters in The Banyan Tree, she was the only one who, despite the heights she had to climb and the depths she had to plumb, by sheer courage and dedication achieved that which she sought. Moreover her satisfaction was topped by happiness.

No-one lives entirely in vain, but the accident of fortuitous wealth can divert and distort the mundane task of careful and caring creation so that that which might otherwise have been achieved however insignificant is ignored and lost forever. The discovery of U-134 and all the opportunity that it represented helped no-one, destroyed a few and injured many, but the same might be said of winning the pools. The experience of others will never deter men or women from seeing for themselves, especially when it involves the promise of a fortune.

Finally, Charles Asprey, the chameleon under the Banyan Tree. His true name is unimportant. Whether he will re-emerge under another is almost irrelevant because by the time that he is needed the task may well require the attributes of another. Asprey might even be too old. One thing is for certain, however. We now know the "how" and the "why". The "when" will declare itself. So if he and his promoters succeed, we shall have only ourselves to blame.

—THE END—